DISCARDE

PRAISE FOR

THE OPTIMIST'S GUIDE TO LETTING GO

"Delightful and heartfelt."

—Karma Brown, international bestselling author of
Recipe for a Perfect Wife

"A delightful treat—Amy's writing gets under the skin of family: how they drive you crazy, but you love them just the same. An absolute joy I am sure readers will take to their hearts."

—Veronica Henry, author of *How to Find Love in a Bookshop*

"Reichert has created wonderful true-to-life characters in a novel of secrets and regrets, loss and hope."

—*Library Journal*

"With charmingly developed characters who are thoughtfully crafted, this story will cling to readers through the final pages."

—RT Book Reviews

"A delicious read full of family and food."

—*Kirkus Reviews*

"Written with Reichert's hallmark humor and heart. . . . Lose yourself in this rich and rewarding read!"

—Pam Jenoff, *New York Times* bestselling author of
The Ambassador's Daughter

"With characters that are as complicated as they are original and a voice that is warmhearted and wise, you will hug this book when you're done."

—Taylor Jenkins Reid, bestselling author of *Daisy Jones & the Six*

"The characters are wonderfully imperfect, and their relationships are recognizably flawed, making their journey around and around—and finally back to—each other immeasurably satisfying. Bravo!"

—Christina Lauren, *New York Times* bestselling author of
The Honey-Don't List

Praise for
The Simplicity of Cider

"Reichert captures the food, relationships, and unique settings of the Midwest at their best. I was absolutely charmed by *The Simplicity of Cider*."

—J. Ryan Stradal, *New York Times* bestselling author of
The Lager Queen of Minnesota

"*The Simplicity of Cider* is the perfect blend of sweet, smart, and immensely satisfying. If foodie fiction is a thing, Amy Reichert is the grand master."   —Colleen Oakley, author of *You Were There Too*

"It's charming, heartwarming, and magical."

—Nina Bocci, *USA Today* bestselling author of *Meet Me on Love Lane*

"*The Simplicity of Cider* is a novel as delicious as cider and as enchanting as magic. . . . This is a lovely book, meant to be savored."

—Karen White, *New York Times* bestselling author of
The Christmas Spirits on Tradd Street

"A lot charming and a little bit magical, Reichert's latest is warm and poignant and romantic."   —RT Book Reviews (4-star review)

"*The Simplicity of Cider* is the ultimate ode to celebrating the dazzling splendor in small things. This will give you more fuzzy feelings than you can count."   —*Redbook*

TITLES BY AMY E. REICHERT

The Coincidence of Coconut Cake
Luck, Love & Lemon Pie
The Simplicity of Cider
The Optimist's Guide to Letting Go
The Kindred Spirits Supper Club

The KINDRED SPIRITS SUPPER CLUB

Amy E. Reichert

JOVE
NEW YORK

A JOVE BOOK
Published by Berkley
An imprint of Penguin Random House LLC
penguinrandomhouse.com

Library of Congress Cataloging-in-Publication Data

Names: Reichert, Amy E., 1974– author.
Title: The Kindred Spirits Supper Club / Amy E. Reichert.
Description: First edition. | New York: Jove, 2021.
Identifiers: LCCN 2020045256 (print) | LCCN 2020045257 (ebook) |
ISBN 9780593197776 (trade paperback) | ISBN 9780593197783 (ebook)
Classification: LCC PS3618.E52385 K56 2021 (print) |
LCC PS3618.E52385 (ebook) | DDC 813/.6—dc23
LC record available at https://lccn.loc.gov/2020045256
LC ebook record available at https://lccn.loc.gov/2020045257

First Edition: April 2021

Printed in the United States of America

1st Printing

Book design by Alison Cnockaert

To Pam—for making me the best brandy old-fashioneds and being Mom's second favorite. Love you!

A single act of kindness throws out roots in all directions, and the roots spring up and make new trees.

—Amelia Earhart

Once in New York, you are sure to be a great success. I know lots of people there who would give a hundred thousand dollars to have a grandfather, and much more than that to have a family ghost.

—Oscar Wilde, *The Canterville Ghost*

1

TWO DAYS, TWENTY-THREE HOURS, and thirty-two minutes. Almost three full days since Sabrina Monroe had last spoken to someone who wasn't a relative. Her record was seven days, four hours, and fifty-five minutes, but still, almost three days was impressive. In her ideal world, she could continue the trend indefinitely, a sweet happily ever after of telecommuting and food delivery.

She sat in the center of a large indoor waterpark, the WWW (Wild World of Waterparks)—or Three Dub, as people had started calling it—the latest addition to the Waterpark Capital of the World. The fake boulders hadn't yet acquired the usual dust and stuck gum, the colors still popped on the waterslides, and the painted murals were not yet dimmed by years of exposure to eye-burning levels of chlorine. With her feet propped on a white plastic chair, identical to the one she sat in, Sabrina stopped scrolling through the news app on her phone when a stack of towels toppled off a neighboring table into a puddle. She scooped them up, draping the wet towels over chairbacks and setting the still-dry towels at the center of the table, then returned to her lounging position before anyone noticed. Her nieces and nephew, Arabella, Lilly, and Oscar, frolicked in the kiddie area, a three-tiered structure of rope bridges, water cannons, and small slides for the little ones not quite ready to brave the twisty four-story flumes. An enormous bucket dropped one thousand gallons of water every fifteen minutes with a clang, a roar, and a rush of wind that blew over a lazy river circling the entire room, where tubes bobbed like Froot Loops and tweens raced around floating adults, who scowled at their rambunctiousness.

It should have been difficult to take her nieces and nephew to a waterpark without speaking to other people, but she had bought the tickets online, then took refuge among the crowded tables while the kids played. Being alone was always easiest in a crowded, noisy location, and no room was louder or more crowded than an indoor waterpark on a rainy holiday weekend.

Within the confines of this humid, echoing warehouse, Sabrina avoided interacting with people by scrolling through the news on her phone. She didn't notice the people who stood up with meerkat attentiveness. She didn't notice the people swiping chairs from other tables. She didn't notice a nearby angry, tattooed chair-swiping victim returning from the snack bar with a giant fully loaded margarita.

Dumb luck had her looking up from her phone at exactly the wrong moment.

She watched as the Refill-A-Rita catapulted out of the tattooed man's hand, centrifugal force and a red plastic lid keeping most of the fire-engine-red contents inside until they collided with the bridge of her nose. Tequila-laden pseudo-strawberry slush exploded onto her hair down to her flip-flopped feet, staining her yellow swimsuit a sunset orange and obscuring her vision with kaleidoscoping stars from the surprising pain. Bent over in agony, Sabrina avoided the unexpectedly aerodynamic white plastic chair that followed the margarita as it arced over her head toward the chair swipers.

A man wearing colorful swim trunks emblazoned with red crustaceans fought back a smile as his eyes inspected the substance dripping from her head, confirming Sabrina's ridiculous appearance. What right did he have to judge her? He had crabs on his pants. As he took a breath to speak, Sabrina broke her no-talking streak.

"Duck," she said, pointing to his white plastic table as a cup of soda soared over them. Caught in food-fight cross fire, the man crouched under it and out of the fray. Now she could do the same.

Sabrina dropped to the ground and scooted to safety, wiping the worst of the overly sweet slop off her face, the alcohol and red dye stinging her eyes. The warring people around her shouted, more food and plastic water bottles skittered across the wet concrete, and soon tables stuttered as bodies shoved against them. The man huddled under his table an aisle over from her. Around them, the babble of water rushing, children screaming, and parents yelling echoed off the walls and windows, amplifying the noise.

From her location under the table, she could spot her charges scampering in the spraying water, oblivious to the commotion at the nearby tables.

Two beefy men shoved at each other like Greco-Roman wrestlers, hairy bellies bumping against each other. Feet stumbled past her table, knocking her phone into a waiting puddle. She snatched it out of the water as her heart raced. Not her phone. She didn't have the money to replace it. She dried it off the best she could on a small, still-clean section of her swimsuit.

A pair of delicate feet stopped beside her table, followed by a cheerful face framed by chin-length bouncing blond curls. The woman's edges blurred into a soft glow as if she stood in front of a lamp. With Ghost Molly, it was barely noticeable. More recently deceased spirits had a blur that made it obvious they were new to the afterlife, helping Sabrina and her mom recognize them.

"Whatcha doing, honey?"

"Hey, Molly." Sabrina wasn't surprised to see her here, in the middle of the brouhaha and unconcerned for her safety as a tray of nachos splattered through her toes—the perks of being ethereal. She'd known Ghost Molly all her life, and she often appeared when Sabrina least expected her. Sabrina scooted over to make room. Between one blink and the next, Molly situated herself next to Sabrina under the table, her arms wrapped around her bent knees, excitement sparkling in her eyes. Sabrina checked her phone, making sure it still worked. So far, so good. She clutched it to her chest, careful to keep it out of the sticky margarita.

"This is bananas. What happened?" Molly said.

"Chair swipers. It escalated quickly." Sabrina's nose throbbed, the pain seeping across her face like water into dry ground. "Why can't people use their words?"

"Look at that cutie-patootie." Molly pointed to the judgmental crustacean-clad man between the chairs and table legs. "Let's scooch over to his table."

Sabrina shook her head. Molly loved shoving her toward men. A rush of warm air hit her face from the giant water bucket, drying the melted margarita coating her face and chest. Her skin started to itch.

"This will probably be all over the internet later," Sabrina said, ignoring Molly's comment. A nearby table was jostled.

Molly smiled. "Will you show me the videos?"

"Yeah."

"Pinky promise?" Molly held up her hand with the pinky extended. Sabrina matched the gesture. When their pinkies touched, it was like sticking her finger in a snowbank. Molly beamed. She loved internet videos.

Khaki-encased legs and sturdy shoes walked by the table.

"Security's here," Sabrina said.

As Sabrina leaned forward to get onto her hands and knees, a glop of slush fell onto her wrist. Gross. By the time she straightened on her feet, Molly stood next to her, too. She wore high-waisted turquoise swim bottoms that cut in a straight line over her belly button and a matching thick-strapped bikini top that ended under her rib cage, leaving only a couple inches of exposed skin between the top and bottom, so much cuter than the margarita-splotched yellow tankini Sabrina wore. It was infinitely easier to wear cute clothes when you could conjure them with a thought. Molly bounced on the balls of her feet while watching the hubbub around her. Some of the nearby people still shouted as the security team separated the warring families.

"This is so exciting," Molly said. "Oh, here comes the cutie." She pointed.

The dark-haired man approached her table with a stack of towels, weaving between the crowded plastic tables and gawking patrons. She wanted to crawl under the table and dig a pit she could disappear into, hiding the melting slush and blossoming black eyes of her embarrassing situation.

"He's the cat's pajamas," Molly said, waggling her eyebrows. "Just how I like 'em."

Sabrina wanted to agree, but her mind threw up every defense. He was going to talk to her, and she would only be able to stare back at him. She started cataloging facts to distract herself. He had thick, wavy hair flopping in different directions, longer on top and shorter on the sides, and a few days' scruff defining his jaw and framing his full lips. Small red patches flanked the bridge of his nose where glasses must usually perch. Later, when she replayed this moment over in excruciating detail, she'd realize he was exactly her type, but for now she ignored it and moved on. He stopped in front of her.

"They take their seating seriously here," he said with a smile.

Sabrina blinked. He'd made a joke about the asinine situation. She wanted to respond with something clever, or at least something not idiotic. Instead, her mouth went dry and she focused on the pulsating pain increasing across her head—anything to distract from her racing heart.

When she didn't speak, he continued. "I thought you might need these." His voice was low and smooth, yet with a touch of roughness, like he had been out too late at a concert the night before or spent the day in the chemical-laden air of WWW. Blue eyes took in her sloppy appearance and stopped on her nose—ground zero of her misery. She pulled her eyes from the wet concrete floor to look over his right ear, close enough that he might think she was making eye contact.

"Thank you." There, that was a perfectly normal response. Sabrina grabbed the top towel and wrapped it around her shoulders to stop more slush from sliding down her swimsuit. Molly stood behind him, signaling that Sabrina should smile by pointing at her own dimpled grin. Sure, smiling like a fool was exactly what this moment needed.

Sabrina ignored her and grabbed another towel to wipe off her face. Not being able to see him gave her time to take a calming breath— in through the nose, out through the mouth.

"Are you okay? I saw that giant margarita hit your face," he said. "I can't believe the distance that flew. I think we have a new Olympic event."

More jokes she'd ignore. Witty banter rarely worked for her; instead it came out as awkward. Even through the terry cloth, his attention burned on her face, adding to the stuffy heat in the waterpark.

"Not great." Sabrina patted the towel carefully around her nose. It hurt to touch the skin. She hoped to hide any bruising, which would be difficult to explain at work, in addition to her Kool-Aid-stained skin. It would take forever to scrub off. There was only one way to handle this. She gulped in some air so she could keep talking. Thinking about it only made it worse. She blurted the first comeback that came to her. "Red's my color."

He laughed at her joke.

He laughed. At her joke.

But was he laughing at her because what she said was funny? Or because she looked funny? Or because she was being so bumbling it was funny? Either way, it was a good laugh that came from his belly, where all real laughs were born. It wasn't a cruel laugh. Those she could recognize.

Molly gave Sabrina two thumbs up. Sabrina struggled to stop a scowl from forming in response. It had been too long since she'd had to ignore a ghost while talking to a non–family member.

"I'm Ray." His lips curved up at the corners, and their fullness didn't flatten when he smiled. She didn't want to be thinking about his lips. She wanted him to go away. She bowed her head, and he kept talking. "Do you want to shower off?"

Shit. He wasn't going away. Sabrina tried to relax the muscles in her body, the ones that wanted her to remain stiff and alert to all potential danger. Peak flight mode.

"I'm going to grab the kids and head out." She pointed in the direction of the giant bucket as it dropped the water and a wave of air blew a loose strand of hair into the sticky residue on her nose. She wanted to say something clever, maybe hear him laugh again, but the words melted on her tongue. Her conflicted body and brain exhausted her.

"You have kids?" Ray said, searching the play area. Good, he wasn't looking at her anymore.

"No." Sabrina said. Molly crossed her forearms to form an X behind Ray's back, making it clear she didn't want Ray thinking Sabrina had kids. Molly liked to worry about things that didn't matter. She gave Molly a quick frown while Ray still looked toward the splash zone. "My brothers' kids," Sabrina continued. "I'm the cool aunt."

There, that was better. She could have normal interactions, even when covered in margarita.

"I bet you are." Ray reached out to pull the hair off her nose. Sabrina winced as even that small touch hurt. "That's not going to look great tomorrow. You should really get ice on it. I'll get some."

Before she could call him off, he headed toward the bar. Sabrina turned to Molly.

"You need to knock it off. I'm trying to have a conversation, and you're being very distracting."

"I'm *helping.*"

"You think you're helping, but you're not. He may not be able to see you, but he can see my reactions. Just shush."

If Sabrina hurried, she could be gone before he returned, ending this awkward encounter. Ray seemed like a nice enough guy, but why bother getting to know someone well enough to get over the Awkwards when she'd be gone in a few months?

2

When Ray returned to the disheveled woman, her lips moved as if she spoke to herself silently. Even stained red, there was something charmingly honest about her. If anything, she didn't know or care about who his family was. With her short responses and lack of eye contact, she probably wanted him to go away. If the situation were reversed, he'd wish for the same, but he wasn't about to leave her without helping as much as he could, even if it meant carrying a towel full of rapidly melting ice through an obstacle course of vacationer detritus. After seeing her rescue towels from a puddle before the food fight, he knew she would have done the same for him.

"Here you are." He held the ice out to her like a peace offering.

"Thank you, Ray." The words came out muffled because of her swelling nose. She grabbed the ice from the top, avoiding his hands. "I'm Sabrina. You said your name. That's mine."

Her brows scrunched together like she was suddenly unhappy.

"Nice to meet you, Sabrina." He put all his charm into his most welcoming smile, the one that got him bumped up a restaurant's wait list or into a property before it was officially listed on the market.

The ice clinked as it settled around her nose, hiding most of her face as she spoke to him. The obstacle would make it more difficult for him to guess what she was thinking, especially since her eyes avoided his.

"I agree." She closed her eyes after she said it.

I agree? Ray clamped his lips together to keep from smiling. He understood now. He made her nervous. That was something he knew how to handle. Putting people at ease, making them comfortable enough to trust him, that was his bread, butter, and celebratory champagne.

"I moved here last fall from New York," Ray said, glossing over Sabrina's taciturn answers. "I haven't had a chance to meet many people outside of work."

Sabrina blinked at him from behind her ice.

When she didn't speak, he continued. "Maybe someone who likes to go out to dinner?" Ray tilted his head down, then looked up at her, putting a see-how-harmless-I-am sparkle in his eyes.

Eyes like maple syrup blinked back at him. Was it surprise? Shock? Horror? He regretted bringing her the ice since it blocked so much of her very expressive face.

"I . . . work a lot," Sabrina said.

Those eyes shifted past his shoulder and twitched into a blink-and-you'd-miss-it glare. He checked behind him, but no one stood there.

"Oh." He paused, thrown by her unexpected answer. "I get that. How about a drink? I work at The Otter Club. Did you know Wisconsin consumes forty percent of the brandy produced? Come out sometime and I'll make you the best brandy old-fashioned you've ever had."

Why did he have to spout such a stupid thing? Now he was getting nervous, too. He never got nervous. She didn't care about random Wisconsin facts. She moved the ice off her face with trembling hands. The skin had started to turn purple. She'd have two huge shiners by morning. It had to hurt. His face had been used as a punching bag before, so he knew what it felt like.

She switched the hand that held the ice to her face and fidgeted with her phone between glances at her charges. Like a trapped rabbit, she was trying to determine the best way to escape while keeping her distance from the big, bad predator—him. He was flipping through his mental file of interesting small-talk questions when she finally spoke.

"I'm not interested in an old-fashioned. My last old-fashioned left me for a craft mocktail."

As soon as she finished the sentence, her eyes closed and she shook her head, a clear sign that she'd said more than she meant to. Now they were getting somewhere.

"Are we still talking about drinks?" Ray asked.

"I'm moving in the fall." Her hand gripped her phone tighter. Her thumb flicked over the screen, but she didn't look at it. "Drinks aren't in my schedule."

Point taken. She wasn't interested.

"What do you do?"

"Journalist. Between jobs." He barely heard the words over the noise of the waterpark.

Sabrina stared at the tables. "I should get going."

She set down her phone and folded a colorful towel before dropping it into a large bag, then did the same to a second one. Hoping it would buy him another minute or two, he handed her a pile of small clothes that were out of her reach. She took the clothes from his hands and shoved them into the tote.

"What brings you to flyover country?" she asked, the words tumbling out in a clump.

"My uncle—well, great-great-uncle, but that seems like a mouthful—he fell ill a few months ago, and I moved here to help." There was more to it, but he could keep his secrets, too. He took a deep breath and looked around him, gathering his next thoughts. "I fell in love. With the area, I mean. The river. I don't know exactly what it is."

At last, her eyes brightened and she nodded.

"It happens to the best of us. The river caught your soul and won't let go."

Ray couldn't have explained it better.

"That's exactly right."

The Wisconsin River wound its way through the city, so a person was never that far from its dramatic shores, with its narrowing sandstone alleys and towering pines of the Upper Dells, the dam downtown where the river's power thundered, or the meandering Lower Dells, where The Otter Club overlooked the water.

She set the ice on the table and grabbed another clean towel.

"That's what I miss most when I'm away," Sabrina said.

It was a starting point.

"That's what drew me to The Otter." She looked confused, so he explained, "The Otter Club. It used to be the River Lodge, but I changed the name when I took it over." She nodded that she followed. She must have grown up here if she recognized the older name. "I look at the Wisconsin River every day. I'd do it for free. Well, almost. A man's got to eat."

Never mind that he had enough saved from his years in real estate; he was here for a fresh start, to pursue the kind of life he wanted, his parents' wishes be damned. Uncle Harry had even helped him buy The Otter Club, investing as a silent partner so he'd have enough funds to make the updates the supper club needed.

Sabrina rubbed the clean towel through her hair and across her skin to remove any of the remaining slush that hadn't dried. She waved at her charges to get their attention. His time was almost up.

"We need to go," Sabrina said. She grabbed a plastic container full of cookies off the table and shoved it at his chest. "Thank you for your help. They're homemade."

Ray nodded and took that as his cue to return to his own table as the kids joined her. With shaking hands, she shoved the rest of her items into a bag, wrapped each child in a dry towel, and led them out in a procession. New guests snagged her table before she was ten steps away, but he still kept staring.

"I know that look." His sister had arrived. Lucy set her gin and tonic on their table and carefully covered a chair in a plush beach towel. Beneath an expensive sheer black cover-up, she wore an equally expensive bikini. He peeled the lid off the container. Inside were neat rows of thin, round cookies that had been rolled in rainbow-colored sprinkles along their edges.

"What look is that?"

"It's the same look you get when you find a property you have to have." Ray couldn't help but smile. It felt similar, too. Lucy continued. "Remember, a romance is so much more than a property."

"Yes, Luce, I'm aware that women are not property."

He selected a cookie and bit into it, the buttery crispness dissolving on his tongue—not overly sweet, with a nice kick of vanilla. It was a damn good cookie.

"You know what I mean. Obsessive research, relentless phone calls, and frequent drive-bys are not going to work here. It will only result in a restraining order."

He picked out another cookie, then held out the container to Lucy. She shook her head no.

"I know how to court a woman."

"It didn't look like it. I don't expect you to be a chick magnet like me, but what I witnessed was embarrassing for our entire family. I'm happy to give you some pointers."

"I'm good."

Ray hadn't dated in over a year—not since his last disaster of a relationship had ended. He'd been too focused on caring for Uncle Harry and getting The Otter Club off the ground. Now that the supper club was going well, he had time to think about other parts of his life. Meeting Sabrina reminded him that he had come for another reason, too. Uncle Harry had always spoken about the people in the Dells as if they were dear friends, people he could borrow the proverbial cup of sugar from at any hour of the day, people who watched out for one another. Not just friends, but neighbors.

He ate another cookie.

It was time to be more neighborly.

3

SABRINA SHOVED THEIR BAG into the trunk of her car while Arabella, the eldest of the trio, helped get the younger kids strapped in. She hadn't stopped to put on her flip-flops, and the warm blacktop rapidly approached blistering temperatures. The shower at home beckoned her, a siren's song so beautiful it would make Josh Groban give up singing forever.

By the time Sabrina was buckled, Molly had materialized next to her in the passenger seat, wearing a crisp white cotton shirt with high-waisted navy-blue pinstriped pants, her hair wrapped in an elegant matching turban. Sabrina could only yearn for that shower.

It had been too much: the margarita, the handsome man with his crabby swim trunks, and Molly shouting encouragement at her from behind him. On a scale from one to ten, her anxiety teetered at a full eight.

Deep breath. Belly out. Belly in.

She had to get them all home.

"What an adorable meet-cute," Molly said. "Hollywood couldn't write a better one. A damsel in distress, a knight with fluffy towels. Take him up on the drink."

"I'm not going to have any drinks with anyone. This isn't open for discussion."

"Who are you talking to, Aunt Sabrina?" Arabella asked from the middle seat in the back. She was the only one old enough to use a regular seat belt without a car seat and was the de facto leader of their little cousin gang, a born dictator and future princess. She kept the younger cousins occupied and having so much fun they never noticed she made the rules. The other two flanked her from their own thrones of safety, Lilly in her small booster and Oscar in his enormous car seat.

"Molly." Sabrina left the waterpark parking lot and merged into traffic.

All three perked up. They loved anything to do with the family secret. She had been that way once, too.

"Tell her we say hi," Arabella said. The other two nodded their agreement.

Molly peeked over her shoulder and waved.

"She's waving hello."

"I'll get to see her first, won't I, Aunt Sabrina?" Arabella said. She scratched her arm that itched from the drying chlorine. They hadn't taken the time to rinse off, so they would all need showers when they returned to her parents' house.

"Probably, but Lilly and you are pretty close in age, so she might beat you." Not to mention that no one in the family was sure if Arabella came from her brother's DNA or Cal's, so she might never get to see Molly. When they'd used a surrogate, they had agreed to never find out whose sperm won the race—though Arabella's amber eyes were just a little too much like her own for them not to be related.

"It happens at pew-berty," Lilly said, drawing out the first syllable. Arabella nodded in agreement.

"When will I get to see her?" Oscar asked, squinting at the empty seat next to Sabrina, trying to see what he never would.

"Oh, honey, you won't. Only girls can see the ghosts," Sabrina answered.

Oscar scowled.

"I want to be a girl."

Sabrina laughed and Molly giggled.

"Times have changed. No boy would have ever said that when I was breathing."

"Give him a few years. It's still a man's world."

Molly tucked one of her curls into her turban. Some days they bounced around her earlobes, other days they curled like vines down her back, but they always looked perfect. Molly might be dead, but she liked to look good.

"Arabella says I'll only see ghosts when we visit Grandma and Grandpa," Lilly said.

"That's true," Sabrina answered.

"Aren't there ghosts in Minnesota?"

"Yes, but another family helps them. Our family helps the ghosts here with their unfinished business. Other families help in other places. That's how it's always been."

"Where do they go when you can't see them? Do they sleep?" Arabella asked.

Sabrina smiled and took a moment to sort out her reply. Since leaving the waterpark, she'd focused solely on what she needed to do next, then the next step, then the next step. Collect the kids, wrap them in towels, get to the car, don't drop anything, and drive. She didn't want to process what had happened lest the mortification send her into a spiral. She tapped her hand on the back of her phone, eager to disappear into the news and other people's problems, but that would have to wait.

"Correct me if I'm wrong, Molly," Sabrina said. "Being visible takes energy, so when Molly wants to rest, she disappears, but she's still there. Molly can go anywhere within a certain distance."

"She can see me in the bathtub?" Oscar asked.

"She would never," Sabrina said.

"Depends on the cutie. Like that Ray might get a visit," Molly said with a wink.

"Why don't you live here, Aunt Sabrina?" said Lilly.

Sabrina licked her lips—they tasted like cheap tequila.

"Because Grandma does such a good job, and you'll be able to help her soon."

Sabrina glanced in the rearview mirror to see Arabella squinting at the front seat, trying to force her eyes to see what they weren't ready to. She wanted to grow up so badly, but Sabrina wanted to tell her it wasn't all adventure and excitement. Kids were mean. She would be different. Though, unlike Sabrina, Arabella thrived on separating herself from the pack. She hoped that continued.

Time to change the topic.

"Arabella, what kind of birthday party do you want?"

"You're planning it?"

Sabrina nodded.

"Now I know it'll be good. The dads aren't good at parties for girls."

"They know that. That's why they asked me. So, what must you have?"

Arabella scrunched her face, giving it proper thought, while Lilly and Oscar had some ideas.

"Dinosaurs," Oscar said.

"Puppies," Lilly added.

"*Octonauts!*"

"*Frozen.*"

"It's Arabella's party, and she gets to choose. When it's your birthday, you can have those things," Sabrina said.

"I want a glamping party."

Sabrina snorted.

"Glamping? Do you even know what that is?"

"Fancy camping with lots of pillows and pretty tents."

"Yes, that's kind of it."

"And fireworks."

"Glamping and fireworks. Got it."

Sabrina eased around the corner toward her parents' home, a large old house just a few blocks from the Wisconsin Dells downtown, where the street was lined with inexpensive T-shirt stores, fudge shops, restaurants, gift stores, bars, and unexpected attractions like Wizard Quest and ax throwing. Ideas for the party tumbled into neat rows in her mind, ready to be put onto paper, then made into reality. She hoped Cal and Brendan were ready for this.

Like Molly, her parents' house was over the century mark. Lined with tall oaks and maples, the street had houses ranging from ramshackle colonials to grander homes converted into bed-and-breakfasts to new homes where older residences had been knocked down.

Sabrina pulled the car into the driveway. Mrs. Randolph's cat sat on the warm blacktop in front of their garage, having found the one sunbeam filtering through the towering trees in the yard. He must have gotten out through the gap in the screen door again, using his head like a battering ram. She reached across Molly to the glove compartment and pulled out a roll of duct tape, threading it on her arm like a bracelet. The kids in the back seat got themselves unbuckled and scampered to the house, ready to tell the tale of Sabrina's blossoming black eyes.

Sabrina got out of the car, and the cat flopped over onto his side as she approached. Blood rushed to her head when she bent over at the waist, sending a new round of throbbing pain to her nose. She gave the cat a quick belly rub and scooped him up, his body limp in her arms like a loose bag of sand. Mrs. Randolph didn't like him outside with the busy traffic on nearby streets, but he staunchly believed the sunbeams were of much higher quality in the driveway. Sabrina had already wrangled him back inside twice this week.

"Come on, Mr. Bennett, time to go home."

Molly followed her, blinking herself from inside the car to Sabrina's side.

"You can't ignore them forever. Those souls need you," Molly said, ignoring the cat. Mr. Bennett didn't like her much, so Molly chose to pretend he didn't exist rather than feel rejected when he hissed at her. They had settled into a truce of mutual ignoring.

"The other ghosts have my mother, and the girls will be old enough soon. They can't wait to join the family biz."

Sabrina tried to squish the cat back through the hole in the screen, but Mr. Bennett didn't care for this plan. It went as smoothly as putting toothpaste back in the tube, but with more squirming and fur. Sabrina gave up, opened the door, set him on the floor, and shut it before he could escape again. Using the duct tape, she sealed the opening. After one attempt to slip back through the hole, Mr. Bennett sat on the other side of the door and meowed his disgruntlement to her. The duct tape wouldn't last long. She'd need to fix the screen.

"You can help Mrs. Randolph but not help a few ghosts with their unfinished business?"

"You know why."

"You aren't a pip-squeak anymore. You can handle annoying ghosts without people noticing. And Ray's no heel. He doesn't seem like the type to mind the occasional visiting specter."

"We aren't going to discuss what Ray would or wouldn't mind. It's not going to happen."

Sabrina didn't want to think about Ray. She only wanted a shower.

"Ray's a good name." Molly's face got dreamy.

"Sabrina?" An imperious voice interrupted her fantasies of hot water and thick lather. Behind her stood a small wrinkled woman. Her gray hair was streaked with strands of dark brown and pulled into a tidy twist. She wore an expensive Chanel suit coat and skirt, and a hazy glow blurred her edges like someone had dragged an eraser around her. Out of instinct, Sabrina stepped back and landed on a sharp stone.

"Damn."

"Language, young lady." The woman pulled herself up taller. Then Sabrina recognized her.

"Madam Hendricks?" She was the grandmother of a former classmate—and had always insisted on being Madam, not Mrs. It was all you needed to know about her and her family. Sabrina sighed and crossed her arms in front of her chest. "Really? Now?"

"So it's all true," Madam Hendricks said as she studied Sabrina with new interest, then held her arms in front of her, inspecting them in the daylight, stretching far enough that her fingertips disappeared into Sabrina's elbow. Sabrina shivered at the icy touch.

Well, shit. Sabrina didn't want to deal with this. She stepped out of reach.

With the Houdini cat problem temporarily solved, Sabrina tossed the roll of duct tape through the car's open window, grabbed her bags from the trunk, and said, "Yep. You're dead. Follow me." Then she walked inside her parents' house with Molly and Madam Hendricks trailing behind like ducklings.

4

RAY'S JUDGMENT IN REAL estate was similar to taste testing cake flavors; he knew instantly if he loved it or if it was too sweet or too dense. That was how it was with The Otter Club when he'd first visited while he was in college. He'd known immediately how he could improve it, what needed to be fixed, and what needed to stay exactly the same. He brushed a hand over the varnished logs that formed the porch railing, absently checking for snags that might give a guest a splinter, but mostly savoring the silence. After the noisy waterpark earlier in the day, he welcomed the quiet, which he'd only have for a few more hours before the restaurant opened.

He took a deep breath. The solitude and peace filled his lungs, the air scented with the rich aromas of dark soil and growing greenery. Surrounded by stately pines and the occasional birch or poplar, the restaurant overlooked a curve of the Wisconsin River and provided diners with expansive views up and down the water until it twisted around a bend, a path it had carved out over thousands of years. The river was wide and slow enough at this point that people occasionally thought it was a small lake or large pond until one of the touring ducks—the vehicle, not the animal—puttered by.

He'd visited last October, on the supper club's final weekend before shutting down for the winter. The parking lot had overflowed with tourists and locals enjoying one more meal before the owner retired and moved to Alabama. At the time, he hadn't really understood how a supper club differed from a traditional restaurant. It was an elusive something understood best through experience, like the sun at the top of Mount Everest or snorkeling alongside a whale shark—every sense was needed to describe it, and even then, it fell short of the real experience. Supper clubs were like that. They demanded time. Time to savor a predinner cocktail or three while noshing on the relish tray, an assortment of raw vegetables, pickles, olives, cheese spread, and crackers, all against the din of clinking silverware and guest conversation. Then came a leisurely meal of grilled steaks with herbed butter served on sizzling metal plates, buttered shrimp sprinkled with parsley, and crispy tender potatoes, probably topped with melting cheese. Then to the bar for an after-dinner drink to end the evening on a sweet note. It was a night out, not just a meal. Since taking over The Otter in the fall, he'd visited several supper clubs around the state, each with its own unique approach. Some had retro (or possibly original) decor, others added modern twists on old classics; some celebrated long histories with colorful stories on menus and family photos on the walls, while others leaned into dark, cavernous settings reminiscent of their prohibition roots. For The Otter Club, he embraced the natural ambience that surrounded it.

After devouring a memorable dinner of prime rib and scallops, he'd stood in this same spot on the restaurant's wraparound porch and nursed a manhattan—that was before he understood the joys of a well-made brandy old-fashioned. While sipping his drink, the dusk draped the autumn landscape in purples and blues, the birds quieted, and he could hear the gentle sound of the river hushing against its banks, an otter splashing into the water, and an owl hooting out a greeting. A sense of calmness settled into his soul, bone-deep; each rustle soothed and eased his racing thoughts. He was content. He wanted to recognize the owls by their hoots, the squirrels by their bushy tails, and the trees by their silhouettes. What would it look like surrounded by white snowbanks or with icy chunks floating past during the spring thaw? What would it sound like with the damp new growth of spring or the dry, crisp air of late summer?

For the first time in his life, he could breathe freely, and not just because the air flowed through his lungs with invigorating ease but because he had found what he didn't know he needed. A place all his own.

His mind returned to the events from earlier in the day. When he'd first spotted Sabrina, picking up towels that weren't hers, it had caught his attention. Sadly, simple niceties were rare enough that they stood out. While she had been anxious and a little awkward, his delight had bloomed when she let a witty comment spill out, a little glimpse of a different side to her. He hoped he'd get to see her again.

"Have you heard from Dad?" Lucy joined him on the porch, dressed as if to close a real estate deal, in a slim black skirt, crisp white shirt, and stylish heels that he knew cost more than a week's stay at most local resorts, her blond hair sleek and straight past her shoulders.

The family was gathering.

"He texted a while ago. The nurses say it won't be long. I'm heading back to the hospital soon."

She set her palm on the center of his back and rubbed. "You doing okay?"

"Dad's still giving me a hard time."

"Do you blame him? He grew up believing the Dells was the tenth circle of hell, devoid of all culture and happiness."

"That's the problem. He thinks I'm throwing away some perfect life, but I know—like I knew when I saw this place—I'm meant to be here. All good things from here on out."

"Now you're starting to sound like Uncle Harry."

"Good. I only hope I'm half as happy."

"Give Dad some time. He'll come around. If nothing else, he understands family responsibility." Lucy paused. "I'm not going to pretend to understand, but I can respect your decision. It's Mom you need to worry about. She hates it here."

"But they seemed to love it the last time we visited together."

"At that fall dance the town throws?"

"Yeah, the Goodbye Gala. It was charming." He was now in charge of the local annual event, since the former River Lodge had always hosted.

"You were still learning how to hold your booze back then. Trust me, it was horrid."

Ray let it drop, but he remembered it differently, enough so that moving here had felt as inevitable as a sunrise. Given enough time, it would happen.

A sharp pain in his hand drew Ray's attention—he'd found a snag in the wooden railing. He studied the sliver sticking out of the meaty part of his palm. Maybe his rosy memory wasn't so perfect, but that didn't make it unfixable. Nine months ago, he'd barely known anything about his uncle. He'd come for some answers and ended up staying when he'd bought the supper club and Uncle Harry had gotten sick. He'd used moving to Wisconsin as an excuse to get away from his life in New York. He hadn't expected to like the old man so much, with his wispy white hair, daily brandy nightcap, and uncanny gift of having a ridiculous story for every occasion—like the time he and his buddies hooked up one of the park's bubblers to a keg of beer and started an impromptu citywide party, complete with a ticket from the local police that he had framed on the wall of his office. The story had gotten even better once Ray had looked up what a bubbler was. Or that Uncle Harry and his brother used to sneak girls into a secret room somewhere in the Jasper home that was once used to hide hooch during prohibition. Ray hadn't had time to find it, yet.

"I'll be fine. I wish there was more time, but I'm grateful I had the little bit I did. He was a good man."

"Are you really going to stay here?"

Ray took a deep breath. Not her, too.

"It's not that I don't respect your decision. I'll miss you." Lucy took a deep breath. "It's just so quiet here."

"That's what I like the most. There's room to get to know people, to know a place, to know myself."

"Is this some quest to find out who you are, and then you'll come back?"

"I'm never going back to New York." He picked at the splinter, breaking off the part on the outside, leaving the larger portion still embedded in his hand. It stung. "This is where I belong. There should always be a Jasper in the Dells, and I'm it now. I've inherited the Goodbye Gala. You know how much I love that."

"Can't you find someone else? Surely the town doesn't expect you to plan it."

"I've arranged multiparty billion-dollar deals. I can put together some dinner and dancing." He grinned, specifically thinking about one bedraggled, kind-of-awkward brunette with amber eyes whom he'd like to ask to dance.

5

THE BACK DOOR LED up a short flight of steps and into the kitchen, which was abuzz with three small children all talking at once as her mom fed them chocolate chip cookies, still warm given the amount of smeared chocolate on the kids' hands and faces.

"Hey, Mom."

Her mom, Jenny Monroe, handed one of the cookies to Sabrina as a greeting, then stopped as she saw who was there.

"Arabella, take everyone upstairs and start a bath. I'll be there in a bit to hose you all down. Tell Grandpa to get towels out for you."

Sabrina shivered again, her elbow still chilly from Madam's touch. Sabrina tried to give Molly her space as if she were solid. Not only was it rude to move through her, but the iciness lingered—a reminder that there was more to the world than most people could see.

"I can do it," Arabella said, standing a little taller.

"I'm sure you can. Part of the fun of being a grandma is giving baths. Now scoot."

Per usual, her mom wore a long, loose summer dress made from thick T-shirt material—the kind found at J.Crew or Talbots that, with proper care, would still look new in twenty years. Today's was navy-blue-and-white-striped on top, cinched at the waist with elastic, then solid navy to her ankles. Bright-white Keds and short ankle socks pulled the look together. She had vibrant white hair, always pulled back into a neat low ponytail, which should have made her gently wrinkled face look older, but instead brought out the pink in her cheeks and her mischievous blue eyes. Everything she owned was ironed, including her underwear and socks. Her mom insisted one was never properly dressed unless properly pressed. Sabrina agreed to disagree.

"That should help your battle-weary soul." Her mom nodded at the uneaten cookie in Sabrina's hand. "Have a seat so I can look at your nose." She licked the chocolate off her fingers while turning toward Molly near the kitchen sink. "Hi, Molly."

At last she faced Madam Hendricks.

"Madam." Her tone was touched with frost.

"I wondered if you were planning on acknowledging me. Perhaps you will tell me why I'm here. Your daughter is useless."

If Sabrina had wondered where the familial mean streak came from, she had her answer. In the Hendricks family, nasty was in the genes.

Sabrina's mom pursed her lips.

"If you don't want to be stuck here forever, you'll mind your manners. I need to help Sabrina first. You think about what you meant to do before you passed away. Molly can help with any questions you have."

Madam sniffed but eyed Molly, who had changed into a kelly-green Chanel suit with three strands of pearls and a pillbox hat. Jackie O. would have approved.

"Sabrina met a boy," Molly said, and grinned when Sabrina scowled. "And he's sweet on her."

Her mom raised an eyebrow while Madam poked her finger through the countertop.

"Molly is usually right about these things. She's the one who pushed me toward your father."

"I know, I know. It was at the Goodbye Gala, and you were at the top of the porch, and Molly pushed you off the steps and into Dad's arms. You've mentioned this a hundred times—and you still think it's romantic rather than dangerous that Molly shoved you down the steps."

Molly stuck her tongue out at Sabrina, who returned the gesture.

"I knew he'd catch her, and that they'd fall in love because he rescued her. I would never put anyone in danger. He'd been staring at her gams for hours. There was no way he would have missed. I'm like Cupid—just cuter."

"That was the first time I saw you poof," Sabrina's mom said.

"We poof?" Madam said.

Molly tapped her lips, then responded. "When we interact with solid objects, it uses up energy, and we don't have enough to stay visible or control where we are. The longer we're around, the stronger we are. Belle can do all sorts of things."

"Belle? As in Belle Boyd, the Confederate spy?" Madam looked shocked.

"Yes. Bit of bitch, too. Stay out of the cemetery. She won't like you." Molly paused. "Anyway, it was a couple of weeks before your mom could see me again. I just floated around having to watch the two of them neck all the time."

"Ew," Sabrina said at the same time as her mom spoke.

"It wasn't all the time. And I didn't know you were watching." Her mom's cheeks turned even pinker.

"I couldn't control where I was," Molly said with a shrug.

"So, about this boy." Sabrina's mom winked at Molly and leaned closer to Sabrina. "Tell me."

"You know those giant refillable margarita glasses? This is what happens when a full one hits your face." Sabrina pointed at her face, which was starting to purple around the eyes.

"That's not what I'm asking about." Her mom poked her fingers at the puffy skin around her nose while Sabrina picked up the ever-present obituary page on the kitchen table. Given their family secret, it came in handy when they had to identify a new ghost.

Sabrina knew what her mom wanted to know. Even with three grandkids making an unholy racket in the bathroom upstairs—and probably starting a small flood—her mom wanted more of them. Her brothers, Brendan and Trent, were definitely done, so it was up to Sabrina to expand the Monroe family tree—and nothing would make her mom happier than expanding it nearby. It was too bad that the thought of dating made her throat close up.

Her mom set a gentle hand on her cheek. "Breathe."

So she did.

Breathe in. Breathe out. Breathe in. Breathe out.

Sabrina repeated it as her mom studied her nose.

"It's not broken, but it's going to look awful and hurt worse for a few days. Keep ice on it."

Before keeping her grandchildren hopped up on sugar, her mom had been a nurse at the local hospital. After long hours caring for other people, she would come home and continue her second shift with her own brood, where there had always been scrapes and bruises to bandage and kiss in addition to her responsibilities to the family profession. Sabrina didn't want that. She could barely manage her own life. Her mom pursed her lips while still studying Sabrina's face.

"Have you called a therapist?"

Sabrina's silence told her everything she needed to know.

"Janie from bridge club adores hers. Says she taught her to be the goddess she always knew she could be. Here's the number."

Her mom handed her a piece of paper. Sabrina didn't need a number or to be a goddess. She needed to get away from the Dells. To get someplace where ghosts couldn't pop out of nowhere and ruin her life. Even Molly, whom she loved like a sister, made normal life impossible with the constant fear that someone would discover her secret.

A loud bang and splash followed by laughter came from upstairs and saved her from having to respond.

"Madam, we'll get you sorted soon. I'd better get up there before we all float away," her mom said, then left the kitchen.

"I'm off to clean this mess," Sabrina said to Molly, before leaving her and Madam chatting in the kitchen.

If only the rest of her life could be washed away like drying margarita and the remnants of her dignity.

Sabrina stripped out of her stained bathing suit while standing in the shower, scrubbing at the red-tinged skin, before drying off and changing into a comfortable summer dress, which was loose and soft against her tense muscles. Looking in the mirror, she smoothed her hair into a ponytail and winced at the darkening skin around her eyes. That would never do for work.

She dug her makeup bag out of her still-packed suitcase and dumped it on the bed for the first time since coming home. She rarely wore more than a tinted lip balm and sunscreen, and maybe a bit of mascara and powder if she had to interview someone for work, but she owned nothing robust enough to hide the emerging purple. It would be worse tomorrow morning when she had to go to work.

She did the mental math on a trip to Walmart. Twenty-two minutes of round-trip driving. Ten, no, fifteen minutes to pick out a concealer. Five minutes to check out. She could be back home in forty-two minutes. She could handle forty-two minutes if she kept interactions with other people to a minimum. Forty-two minutes, then she could crash on her bed and shut out the world.

Next she grabbed her key chain and wallet, which contained a few dollar bills and her credit cards. All her tips went into the giant cheese-ball jug on her dresser.

As she settled into her car, she could see Mrs. Randolph's door bulging where she'd put the duct tape. Every few seconds it would expand like it was breathing. Mr. Bennett was attempting another prison break.

She added a stop at the hardware store to her ticking clock. Sixty-five minutes.

:◦⟩꠹♡⟨◦:

SABRINA HAD MADE GREAT time, catching all the green lights and avoiding slow drivers. A parking spot had waited for her near the door, and she already had the perfect concealer picked out, designed for maximum coverage. She'd even completed a quick search online for reviews to make sure it met the claims on the package—it did.

Internet research had always been her strength as a journalist. That, and the writing. She loved how the right words could reveal truths. It was the pushy part she hated, the way her mouth went dry and her stomach twisted every time she reached for her phone to call a source, the furiously thumping heart and flooding sweat when she met someone for an interview. Those should have been all the signs she needed to know she'd picked the wrong career. But that would mean admitting she'd amassed debt and wasted six years of education on a specific job. She wasn't qualified for anything else. If she could be left alone with her computer, she'd be fine. At her last job, back in Washington, DC, she hadn't even hidden it. It wasn't layoffs that had gotten her fired; she'd missed one too many deadlines because she'd spent too much time scouring the internet rather than making a few quick calls. They'd lost out on an exclusive, and she'd lost her job. But how else was she going to get out of her hometown? She just needed enough money to make a dent in her bills and a new job as an excuse to leave.

Clutching the smooth tube of concealer, she joined the shortest line—only one person. Giddy with her success, she turned to pick up a candy bar. Standing right behind her was Ray from the waterpark, fully clothed, wearing glasses, and even more attractive. She couldn't leave or switch lanes. She was trapped. Maybe he wouldn't recognize her now that she was showered and less red. Snatching a Twix while keeping as much of her face turned forward as possible to avoid him, she couldn't resist a quick glance.

He was staring right at her, and recognition lit up his eyes. A genuine smile joined it, as if he was truly glad to bump into her.

"Hey," he said. "Glad you're all right. Your cookies were amazing. I wondered how I'd find you to return your container. I'll have to start carrying it for when we run into each other again."

Again? She hoped not. How did he have so much to say? Did he expect her to respond in kind? Wait . . . he had been thinking about her? Against her better judgment, that pleased her.

The cashier had scanned her two items, so she used that as an excuse not to answer him, instead pulling out a credit card. A few singles that had been jammed in next to the card fell to the ground. She just wanted to pay and leave. She quickly tapped her credit card before picking up the dropped bills, forcing a tight smile. Was that enough of a response?

The cash register made a sad beep, and the cashier turned her head to the screen.

"I'm sorry, your card was denied." She said the words the same annoyed way a frustrated parent might scold the ice cream shop worker who didn't add enough sprinkles to their spoiled child's sundae.

Sabrina's heart chugged, and a line of sweat formed on the back of her neck.

"I'll try again."

This time she shoved it into the chip reader. Maybe the tap didn't work? Or there was a blip in the system somewhere? But the growing pit in her stomach knew better. She'd relied on her credit cards too much in DC. Did it have to catch up with her right here? This time, she and the cashier both stared at the screen, while Ray tactfully studied the gum selection. She wanted to pretend he wasn't there, but he was like a giant handsome elephant in a tiny room.

The sad beep dinged again.

"I'm sorry. Do you have a different card? Cash?"

She looked at the two bills wadded up in her hand.

"Here," Ray said, his card extended toward her.

Oh my God. He was going to buy her things, acknowledging that he was fully aware that her card had been rejected. Her wobbly knees made it clear she needed to leave before she lost all muscle control, but the good manners drilled into her by her mother won out.

"No, thank you." Sabrina hoped she'd said the words loud enough.

She couldn't meet his or the cashier's eyes. With her gaze on the ground in front of her, Sabrina left the store, bumping into one other shopper on the way to the exit. She should have known better than to tempt her luck today. Bad things always happened to her in the Dells, though it seemed so much worse with a handsome stranger as witness to her humiliations.

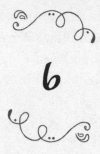

6

RAY BREATHED THROUGH HIS mouth as he stood in the doorway
of his uncle's hospital room. Hospitals smelled the same, no matter
where they were, the same antiseptic odor covering up the sadness
and heartbreak, suffering and hope. It could have been lilacs bathed
in rainbows, and Ray's mother, Claire Jasper, would still make the
same pinched expression as she looked around the small hospital
room where Uncle Harry lay flanked by Ray's parents and beeping
machines. It wouldn't be long now. His liver had finally flown a
white flag after a lifetime of rich foods and frequent brandy, and it
wasn't pretty. Sometimes he'd be lucid, and other times he wouldn't
know where he was or who was there.

"Ray." Uncle Harry whispered his name when he saw Ray in the
doorway. His parents turned to face him, his mother's lips tightening
further. Ray ignored them.

"Uncle." He grasped Uncle Harry's hand. It was cold, as if the
blood couldn't be bothered to travel that far anymore, the skin yel-

lowish and bruised. Ray willed the heat to transfer from his hand to Harry's. "I learned that Wisconsin has three times more bars than grocery stores." Harry was the one who'd encouraged him to learn more about the state's food and drink if he was going to own a restaurant. He struggled to think of anything else, his mind blank except for the one topic he had to tell someone about. "I asked someone out for a drink. She shot me down, but I'm hoping she'll give me another chance."

Uncle Harry's lips turned up a bit, even as his lids slid shut and he dozed off. Ray kept holding his hand. He wanted to tell him all about meeting Sabrina and her cookies, which he'd already eaten half of, wanting to get to know her more with each taste. Uncle Harry might even know her.

The room stayed quiet for an entire thirty seconds before his mother started.

"What nonsense is this about meeting someone? Don't tell me you're dating," she said.

"Okay, I won't."

She sniffed, then frowned. Ray enjoyed it. His mom was too invested in his love life.

"Once we get back home, we'll have dinner with the Sullivans. Their daughter just finished at Wesleyan. Or was it Sarah Lawrence? One of those. We'll have that duck dish you like so much. Maybe open up a few special bottles from the cellar. What do you think, darling?" Claire said, turning to her husband.

"That sounds lovely," Raymond Jasper III said, smiling at his wife, though Ray was certain he hadn't heard one word. His dad operated on a Pavlovian response, honed over forty years of marriage. When his wife said "darling," he said "That sounds lovely." She was going to do whatever it was anyway, no matter what he said, and it saved him hours of tedious conversation. It worked most of the time. Ray had vowed years ago to avoid a similar fate.

"I'm staying here, so unless the Sullivans' daughter wants to come to Wisconsin for dinner, I'm going to miss it."

"You're being absurd. Tell him he's being absurd, darling."

"That sounds lovely."

Ray bit his lip to keep from laughing. This was not one of those times when the standard answer worked.

Claire huffed.

"Raymond Jasper, I need you to back me up on this. Ray needs to come back to New York, not fritter his life away at the end of the world."

"Mother, this is not the end of the world. We have the internet and electricity, even running water. There's nothing left for me in New York."

"Your career is there."

"My career can be wherever I want it to be. I want it to be here, at The Otter Club."

"What am I supposed to tell people?"

"Make up whatever you want."

"We are not going to support this little hobby."

Ray clenched his jaw.

"I can support myself. The restaurant will be in the black soon. I might not have loved real estate, but I was great at it. I know a good investment."

"Raymond." His mother's tone made it clear that his father was to deploy the next stage of their two-pronged attack.

With a sigh, his dad stood and walked to his wife's side.

"We'll sell the Jasper properties here, then you'll have no reason or place to stay." He paused. "Including his house and Harry's half of the restaurant."

Ray's mouth dropped open. Jaspers never sold land unless they meant to make a tidy profit.

"You can't do that. I'm living there, and it's in Uncle Harry's name."

"And soon it will be in mine. We're his heirs, being the closest living relatives," his dad said.

"We'll sell it all to get you back home," his mother said.

Ray frowned. He didn't have enough cash to buy out the other half of the restaurant—he'd used most of his reserves on improvements, leaving just enough for living expenses while the restaurant found its footing. Every part of the Jasper legacy in the Dells would be gone if his parents went through with this.

"I'll buy it." He'd find another investor.

"You don't have the money," his dad said, his tone sad, like he didn't enjoy manipulating his son that way. "We won't sell to another investor. You'll have to sell to us or default."

"Why are you doing this?" Ray asked.

"We know that going back home is best for you," his mother said.

What did they want from him? To take over the family's business, Jasper Holdings? Lucy wanted it, not him. Ray had to find a way to keep the house and the restaurant, at least. With the house, he could do what he'd come here to do. Ray scrambled for something, anything, to make his parents change their minds.

"A Jasper always needs to be in the Dells," he said.

"That's Harry talking, not you," his mother said.

"That's enough, Claire," his dad chimed in. "Ray is an adult, and he's right about one thing. There's a family obligation to represent our interests here. The Jaspers are leaders, wherever they live. If you can demonstrate that to us, then we'll consider selling Harry's portion of the restaurant to you. But you'll need to find the money."

"How am I supposed to prove it to you?"

"Your restaurant hosts that annual hoedown, doesn't it?" his dad asked.

"The Goodbye Gala." Ray nodded.

"Yes, that one. Show me you belong here instead of taking over Jasper Holdings," his father said. His mother opened her mouth to protest, but his dad held up his hand to stave off her comments. "Let it go."

She got up and left the room, her tiny heels clicking like precise hammer strikes to his temple.

"Thanks, Dad."

"I didn't do it for you. Your uncle Harry was a good man and they loved him here. His legacy shouldn't be forgotten. That's on your shoulders now. Do the family proud."

His father left the room to join his mother. Ray looked down at Uncle Harry's shrunken form under the thin hospital blanket, the machines' beeps a metronome for his racing thoughts. Where to begin? He had no idea what invisible benchmark his dad could have in mind, but he knew he had to find it. Planning the gala was already a huge challenge—he had only attended the event once in his life. He needed help—someone who knew the area and the other local businesses. His staff would do the food, but a successful event needed more. He knew his future lay here in the Dells, but first he would have to pull off a successful event to earn that chance.

1

THE NEXT DAY AT work, Sabrina ducked into the staff bathroom as a horse tail of sleek blond hair swayed ahead of her. Erika Hendricks. Heiress to the Real Dells Ducky Tours, granddaughter to Madam Hendricks, local socialite (if one could be considered a socialite in the Wisconsin Dells), and childhood tormenter. Erika never missed an opportunity to exert her superiority over Sabrina, but Sabrina didn't intend to give her a chance today. The chill from the cinder block wall seeped through her white polo shirt as she leaned against it. With the sun shining and a full schedule of tours, it was going to be too good a day to let it be ruined by that spoiled harpy. Sabrina counted to sixty as she retucked her shirt into her navy-blue shorts, unnecessarily smoothing the material, and straightened her bright-yellow bucket hat, pulling it tight onto her head like a fisherman in a rainstorm. She pulled out her phone, opening the news app and clicking to the top stories. A flood in Southeast Asia, an early-season hurricane brewing over the Atlantic, another politician said something stupid. Oh, look, a mama cat had adopted some baby raccoons.

Deep breath.

Pulling the hat farther down her forehead, Sabrina yanked the door open, squinting at the bright sunlight from under the hat's brim. Most of her coworkers hated the childish hat, complete with a rubber ducky insignia, but Sabrina liked it. It added an extra barrier between her and the world around her, a mini portable shelter. Logically, she knew that made no sense, but psychologically, it was like carrying around a roof. Add to that her essential dark sunglasses and scripted talking points and she was well armed for a day of speaking aboard duck boats full of strangers. With luck, she'd leave with a couple hundred dollars of cash on top of her daily wage. After the horror of Walmart, she needed every penny.

Tourists stood in long winding lines, ready to buy their tickets and hop onto the next available duck that waited next to the loading chute, where guests would board the amphibious vehicle. Ducks carried twenty passengers, plus herself, with a hopper seat for an additional two, but she only let kids sit up there—adults made small talk. Each vehicle was navy blue with a white canopy over the seats. On both sides and on the top were large yellow ducks wearing the same hat she wore. Its name was Ducky. Ducky the Duck.

Sabrina stood in the shade of the garage near the bathrooms where the mechanics kept the boats in working order. Each one was an actual duck boat used in World War II, so keeping them running was a major investment every season. It was time to get hers in line for tours.

"P. S.," a nasally voice said, slurring the letters together so it sounded like "piss." Erika. Of course, she would use Sabrina's hated middle school nickname—short for Psycho Sabrina, because kids sucked. Suddenly light-headed, she shoved her sunglasses onto her face so Erika's shiny hair wouldn't blind her, bumping her bruised nose in the process.

"Erika." She had to choke out the name, but Erika didn't notice. She never listened to anyone.

"Mother said you were working here this summer. It's always nice to have older employees who won't be out socializing every night." Erika didn't look her in the face, instead surveying the area around them in case anyone more interesting appeared, her black sundress— absorbing all the light, just like its owner—the only sign that Erika grieved for her grandmother's death.

Sabrina stayed silent. What was she supposed to say? Erika was right. She wouldn't go out at night.

"I'm higher management now, so I'm taking over scheduling. Let me know if you have any conflicts." She smirked under her tiny, straight nose, which was definitely different from the one she'd had in eighth grade.

Erika paused, either to give Sabrina a chance to respond or merely to make her squirm in the silence. Sabrina counted her breaths. *One, two, three.* But the silence became too much, and good manners won out. Death was not something her family ignored, no matter how much Sabrina wished they would.

"I'm sorry to hear about your grandma. I'm sure she'll be missed."

Her mom had told her what had happened when she'd gone to the Hendrickses' home with Madam's specter in tow.

"That family," her mom had said. "They wouldn't believe in gravity if it didn't keep them on the ground. I finally barged into their house and dug the family diamonds out from behind a loose brick in the attic. They would have taken the house apart board by board before believing she told me postmortem where they were hidden."

Erika had already taken a swing with a sledgehammer to the bedroom wall."

Now Erika rubbed those same diamonds, sparkling on her ears, and pursed her lips. "You didn't know her."

Sabrina blinked. So much for social niceties.

"I should . . ." Sabrina pointed to the duck, the one excuse Erika couldn't begrudge her. Sabrina stepped into the sun, and Erika gasped.

"What happened to your face? Take off your glasses."

Sabrina eased them off her face, her eyes dropping to Erika's shoes rather than make eye contact without the barrier of her glasses. Erika's tanned and perfectly pedicured feet—the nails were painted a burnished gold—wore slide sandals, but not just any sandals. Gucci. They were a soft-pink stitched leather with two golden Gs marking the top of each shoe. Before Sabrina could rally for an actual response, Erika kept talking. Her nose crinkled as she studied Sabrina's bruised eyes and nose.

"Don't you have any cover-up?" No, actually, she didn't. Like gremlins, the humiliations found ways to keep multiplying off each other. One humiliation had become three. At this rate, she might as well stay in bed tomorrow because the sky would definitely be falling on her head. "You can't go out looking like that. You'll scare the children."

At her waist, the two-way radio that Sabrina carried crackled to life.

"Sabrina, you coming?"

She pushed a button on the side. "On my way."

Sabrina shrugged at Erika. What was she supposed to do? The tour was ready.

"Ugh. Put your glasses back on and try not to turn around on the boat. If I get one complaint, I'll refund their money and take it out of your check."

Sabrina nodded, but before she could escape to her duck, an old man materialized next to Erika, pale skin hanging from his face, which must have once been full and flush with vigor. Thin white hair stood up on his head, decorating patches of shining scalp like snowdrifts, and a telltale hazy glow even more pronounced, like fog around a streetlamp. She twitched at his sudden appearance, drawing Erika's attention back to her.

Not now. Please, not now.

Erika's eyes narrowed and focused on the spot where Sabrina's eyes had strayed. Out of practice in ghost ignoring, she shoved her glasses back on. After years away from home, she had lost her ability to play through a ghost's sudden appearance, and this one didn't make it easy.

"*Giorno boxis! Mulleigh kluf!*" He shouted nonsense over and over at her, flailing his arms like Kermit the Frog. The new noise and Erika's scrutiny were too much. She stepped toward the duck chutes, putting her hand into her pocket to rub her phone's screen like a worry stone. If she didn't get away, Erika would have more grist for the town's gossip mill. People loved anecdotes about her family's latest wacky behavior. Her mom was immune—too many people had been helped by her at the hospital—but Sabrina was more than fair game.

"I can't help you," Sabrina whispered to the ghost, hoping Erika wouldn't notice.

Sabrina kept her eyes on the ground, speed walking toward her duck, the old-man ghost pointing at himself.

"*Razz unco. Razz unco.*" His arms waved so much she could almost feel the wind, and his voice warbled as the gibberish tumbled out. His persistent actions were weak. He must have been quite ill when he had passed.

"What was that?" Erika said.

Sabrina kept walking, the ghost barely keeping up with her. Panic flooded. She couldn't give a tour with him shouting in her ear. She stopped, hoping she was out of earshot of Erika.

"I can't help you. Go see my mother, the other glowing person." Ghosts were drawn to Sabrina and her mom like ships caught in a tractor beam, and, according to Molly, they glowed a welcoming blue. No matter where in the area Molly was, she could tell where Sabrina and her mom were. Clearly this new ghost didn't get the idea, as he kept yammering. Where was Molly when you needed her?

"Who are you talking to?" Shit. Erika had followed her.

"Myself," Sabrina mumbled. She shoved her hands deep in her pockets, and the air grew heavy around her, pushing her down. She struggled to stand against the weight of it, making her breath short and her legs wobbly. There was nowhere to go, and the garbling ghost wasn't helping.

"We can't have our drivers talking to themselves, P. S. If you can't at least pretend to be normal, then this won't work." Erika looked like she had more to say, but her phone buzzed. With a quick glance at the screen, she looked over her shoulder toward the office. "Get it together. And get some makeup for tomorrow."

Erika walked away, pulling the suffocating pressure with her. Sabrina took a deep breath, then another. Counted to ten, then to twenty, then to thirty. She could see tourists lined up on the other side of the duck, ready to board once she got there. A little girl wearing a rainbow dress and a unicorn hat peeked at her through the railings. Sabrina needed to pull it together. She couldn't melt down in front of that little girl. *Focus on her.*

She was okay.

Her stomach wasn't going to turn inside out.

Her legs weren't going to crumple.

Breathe in.

Breathe out.

She climbed the stairs leading to her empty duck, leaving the ghost on the ground behind her.

Her duck was named Normandy, but she called him Norman. The navy-blue vinyl-covered seats were narrow and tattered in places even though she'd done her best to mask them with navy-blue duct tape. Duct tape could only do so much, even on a duck. Each seat had barely fit the two slim soldiers they were designed for, let alone the widening Midwestern behinds that would soon occupy them. It was snug. The one-hour tour wasn't known for its comfort or first-class accommodations. Even so, nearly every tour of the day would be full.

She stepped into the driver's seat. The steering wheel was much larger than a car's, and the spare dashboard had a few shafts and dials not typical in a road-traversing vehicle. Coming out of the floor were a gear shift and shaft that lowered and raised the wheels when she needed to go in and out of the water.

The job was perfect for her. Driving and reciting the pun-filled speech took so much concentration, she didn't fixate on the duck full of strangers behind her, not until the end of the day, when she could collapse onto her bed.

She turned the key, and the engine roared to life. As she maneuvered the duck into the chute where Norman would get his first batch of passengers for the day, including the little unicorn girl, the new ghost appeared in the hopper seat next to her. This was not good. "Look, I can't help you, but if you don't know where to go, sit there and I'll get you to my mom later."

While she didn't understand him, he seemed to understand that she meant to help. He quieted down and sat on top of the folded hopper seat. Or appeared to sit, since he wasn't really there. Who the hell knew?

One of the other employees, Joy, who worked the passenger management side of the operation, nodded at Sabrina to see if she was ready. Sabrina slid the headset on over her hat and nodded back.

Let's do this.

"Good morning and welcome to the Real Dells Ducky Tours. As you board, please get seated quickly, with two people per seat. It's a full tour, so every seat needs to be filled." The passengers squashed themselves into the bench seats, with the little unicorn girl right behind the driver's seat next to her dad. An older man studied her, and she girded herself for the inevitable comment.

"You sure a little lady like you can handle this? Let me know if you need a hand."

Har, har.

Sabrina had learned long ago to ignore the comment as if she hadn't heard. There was always at least one person, predictably an older man, who made some sort of reference about a woman driver. Usually the comments came at the beginning or end, but one annoying fellow had made them anytime the duck hit a bump—which happened all through the tour, as ducks didn't have great suspension.

"Welcome to Norman. He served during World War Two and has

a few bullet holes to prove it. He was used to ferry supplies from the boats off the coast to the beach at Normandy. Anchors aweigh."

She slid into her seat, pressed the clutch, and released the brake as she shifted into first gear.

"Norman is thirty-two feet long, nine feet high, seven and a half tons, and can go fifty-five miles per hour on land and twelve knots in the water, but yesterday I had him up to five hundred miles per hour right off the edge of this cliff." Sabrina zoomed the duck down a steep hill as a mix of groans, laughs, and a squeal from the unicorn girl let her know they were paying attention. "And do keep in mind, if you fall overboard, remember to grab the person next to you. I don't stop for just one."

She settled into her monologue, driving the duck as if it were a perfectly choreographed musical number. Recite the line, move the stick shift, drop the punch line, hit the gas, swoop down the hill. Stomp, kick, turn, sashay, jazz hands. Kick, ball change, kick, ball change.

It was early for her brain to go rogue, but it had been a rough morning. If some mental ridiculousness got her through, she'd gladly accept it. Survival for her was about countering harsh reality with any levity she could muster.

The white-haired ghost sat next to her, wild-eyed as they dipped into the Wisconsin River, and she adjusted the correct crank to pull the wheels up and then engaged the motor.

"I've just disengaged the wheels, so if you look over the side, you'll see them slowly sinking to the bottom." She paused to let them groan.

Settled into cruise control, she let the tour routine take over. The layered sandstone that lined the river ranged from light gray to orange-brown depending on its composition. Growing from any crack or crevice that could collect enough soil to hold roots were small scraggly trees, weeds, and the random stubborn pine, as if growing off the wall made them more daring than their brethren, which were perched on top like erratic hair. The flaky layers of stone—worn from water, wind, and roots—resembled a croissant and looked like you could peel back each one and pop it into your mouth. The imagination liked to assign shapes and meaning to nature's random beauty—like a giant piano or observant hawk.

Toward the end came her least-favorite part of the tour. The shakedown. But it was also where she made the biggest dent in her towering debt. Stopping Norman at a quiet, secluded spot, she turned off the engine.

"Okay, people, as you know, we at the Real Dells Ducky Tours are struggling college students trying to avoid a mountain of debt."

Too late for her.

"Most of our income comes from the generous tips of our hostages—I mean *guests*. I'm going to pass around this jar, and when it hits the line, we can head back. For those of you interested in more than the satisfaction of paying off my student loans, for five dollars, you can get a stack of Real Dells Ducky Tours historical postcards, complete with fun facts about the beautiful sites you've seen today, including this very rare postcard of Norman and me. This is the only place you can buy this fine collectable. They don't sell on eBay, I've tried. I mean, I've checked."

Ugh. Everything about this felt icky. It must have finally crossed a line with the new ghost, because even he disappeared. She was a bit envious of him. Other ducks were parked nearby, with their guides giving the same sad performance.

The jar made its way around the duck, filling with mostly singles, but a few generous or sympathetic guests gave her five dollars. Every bit counted. When the jar made its way back to her, she fired up Norman and headed back to camp.

Sabrina could make it through the day. Then she would make it through tomorrow. She could make it through this summer. Five more tours in the day to go.

8

THE SUN SHONE. THAT was the only good thing Sabrina could say about her day. Between Erika and that rambling old ghost, her nerves were fried. At least her mom and Molly could help with one of the problems.

Her mom puttered around the kitchen, making her nightly tea for herself and Dad, Doug Monroe, while Molly touched the red burner with her finger.

"Will you stop that?" her mom said. "I know you can't feel it, but it's still hard to watch."

Molly laughed and pulled her hand away.

"It keeps things interesting," Molly said. "Hi, Sabrina."

Sabrina's mom turned to face her. "Hello, dear. Would you like a cup?"

"Yes, please." Sabrina sat at the table and pulled the obits toward her. "Have either of you seen a new ghost? Old man, white hair?"

Her mom set the tea in front of her, the soothing chamomile scent relaxing her tense face muscles. She took another deep breath. Better.

"I haven't. Molly?" Molly shook her head and joined them at the table. "Did he tell you his name?"

"He could only speak gibberish."

Her mom rubbed Sabrina's back and looked at the obit page along with Sabrina. "These are today's, so depending on when he died, he might not be in them yet. It can take a few days."

Sabrina scanned the page and didn't see anyone who matched the man she saw.

"Gibberish, you say." Her mom sipped her tea. "He must have been really sick."

"He should be able to speak eventually," Molly said. "It might take some time to get real information from him, but he'll get there. We'll keep trying."

"What about Mr. Garnham?"

Her mom frowned. "No, he's fine. I spoke to him this morning."

Sabrina sighed and held up her phone. "Maybe he knows."

"Of course. I'll call him."

She grabbed her own phone and called. Her mom had him as one of her favorites. As the owner of the local funeral home, Mr. Garnham was one of the few people in town who knew the family secret—there was a lot of crossover between their jobs.

"Hi, Alfie. How are you? . . . I'm fine . . . I'll tell Doug to call."

Sabrina flicked through the news on her phone while her mom made small talk. Conversations were never efficient in this town.

"So, Alfie, I'm calling for a reason. We have a new one and I'm not sure who it is . . . Oh no . . . That'd be great if you could send a photo. Thanks, Alfie."

Before her mom set the phone down, it pinged with an incoming photo. She held it up for Sabrina to see.

It was close. If he had whiter hair, and a gaunter face. She squinted.

The blue eyes were the same, as was the strong chin. The picture was followed by his obituary, which hadn't been printed yet.

Harold James Jasper.

"That's him."

Molly and her mom leaned over her phone.

"Such a shame," her mom said. "He'd been sick for a long time, so that explains quite a bit. I wonder what he needs?"

Molly covered her mouth, and her eyes sparkled with tears. While the community didn't know about her, she had known most of the local residents since they were children, so deaths were always hard on her. As far as Sabrina knew, Molly attended most of the town's funerals. Was it the loss of their presence that upset her or that they managed to move on to somewhere Molly couldn't go? Sabrina couldn't say.

"I'll have to go to the funeral. Your father and I knew him. What a character," her mom said. "He once let a goat loose in Noah's Ark. It was after hours, but the poor thing left droppings everywhere and tipped over all the garbage bins."

"Poor goat."

"I think it had the time of its life, or at least it ate like it did." Her mom patted her hand. "Don't worry, the goat was fine."

Sabrina stared at the photo. There was something familiar that she couldn't identify. She shook her head. It would come to her eventually.

For now, she just wanted to feel better.

"Dinner will be ready in an hour—your dad's grilling burgers. Bring your appetite because he bought way too much for three people."

"Maybe she can invite Ray," Molly said.

"I will not be inviting anyone, even it if means I'm eating burgers for a week."

Sabrina could tell her mom and Molly weren't going to let it go. She'd have to leave and knew the perfect way to kill an hour and improve her day—it had worked since high school. In her room, she grabbed two five-dollar bills from her tip jug, notecards, and a pen, then headed to the library.

:ᴄᴊᴊ˚ᴠ:

RAY STACKED TWO MORE cookbooks onto a nearby table at the local library, careful to square them so they wouldn't topple and disturb the serene afternoon. Deep in the 600s, he'd discovered a trove of regional cookbooks, which he planned to scour for Wisconsin recipes he wanted to master. First up was a beer-cheese soup. Already thinking about the different cheeses he wanted to try, he picked up his stack and headed toward the checkout, not noticing the leg sticking out from the N-through-T row of fiction. Instinct pulled back his foot as soon as it encountered uneven ground, but his other leg had already lifted off. His only option was to crumple sideways or risk hurting the leg's owner. Books flew out of his hands and slid across the floor—literary blood spatter. His left elbow caught the brunt of his weight, shooting pain like lightning up his arm. Damn. He needed that arm.

"I'm so sorry," said a now-familiar voice.

He pushed his glasses back into place, looked over at the woman speaking to him, and smiled. Sabrina. She was on her knees next to him.

"Hey," Ray said, pushing himself up and moving his arm to test the extent of damage. He could move it, though it smarted when he extended it fully. It would be tender, but nothing permanent. Now he could focus on what was important—Sabrina in front of him.

"You okay?" she said.

"I'll be fine once I get some ice on it."

Surely she could see this was some kind of sign. Three random meet-ups, even in this small town, showed they had something in common. The universe wanted them to get to know each other.

She sat back on her heels, adding more distance between them—clearly not seeing the same message. She slid some paper into a book and set it back on the shelf. He noted the title, but didn't comment. If she was up to something, he could figure it out later.

"Let me help," she said, picking up some of the books he'd dropped. There were more notecards in her jeans' back pocket.

She retrieved the few books nearest him. Careful not to touch him when she set the books in his hands, her eyes scanned the titles.

"I like to try new recipes. I'm mastering Wisconsin cuisine." Ray wanted to keep her talking, discover more about her and why she kept popping up wherever he went.

"Wisconsin cuisine? Is that even a thing?" Sabrina asked.

He smiled. "Have some state pride. You know, kringle, booyah, fish boils, cheese curds. Do you have a favorite?"

Sabrina took a few breaths before responding.

"Kringle . . . and anything with cheese." A tiny smile curved her lips.

"Then I'll start there." Ray smiled, hoping she'd relax around him. "Can I count on you to be a guinea pig? I'll need someone to tell me if I get it wrong."

"Sure?"

She didn't look sure. She rubbed her hands over her arms and checked over her shoulder as if confirming that the path for retreat was clear. He didn't want to make her uncomfortable.

"Thanks for helping pick up the books. I'd better check these out. See you soon." He pointed to the circulation desk.

"Sorry again. For tripping you."

"Always a pleasure to see you, even if I get a few bruises."

She glanced up at him, her own bruises surrounding her eyes.

"Seems to be a theme with us," Sabrina said.

Her hands shook slightly before she shoved them into her pockets.

He unsettled her, but not enough that she couldn't crack a joke. Progress.

Seeing her chance, Sabrina waved and escaped before he could say anything else. He waited to make sure she was really gone, then set his books on the floor, stretching his arm again in the process to test for a more serious injury. He slid out the book that Sabrina had been holding and opened it up to the piece of paper.

It was an anonymous note for whomever checked out the book next along with five dollars.

Here's a treat for someone with exceptional taste in books.

Sabrina was leaving surprises for readers in books. With her rejected credit card, he doubted she had the spare money, but she did it anyway. Why?

She was a breath of fresh air compared to the women his mom set him up with. Ever since he'd first seen Sabrina covered in margarita, a tension had eased inside him. He could breathe, just like when he stood outside on the deck of his supper club. And somehow each new detail he uncovered about Sabrina intrigued him even more.

9

"I'M HOME!" SABRINA SHOUTED as the screen door slammed behind her and she pulled herself up the handful of steps into the kitchen. Since seeing Ray at the library, she'd managed to have a few long but uneventful days at work with no surprise run-ins with Ray or his adorable glasses and easy smile. Sigh. Between that and the embarrassing Walmart incident, she could never see him again. So far, so good.

In the kitchen, her mom, wearing a navy-blue-and-white-gingham sleeveless dress with its collar turned up and a white sweater wrapped around her shoulders, looked ready for a night of drinking gin rickeys at a country club. Molly wore the same outfit, except in bright-pink-and-white gingham and with a faint blur around her. Both sat at the kitchen table with another woman. The hazy third woman was in her midfifties, with unnaturally red hair, light brown and gray at the roots, that clashed with a thin pale-pink cotton dress similar to a hospital gown. Her arms waved as she spoke, while her mom and Molly listened closely to her story. Sabrina wanted to flop onto her bed, but that was clearly not going to happen.

At the stove, her dad stirred a pot with a wooden spoon, oblivious to the side of the conversation he couldn't hear. Sabrina kissed him on the cheek and peeked into the saucepan. Homemade fudge sauce. Her favorite. She stuck her finger in it and sucked the chocolate off.

"There's ice cream in the freezer. YOLO-gurt, right?" her dad said.

Sabrina rolled her eyes but gave her dad another kiss.

"Who's that?" Sabrina whispered to him. She planned to get up to her room before her mom could wrangle her.

"Don't be rude, dear," her mom said. Too slow. "Mrs. Smoot just arrived and is telling us about her husband. She suspects he's been unfaithful and plans to catch him in the act."

Great. A paranoid ghost. That always went well.

"I'm going to bed."

"No, you're going to pull up a chair and be polite to our new guest."

Molly's and Mrs. Smoot's faces reacted as each of the Monroe women spoke, following the back and forth. Her mom's eyebrow rose—just the left one, but it might as well have been a loaded pistol holding her at gunpoint. Sabrina pulled out the last remaining chair and plopped into it. Molly gave her a sympathetic smile, then returned her attention to Mrs. Smoot.

"You were saying?" Molly said.

"Well, I know the bastard has been seeing someone else for years. I mean, I was in the hospital for cancer and he couldn't stop philandering. He would sneak out when he thought I was asleep, and when he returned, he would smell like he'd bathed in drugstore perfume. I was dying, but I could still smell. I've never been able to catch him at it, but now . . ." She motioned to herself.

"Sometimes it takes a while before you can control what you're wearing," Molly said.

"Is that why I'm still in my hospital gown and you're straight out of a magazine?"

"I've been around a lot longer. I have more control over the razzle-dazzle of it all."

"Will I be able to slap him? I'd love to give him a good solid whack before I go. That would be satisfying."

Molly frowned. "Touching things is tricky. It takes a lot of energy and concentration. Maybe in a few years you could, but even I can't do much. When I do, they can't see me for a week or more, so I only do it when absolutely necessary. You wouldn't even be able to poke him in the face."

Mrs. Smoot scowled. "Then how will I make sure he knows that I know? Make him feel my pain?"

"Mom can do it." Sabrina said. If she had to sit here, she was going to make the most of it.

"Sabrina, I am not going to slap people," her mom said. But Mrs. Smoot seemed to love the idea and nodded to herself, probably imagining her husband's expression of shock when a strange older woman smacked him unexpectedly.

"You will if it's what she needs to move on." Her mom narrowed her eyes at Sabrina. She knew that Sabrina was right—her mom was committed to the family calling and would do anything short of a felony—and even then, it depended on the crime. She'd seen her mom collect dog poop at the park into a paper bag, set it on a porch, and light it on fire. A slap was nothing. It would almost be worth following her around with Mrs. Smoot so she wouldn't miss it. Almost. A wave of exhaustion hit her, draining all her energy at once, like someone had pulled the plug on an inflatable mattress.

She couldn't sit at this table for one more second. It was like this sometimes. Life would roll over her like a boulder she didn't see coming. Too many good days in a row could do that—make her think she was in control. She could almost hear her brain laughing at her naivete. She stood, and her mom gave her the eyebrow again.

"Spoons are gone," Sabrina said, and shuffled from the room. The conversation continued as she left, but she no longer cared to listen.

She'd played her get-out-of-jail-free card. "Spoons" was their code word for when she needed to retreat. Spoon theory was the best way to describe how a day could sap her energy. Everyone started each day with a number of spoons, some people started with more than others. Every activity used up a certain number of spoons, and when they were gone, then the energy was gone for the day. For Sabrina, everything required a lot of spoons, and she didn't have many to begin with. Using the railing to get her body upstairs, each step felt higher and steeper than the last. At the top of the stairs, she looked toward the bathroom at her right. A shower would feel amazing, but she might not have enough energy to finish. She wanted dark and quiet and silence. In her room, she pulled her blackout drapes closed, shut her door, and flopped onto her bed, her work clothes still on, sunscreen and dried sweat from a day in the sun still sticky on her skin. The tiniest amount of light seeped under the curtains, just enough to see Molly when she appeared next to her bed.

"Hiya, hon. You okay?"

"Bleh." She pulled the covers back. "I need to refuel before I do it all again tomorrow."

Molly nodded.

"That Mrs. Smoot is vengeance on fire. I'm not sure one slap will be enough for her." Molly set her hand on Sabrina's arm. It was weird how she could almost feel the warmth under the chill, but she'd decided long ago it was her brain tricking her. "Anything else happen?"

Sabrina rolled onto her side. How did Molly always know?

"Ray. I'm so stressed about running into him again."

Molly didn't even try to hide her smile.

"It's not going to happen," Sabrina said.

"Why not? He's perfect."

"You don't know that. He could steal candy from children and kick puppies."

Molly rolled her eyes and ignored her comment. "Did he see you? Did you talk? Did he flirt?"

"So much worse. I tripped him at the library a few days ago." Sabrina told her all the details. "Every time I see him, something horrible happens to me. The way it's going, the next time I see him, all my clothes will unravel."

"One can only hope."

"Molly!"

"I only mean it's been a hot minute since you've been with someone. It's healthy."

"Not for me."

Molly pursed her lips, but Sabrina didn't want to give her a chance to respond.

She didn't want to relive Charles and how just when she'd thought she could trust him, he'd left her for an up-and-coming environmental lobbyist. The next week, she'd lost her job and had to move home.

"You want to watch something?" Sabrina's voice came out scratchy, as if it had been held just as taut as the rest of her body.

Molly nodded, and her curls bobbed. "You still haven't shown me the waterpark video."

She should have known Molly wouldn't forget.

She settled next to Molly, covering her legs with the purple bedspread she'd had since high school, pulling her laptop closer. As she had predicted, the video of the brawl was online. Several actually. She pressed Play. As it started, her dad entered her room, handed her a bowl of ice cream drowning in fudge sauce, kissed her on the head, and left. What must it be like to live in a house where half the action was invisible? He was a special man.

She dug into the already melting ice cream and scooped out a dripping spoonful. The hot and cold mixed in her mouth, chocolate and vanilla, sweet and a touch of bitter from the dark chocolate. The perfect balance of opposites.

An ad played, and Molly watched it with as much interest as any other video, captivated by the images on the small screen. Sabrina let another spoonful of ice cream melt on her tongue, studying the room. It was exactly the same as when she'd left eleven years ago, down to the faded poster of two hands cupping an apple, now more pink and gray than vibrant red and black. Next to that was a poster of Hogwarts at night, the lights twinkling. She used to fantasize that she could go there—where seeing ghosts would make her not an outcast but just like everyone else. Sadly, she wasn't that kind of special, and no owls had ever flown down their chimney.

While she had always come home for holidays, she'd never stayed long enough to update the decor, and her parents must not have wanted the task of cleaning out her things.

"It's starting," Molly said, pointing at the computer screen. There was the waterpark. A woman in a baggy swimsuit dragged a chair away from a table, and then Sabrina noticed her own head. It all happened quickly. The margarita hit her face, then Ray approached.

"There's the meet-cute!" Molly clasped her hands under her chin.

He did look good, even in this shaky footage, during the fraction of a second before she yelled at him to duck. Then they disappeared under their respective tables as cups and bottles flew and people dashed past the camera, either avoiding or getting involved in the tussle. It wasn't the most attractive side of humanity. Such a mess over a few plastic chairs.

The video ended when security arrived, cutting to black.

Sabrina closed the window on her computer.

"Such a cutie-patootie. You need to see him again." Molly said.

"Absolutely not."

A few years ago, and in another city, the answer would have been a quick yes. She'd wanted to find her someone, the person she could drive to the airport and who would surprise her with well-timed cups of coffee. But not anymore, and definitely not here. Like tube tops and Bloody Marys, romance wasn't for her. She'd be gone in a few months anyway. This meet-cute would never advance to the next stage, which was best for everyone involved.

"Go have that drink. He's asked you twice now."

"I'd rather sashay naked down Main Street."

"I did that once." Molly's eyes twinkled.

"It doesn't count when no one can see you."

"Still a thrill." Molly winked. "Meeting up again is what always happens next. You've met, you've casually bumped into each other, and now it's time to admit there's a connection. That's how it works."

"Life is not a movie."

"It should be." Molly crossed her arms with a "Humph." Sabrina scraped up the fudge around the edge of the bowl, licking it off her spoon.

"Can we watch one?" Molly asked, breaking into Sabrina's food-born revelry.

Sabrina nodded and flicked through the different streaming services, waiting for something to catch Molly's eye. This was the routine. Sabrina would flick, and Molly would say when to stop, like some sort of bizarre movie game show, where the prize was two hours of frothy, romantic fun.

"Ooooh, that one looks good."

"*Crazy Rich Asians*? Have you seen it?"

Molly shook her head. "I'm in the mood for something new. Isn't this about a regular girl who falls in love with someone rich, but his family doesn't approve?"

"Yes."

"I'd like to see a version of that where it works out."

Sabrina only knew pieces of Molly's past. She knew that Molly had been engaged to someone from one of the wealthy families in town and they hadn't approved of her, which was absurd. Molly made Jennifer Garner look like a grouch. Her fiancé had gone away, and Molly had become sick and died shortly after. She'd been a fixture of their family ever since. All Molly wanted was to see him again, but according to her mom, he'd died decades ago, so Molly was stuck. Sabrina never asked for more details, and it never seemed polite to ask. Her mom told her that her great-grandma and grandma had tried for years to help Molly move on, but they'd all given up.

Once the movie started, Molly's eyes sparkled. Her happy place was watching a story about how wonderful love could be. She never tired of them. Never got bored with the predictable nature. Sabrina wished the world really could be made better with a little more love.

With her laptop still open on her lap, Sabrina scrolled down to see the growing comments on the waterpark video, which had already racked up thousands of views. She paused on one. It was a GIF created from the video—a zoomed-up shot of her head snapping back as the margarita hit it. It played on repeat, over and over, and each time, her face throbbed with remembered pain. Who knew a person's life could be digitized into a two-second clip? One shot to the head after another, for all the world to see. She closed the window.

In her e-mail, she had ten new messages. Nine were junk, and the tenth was a bill reminder for her student loans. Her stomach clenched at the amount due. Since moving home, that had become the permanent state of her stomach. The only difference was how tight a grip. And that number was spread over the next thirty years. Thirty years of stomach-clenching payments for a journalism degree she wasn't using anymore. When she was being honest with herself, which she tried to avoid, it had all been a bad idea. She had no business being in an industry where so much depended on speaking to people. Even away from the Dells and without the added complication of spectral visitors, she couldn't change her personality. She was who she was. No wonder she'd been fired from five jobs.

She did miss the writing.

Opening a blank document on her computer, she sat with her hands poised over the keyboard, wanting to write about something, but not knowing where to begin. What mattered in the world? She had nothing to say, but a desire to say something. She reached over to her nightstand, where she kept a small notebook with story ideas. Stuffed in its pages was a sticky note with the contact information for the local therapist her mom had mentioned the other day. If she were home in DC, she'd call her therapist, schedule an extra session, get her mind in a better place.

She shoved all the papers into the notebook. She couldn't see a therapist here. It would be one more connection tying her to this place. One she couldn't pay for with money she didn't have. Seeing a new therapist felt permanent, like growing roots. She didn't want to take root here when uprooting again was too difficult. If you did it too many times, a plant could die.

She shut the computer and leaned back into her pillows, escaping into the movie where people had money and love won out in the end.

10

A SPLASH OF HOT grease singed Ray's arm. His other arm held a phone to his ear.

"Damn," he said, scurrying to the sink to douse it in cold water. The pain eased as the cold water washed away the burning oil and chilled the sore skin. He should have known better than to cook cheese curds with one hand.

"Excuse me?" said a voice on the phone.

Dammit. He had finally gotten hold of the best pork supplier in the state. After fifteen unreturned phone calls, he had been about to give up when Steve, the owner, called.

"Sorry. I burned my arm."

"If you're too busy . . ."

"No, no, it's a great time." It was the perfect time. The Otter Club was closed on Mondays to give everyone a break after the busy weekend. It was also his day to play in the kitchen without annoying his staff, which meant no one witnessed his stupidity. They already teased him enough for his sloppy attempts at cooking. They didn't need to know when he burned himself. "I've been hoping to talk to you about ordering some hogs. My chef says you're the best."

There, flattery should get this call back on track. Who didn't like a compliment?

From across the kitchen, which was large enough to contain two sink areas, every appliance a chef could want, and gleaming lines of stainless-steel counters and shelves—all of which were used to their limits on a busy Saturday night—he could see the oil bubbling like a Holiday Inn hot tub.

Dammit again. He had forgotten the curds.

At least he didn't swear out loud this time.

He rushed toward the fryer, where the charred hulls of his latest attempt at the perfect deep-fried cheese curd floated like sad empty water bottles, bumping against the sides with nothing weighing them down. He lifted the basket and dumped the remains into the garbage, where the hot debris burned a hole through the industrial black plastic, dropping through into the unlined can underneath. Now he'd have to take out the garbage, clean the can, and replace the liner. He couldn't leave the mess, or evidence, for his crew. He'd do that later, after he convinced Steve to sell him some pig.

"Yeah . . . we're sold out."

It had been the same thing from the microgreens guy he'd called and the farmer raising Wagyu-style cattle. When he finally talked to a person, they were sold out for months, maybe years. He needed the best of the best for the Goodbye Gala to ensure it was better than previous years.

"Steve, what can I do to make this happen? Do you have part of a hog you haven't been able to sell? A premium to be moved up the list? Cost is not an issue."

His stomach clenched at the idea. He'd sell off his retirement if necessary.

"I'll see what I can do and get back to you. Tell Rick I said hi and he owes me."

Hallelujah! At last something was going right.

"Thank you for your time, Steve."

Ray set down the phone with a smile and surveyed the kitchen, which had not heard the good news and cleaned itself.

He might as well take care of the garbage can mess.

When he returned from the dumpster, he washed his hands and stood in front of his station, studying his setup. He had cheese curds that were room temperature, fresh from the store this morning and still squeaky when he bit into them, which he did now—the *squeak, squeak* keeping time as he plotted what to do next. In a line, he had the curds, flour, and a beer batter—a simple mixture of Spotted Cow beer, flour, salt, pepper, and a dash of cayenne—each in its own tray. After his first failed attempt, flour and batter droplets surrounded his assembly line. With a quick wipe, he erased the worst of it and returned to his project. Obviously, the first batch hadn't worked because he had overcooked them. He couldn't be distracted. *No phone calls this time. Stay focused on the goal.*

Taking five curds, he rolled them in the flour, shook off the excess, and dropped them in the batter. Using a wire spider strainer, he lifted them out, allowing the excess to drip off, then carried them to the deep fryer, leaving a trail of drips along the floor. He rolled the battered curds out of the spider and into a waiting fryer basket, then lowered it into the oil, which hissed and spit as the food made contact. The curds rolled in the oil, going from pale to golden to brown. Just as the first bit of cheese started to poke out the side, he lifted the basket and let the oil drain for a few seconds before dumping the nuggets onto a paper towel–lined plate.

He picked up the first one and pulled it apart, the cheese stringing between his fingers like a rope suspension bridge. Good. That was the consistency he wanted. He had worried that room-temperature curds would explode out of the batter before they turned golden, but these had stayed put. Wrapping the stringy cheese around one half, he popped it all into his mouth and chewed, closing his eyes to focus on the flavor. The batter was crispy, like tempura, but it didn't have much flavor other than beer—which was fine, but not what he wanted. It added a malty bitterness that didn't balance right with the cheese. He wanted everyone to love these curds, not just beer fans. And it didn't have the crunch he wanted. It was too tender, which meant perhaps a batter wasn't the route to go. Maybe breadcrumbs would give him the texture and structure he craved. But the cheese— the cheese was perfect. Melty, stringy, yet still retaining a bit of the squeak that made fresh cheese curds so special. It would be easy enough to get the supplies from a local dairy or even the grocery stores. In Wisconsin, great cheese was easier to find than a bagel in New York.

He ate another one. The cheese itself was salty. What would work with that? Something with a little sweetness? Like a Wheat Thin or a graham cracker? He could mix crushed graham crackers with breadcrumbs for his next attempt.

He wrote down his ideas and what he liked in a small, smudged notebook on the end of the stainless-steel counter, then proceeded to batter and fry the rest of his cheese curds. They weren't perfect, but they were still deep-fried cheese.

"Ray? You here?" his sister called from the main dining room. He took the paper towel–lined plate of fresh-out-of-the-fryer gooey goodness and pushed through the swinging doors to join her, the heat from the cheese curds transferring through the porcelain. She stood behind the bar, pouring herself four fingers of his best Scotch.

"That's a Benjamin of booze you're swilling there."

She took a big sip, closing her eyes when she swallowed, as if gulping down cool water. When she opened her eyes, she studied Ray's appearance, taking in his flour-smudged black pants and grease-spattered white shirt.

"You can't go like that," Lucy said.

Ray checked his clothes, his brow scrunched, as he set the plate of cheese curds on the bar surface.

"The funeral?" Lucy said. "You forgot. Too busy with your latest experiment?" She picked up a curd and popped it in her mouth. "What is it?"

"Beer-battered cheese curds. They aren't there yet." Ray unbuttoned his white shirt, took it off, and swiped at the white smears on his legs, removing the worst of it. Lucy took another gulp as she rolled her eyes. "And I didn't forget forget—I lost track of time."

"You're a mess." She drank again, then ate another cheese curd. "They're good."

Ray smiled. Lucy didn't give compliments often, especially with anything regarding Wisconsin, though she was the most receptive to his culinary exploits.

"Mom will flay you if you show up in a T-shirt." Lucy said.

"I have a spare dress shirt in my office."

"I bet you have at least two full suits in there." Lucy set her drink on the counter and grabbed two more cheese curds.

Ray shrugged.

"Old habits die hard. Today it's paying off."

He picked up her glass and sipped. It was great Scotch. More than twenty years old and smooth—or as smooth as any whiskey could be. He winced as it burned going down.

"Can't take your booze anymore?"

"More of an old-fashioned drinker."

"That's right, you water them down into a kiddie drink here."

Ray smiled. "What's not to love? Old-fashioneds are a little sweet, a little bitter, with a cherry on top. It's life in a cocktail. I'll make some after the service. Uncle Harry would expect nothing less."

Lucy frowned and swirled the last bit of Scotch around the ice in her glass.

"You aren't going to convince me to stay, too, but I'm glad you like it here. You seem happy."

Ray looked at her, feeling decidedly unhappy. Playing in the kitchen had been a much-needed distraction. Uncle Harry had only been gone a few days, but the pit that was left was real and permanent. Lucy saw the thoughts pass over his face. She could always read people, especially him.

"I know you're not happy right now, but you were, and you will be again. And maybe there might be a brunette to help that along?" Ray wasn't ready to discuss his interest in Sabrina with Lucy. She let it slide. "As much as I tease, Wisconsin looks good on you."

"Wisconsin makes everyone better." Ray grinned.

Lucy nudged his shoulder with hers. "Will you keep the house?"

"Do Jaspers ever get rid of property?" He sighed. "Assuming Mom and Dad let me." He met her eyes, and she understood—their parents' manipulation methods didn't vary much. "They're holding The Otter hostage, too. I can't lose it or the house. There's so much history there. There are boxes in the attic that haven't been opened in decades. That's our family. There are answers in those boxes."

"To what?"

Ray hadn't shared with anyone what he had discovered in New York. Coming to the Dells had always been about more than helping Uncle Harry, and now it was time to get back on track in case his time ran out.

"I don't know yet."

Lucy narrowed her eyes. She knew he wasn't telling her everything, but she'd have to deal with it.

"Fine. Keep your secrets for now. You'll tell me eventually."

Lucy was right. He could never keep secrets from her, but he wasn't ready to share this mystery yet, not until he'd discovered some real answers. With his restaurant held hostage, he needed to rescue that first.

11

Sabrina hadn't set foot in The Otter Club for years. Thirteen years. The night of the Goodbye Gala—the town's celebration that the summer season was over—and the same night she'd vowed to escape the Dells and her family's secret and only return for short visits.

Boy, had she screwed up.

Growing up, it had been known as the River Lodge, not The Otter Club. As she and her parents walked into the log-cabin restaurant, complete with vaulted ceilings supported by log rafters, it was clear only the name had changed. Taxidermy animals still cluttered every spare patch of wall, and above the bar hung a large wooden canoe where wineglasses hung like stalactites. The wood glowed like a cozy fireplace on a chilly winter night.

Her dad fought his way to the crowded bar as her mom added their name to the waiting list. Sabrina studied the nearby animals to appear busy while she stood alone in the crowded waiting area, keeping her eyes to herself, not wanting to make eye contact with anyone, especially someone she might know. Her hand was hovering over her back pocket, where she had her phone, when something about the animals caught her eye.

She was wrong. More than the name had changed.

Many of the animals had new accessories. The stuffed squirrel had a tiny jar of Nutella. A beaver wore a delicate pair of wire-rim glasses and had a copy of *The Dam over the River Kwai* tucked under his furry arm. A trio of mice played poker, with one of them hiding an ace behind his ear. She smiled at this new touch of whimsy—a perfect fit for the supper club atmosphere because it gave the guests plenty to discover over the long evening of cocktails, socializing, and dinner.

As supper clubs went, this was a good one. The beautiful setting overlooked a wide part of the Wisconsin River she covered on her Ducky tours and created a peaceful environment where guests didn't mind waiting a couple of hours for a table. Plenty of picnic tables and Adirondack chairs encouraged patrons to wait outside, where the wait seemed shorter.

Her parents found her at the same time, her mom with a buzzer that would let them know when their table was ready and her father with three brandy old-fashioned sweets. Perched on the edge of her glass was an orange slice speared by a toothpick and topped with a dark-red cherry. She popped the cherry into her mouth and chewed. It was a good one, not the plasticky kind. This one burst on her tongue in a sweet bomb of flavor, with a boozy kick letting her know it had been soaked in brandy.

"Where should we go?" her mom asked.

"The porch has rocking chairs," her dad said. "We can pretend to be old people."

"You are old people," Sabrina said.

He led their trio in the direction of the promised chairs. She liked her parents, and under different circumstances, she'd happily live near them forever, meeting up for family dinners. It made her sad that they would never have that future. Her parents settled into a double rocking chair, holding hands between them. They were terribly cute. Goofy and a little eccentric, but cute.

Once, she had hoped to have the same thing, but with her inability to have a normal relationship with anyone, that seemed unlikely. She stood at the railing, which had been smoothed by years of diners and a thick coat of fresh varnish. She sipped her old-fashioned. Sweet and light, with notes of orange and the herb-spice flavor of bitters, all of it balanced with the subtle burn of brandy. It tasted like Wisconsin. It tasted like home. She had tried to order a brandy old-fashioned in DC, and she hadn't gotten this. Nowhere else made them quite right—and The Otter Club's version was a perfectly executed classic.

:᠅ⱸᏈᏋ᠅᠅

DINNER WENT BY SLOWLY, her parents chatting with half the people in the dining room. At one point, her dad actually got up and made rounds, like a movie producer working a room. Instead of making deals, he sold them all insurance. Between her mom, who was a former nurse, and her dad, they knew everyone, and her mom made it work despite the awkward moments when she was helping the recently deceased.

"I'm heading to the bar," Sabrina said, sliding her backpack onto her shoulder.

Her mom nodded and said, "Have them put whatever you order on our tab."

Of course, so she wouldn't spend money on something as frivolous as an after-dinner drink.

At the horseshoe-shaped bar, an empty stool was tucked at an awkward angle by the cash register, making it difficult for whoever sat there to speak to anyone but the bartender. Perfect for her. She slipped onto it and grabbed the drink menu. After this week, she wanted something ridiculous and decadent—a Pink Squirrel—almond and cocoa liqueurs blended with ice cream.

"Sabrina?"

Behind the bar and right in front of her was Ray from the waterpark. Shit. She had forgotten he might be here. What fresh disaster would unfold tonight?

Maybe a little part of her had hoped she'd see him here. But just a tiny part. The same foolhardy tiny part that had thought that drenching her brown hair with lemon juice would turn it blond or that Instagram stalking Charles post breakup and accidentally liking a photo after she had drunk a bottle of wine was a good idea.

Ray would want to chat with her. She looked at her parents' table and considered returning there, but more people had pulled up chairs. Was that the Shores? And the Bartons? The Garnhams? They all had kids she'd gone to school with. Ray waited for her response with a patient, slightly crooked smile on his face. And those dark-rimmed glasses. Sigh.

She pulled out her binder, pens, and stack of sticky notes and set them on the bar in front of her. Maybe he'd get the hint that she didn't want to chitchat.

"Hi, Ray."

"Are you here for your promised old-fashioned?"

She shook her head. "I've had two. How about a Pink Squirrel?"

"I make the best."

His smile stretched further. How could a person be that happy all the time?

"I bet you make the best everything."

"I'm still working on my cheese curds."

His cheese curds? Was he saying that because she had mentioned them the other day?

With easy movements, Ray added the ingredients to the blender and sent it whirling. He poured the cotton-candy-pink concoction into an enormous glass nearly the size of a fishbowl, piled the whipped cream impossibly high, then drizzled more of the pink liqueur on top. It was gorgeous. He slid it in front of her on a napkin that was already getting soaked as the glass overflowed.

"I got a bit carried away."

"Add it to my parents' tab. They're the loud table."

"This is on me." He wiped his hands off on a bar rag, keeping his eyes on her as she took her first sip. "Your face is looking good."

She coughed on the sweet drink. "Excuse me?" Did he actually just say her face looked good? How was she supposed to take that?

"That didn't come out right, did it? I meant most of the bruises have faded from the margarita attack. I can barely tell. I noticed them at the library, but didn't get a chance to say anything before you left. Does it still hurt?"

Whew. Classic misunderstanding. She could certainly relate to words not coming out as intended. She touched her nose.

"It's better, but still tender. I use concealer. Yellow-green is not a good look." She grimaced as she remembered the Walmart incident, but he didn't comment on it. She appreciated that.

She sipped her drink. The cold ice cream felt great on her tight throat, creamy with a sweet almond taste followed by a kick from the booze. She took a longer sip. "It goes down a little too easy."

Ray smiled, and she could tell he tried not to make the obvious that's-what-she-said joke. She focused on her drink as Ray lined up glasses and added simple syrup, an orange slice, a cherry, bitters, and some brandy. Then he muddled them all, leaving them as is so they were ready to be finished when an order came in for an old-fashioned, which happened a lot. Watching him work soothed her, like staring at waves hitting the shoreline. He had an energetic efficiency, taking new orders as he made previous ones, always a step or two ahead.

As he made drinks, she went over her notes for Arabella's party. She'd been passing along lists of businesses for her brother to contact. Once he had something booked, she marked it as complete. The tents, squishy pillows, and beanbag chairs were lined up. They'd decided to have the party on the Fourth of July in combination with their traditional gathering, since the family would already be together and Arabella wanted fireworks. They could watch the fireworks from the fancy tents, eat fancy foods, and lounge on fancy pillows. The pillows had been the trickiest because her brother and his husband didn't want to buy dozens of them, so they'd decided to borrow all the pillows from their homes and their friends' and cover them in satin and faux-fur blankets. Same effect, much cheaper. All that was left was the food, and most of that could be prepared by the family. She jotted down ideas for fancy kid-friendly food, like puff-pastry-and-cheese pinwheels and dainty chocolate tarts.

Each idea was written on a sticky note and neatly stuck to a plastic sheet inside the binder. She'd give the ideas to her brother and would toss the ones Arabella rejected. Once the menu was set, she could add the name of whoever would make the item onto the same sticky note. It was an easy way to control such a fluid list.

As she brainstormed, Ray kept checking on her to see if she was still there—a quick glance, so fast that maybe he didn't think she'd notice, but she did. And each one eased the tightness in her stomach. It was almost peaceful sitting in the crowded bar, sipping her Pink Squirrel, organizing her lists, and watching him work. She hadn't reached for her phone once.

A waitress came to the bar and spoke to Ray, then he followed her toward the kitchen's swinging doors. The couple next to her left when their buzzer buzzed, letting them know their table was ready.

"I heard you were back in town," a male voice said behind her.

Sabrina wanted to melt away, even as her body swiveled to face the voice.

"Bobby." Her voice squeaked as she said it. The last time she'd been in this building, she had been with Bobby Meltzer, heir to most of the waterparks in the city and her high school boyfriend. He appeared mostly the same, softer around the middle with shorter blond hair. The extra weight filled out his cheeks, smoothing the wrinkles like the body's own Botox. He was still cute, especially when he smiled his toothy grin at her.

"I just finished dinner with my parents," Bobby said. "They're talking to everyone around them, so I took that as my cue to get a fresh drink."

He sat on the empty stool next to her, forcing her to turn uncomfortably so she could look at him without twisting her neck, her knees bumping a wooden support beam under the bar.

He had been her first love, and her first heartbreak. She sucked up another long sip, hoping to bring back the calm. Seeing him was like being seventeen again.

"It's good to see you," he said once he ordered his Scotch. Sabrina never understood the appeal. She'd keep her ice cream drinks.

He nudged his stool as close to hers as possible, until their knees bumped under the overhanging edge of the bar. He kept his there.

"It's been a while," Bobby said, setting his Scotch onto the open page of her binder, letting condensation slide onto her pristine notes. She moved his drink and closed the binder so he couldn't do any more damage.

"Yeah." In high school, she would run her hands through his golden hair and twirl the loose curls around her fingers. The curls were gone now, leaving it looking more prickly than soft.

"Sorry about that." Ray had returned. "I brought you a treat from the kitchen." He set a basket in front of her, filled with golden balls that oozed orange cheese. "They're my cheese curds. Let me know if they meet your standards. Did you know that it used to be law in Wisconsin that every meal had to come with two-thirds an ounce of cheese? Even dessert."

Bobby grabbed a nugget.

"Thanks, dude. We'll let you know how they are."

Ray's eyes flicked from Sabrina to Bobby and back, noticing the closed binder. His head tilted to the side as he tried to figure out what he had missed.

"Ray, this is Bobby Meltzer. Bobby, this is Ray . . . I don't actually know your last name."

Sabrina could manage good manners when the situation dictated it. It was like reading lines from a script.

"Jasper. It's Ray Jasper. The fourth, but who's counting other than my parents?"

Shit. Ray was Raymond Harold Jasper IV, one of the surviving relatives from Harry's obituary. Ghost Harry was related to Ray. His family had been around as long as hers and Bobby's and Erika's, the only difference being they owned most of the town. Sabrina reeled as her mind sorted this new information. Maybe Harry wanted her to tell Ray something, but she couldn't do that. He couldn't know about her family. Her throat tightened.

"You're the new owner. My dad said you had moved in with your uncle and bought this place." Bobby chewed a cheese curd as he spoke. "Are you sticking around now that your uncle is dead?"

Ray frowned, but Sabrina didn't notice Bobby's tactlessness, since she was still processing this new information.

"I'm so sorry, Ray. Harry did a lot for the town," Sabrina said. She finally picked up a cheese curd to taste, wondering what Harry needed help with. She'd have to work that out later.

Ray focused on her, his blue eyes softening. "Thank you."

"Thanks for the curds, man. They're good," Bobby said, and turned his full attention to Sabrina. Ray definitely scowled, but another customer arrived at the other side of the bar.

The cheese curd was good, crispy and a little sweet, a nice foil to the salty cheese. She liked the crumb breading better than a batter, making them among the best cheese curds she'd ever tasted.

Bobby set a hand on her knee, and she stopped chewing. This was not happening. She swiveled her stool away from him, breaking the contact.

"Now, where were we?" Bobby smiled as if nothing had happened.

It was familiar and alarming at once, flooding her with memories of when they had dated, how he had always found a way to gloss over potential problems. She had reveled in his attention back then, so she'd let it slide. Before she could decide what to do, his phone buzzed. A small frown flitted across his face, then he set the phone down, returning his hand to her leg, higher up this time. Sabrina swiveled her stool again but couldn't turn far enough to break the contact without drawing attention to them. The phone buzzed again.

"Everything okay?" Sabrina asked.

"Yeah. Just a friend." Bobby gave her his full attention. "Are you going to be around all summer?"

She sipped her drink, scrambling for how to respond to his words. The alcohol was making her head numb. "I'm waiting to hear about a new job, and then it's back out east."

"We should get together while you're here. Talk about old times." He leaned in closer, pushing back the strands of hair on her shoulder, letting his fingers linger on her neck. She leaned away. "I have my car and could drive you home tonight. No reason for us to wait for our parents."

She was not getting in his car. Been there, done that. His phone buzzed again. He ignored it. It buzzed again.

"You should get that," Sabrina said.

Bobby looked at his phone, then sighed, punching in a response. She took the distraction as her chance to escape.

"Feel free to leave," she said under her breath, not caring if Bobby heard her.

She slid off the stool, doing her best not to rub against Bobby in the tight space, and speed walked to the restroom. Perhaps Bobby would be gone by the time she returned so she could finish her drink in peace. But when she emerged, he was waiting for her in the dim, empty hallway outside the bathrooms.

"I gotta go," Bobby said, then grabbed her face and kissed her, smashing his lips into her teeth. He tasted like Scotch with a kicker of cigarette smoke. Sabrina shoved him away. "Why did we ever break up?" Bobby asked. Sabrina recalled exactly why—and nothing had changed. "I'll text you."

Sabrina didn't move, and he didn't wait for a response, turning and disappearing toward the front door. Sabrina wiped her lips and returned to her stool, stunned by emotional whiplash. She stared at the nicked and worn wood of the bar. Bobby was a big part of the reason she'd moved away. Drained after his abrupt exit, it was how she had felt during their entire relationship—dizzy and exhausted from the attention. Was it the effort of being normal in his presence? The fear he'd reject her again? She stared at nothing in particular, in shock from the whirlwind.

Sabrina closed her eyes, trying to let the people around her disappear into background noise. Logically, she knew they weren't paying attention to her, but her brain told her they all knew Bobby had kissed her. Their judgment weighed on her, crushing her lungs and spine until she wanted to slide off her barstool and disappear into the floor.

"You okay?" Ray asked, interrupting her mental meltdown. His voice lifted her. She let it. "He seemed a little handsy."

As her attention returned to the present, she saw that Bobby had left his bill for the most expensive Scotch on the menu—sixty-five dollars. That was half her tips from yesterday. With a sigh, she pulled out a wad of twenties, but Ray snatched the slip of paper away before she could add her money to it.

"I'm not taking your money. I'll add it to his parents' tab."

She nodded her agreement and sucked up the last of her Pink Squirrel, letting the creamy almond drink dull her senses.

Ray pushed his glasses up his nose.

"You can do better," Ray said. "Who do you think was summoning him? His parents are already here."

As he spoke, he wiped the counter and refilled straws and napkins, all without looking away from her.

"Old boyfriend. Not really sure what that was all about," Sabrina said.

Ray gave her a look that said *We both know what that was about*, but he was gentleman enough to not say it out loud. She opened her binder back up and returned to brainstorming, letting the straight lines of the sticky notes and the satisfaction of checking items off a list soothe her mental chaos. Controlling something, no matter how small, always helped. Arabella's party was a perfect balm.

"What's all this?" Ray asked, pointing at her binder.

"My niece's birthday party. I'm helping my brother. I plan it, he executes."

"Seems like a bit much for a little girl's party. Cake, balloons, maybe some pizza and a few games. Done."

"When was the last time you attended an eight-year-old's birthday party?"

"When I was eight."

"Things have changed. It needs to be Instagrammable now so you can make everyone else jealous of your party planning." Sabrina shook her head and muttered under her breath, "Cake and balloons."

"You're good at this? You like doing it?"

Sabrina looked at her color-coded and perfectly organized binder.

"I am and I do. To a point. I don't make the calls. I give my brother options, and he does that part."

Ray studied her, then leaned on the bar. "I could use some help."

"With what?"

"The Goodbye Gala. It's my first year hosting, and it needs to be perfect."

Oof, the gala. The last thing Sabrina wanted to do was organize one. Just being here was enough of a reminder.

"Have you ever been?" Sabrina asked.

"Once, in 2007."

Sabrina paused. She had been there that year, too.

"I remember that one." It was all she could manage as the memories sprang to life in her head, playing like a film projector she couldn't ignore.

"You were there?" Ray asked.

Sabrina nodded.

"I wonder if we saw each other."

Sabrina only shrugged. That night, she had only noticed Bobby. Her hands shook at the thought.

"Sabrina? Still with me?" Sabrina's eyes met Ray's, his head tilted as he dried glasses and set them in neat rows. "I lost you for a moment."

"Sorry."

"No need for apologies. I owe you a life debt from saving me during the waterpark brawl."

Something in her eased a bit. More orders came in, and she watched him mix and blend drinks. When he returned, he slid another Pink Squirrel in front of her.

"What's this for?"

"A bribe. Help me, please."

"You'll need more than an ice cream drink. You don't know what you're asking." Sabrina shivered at the idea of having to talk to all the different businesses, the hours of phone calls, the days of directing people like a drill sergeant, though there would also be a lot of lists. And binders. And sticky notes. She loved sticky notes. Never mind that it would mean she'd have to stay until October. She had hoped to be gone by then.

"Name your price," Ray said.

Sabrina sighed. What would be a ridiculous enough number that he'd never consider it? She wrote a number on a napkin and slid it to him, waiting for him to snort at her audacity.

"Done."

What? She wasn't actually going to help him—though that money would make a nifty dent in her student loans.

"I wasn't serious. I can't help you. I already work sixty-hour work-weeks. And . . . I can't."

"I'm absolutely serious. I need help more than I need money at this point. Please, save me."

A customer needed his attention, so he turned from her, and she thought about how life-changing that money would be. She wanted to agree, but she couldn't do it. She needed to stick to her plan. Work hard, save money, pay down her debt, get out of town. She had it all laid out in her spreadsheets. Even if the idea of spending more time with Ray made her tingle in the best way. Especially because of that.

He must have read her face because when he returned, he said, "Just think about it. That's all I ask for now. Here's my number." He'd written it on a napkin in neat, precise digits. She tucked the napkin into her pocket.

"I'll think about it, but don't get your hopes up."

She'd started to smile when Mrs. Smoot appeared next to her, her eyes tight with rage.

"That's him, that's the cheating bastard canoodling with his cheap floozy. Slap him! Tell him Karen knows he was sleeping around while she was dying in a hospital bed."

Mrs. Smoot pointed at a couple a few stools up from her. The man had dirty-blond hair, brushed back from his forehead and gelled. If he were caught in a rainstorm, the chemical runoff could cause an environmental disaster. His black button-down shirt had three too many buttons undone, but the woman at his side didn't seem to mind as she giggled at his every word, flipping her streaky brown hair over her shoulder, exposing a hot-pink bra strap. She wore heavy eye makeup that burrowed into her wrinkles like ink spilled onto carpeting.

"Who's Karen?" Sabrina said the question out loud before she remembered where she was. Ray tilted his head at her but was distracted by a new customer.

"I'm Karen, obviously. Go now," said Mrs. Smoot.

"I'll get my mom." Sabrina whispered the words hoping no one would notice.

"Quick, they're leaving. You have to do it now. Go."

Her shouting got louder, clanging on Sabrina's nerves. She'd had enough of tonight. She needed to get away from everyone. She slid off her own stool and turned to leave.

"You can't leave. Help me. Help me." Mrs. Smoot started to glow red around her edges. Sabrina hadn't known ghosts could change colors.

Sabrina sighed, gripped her still-full Pink Squirrel around the stem of the enormous glass, and stepped in front of the happy couple. The ice cream drink slid in her palm, and a bit sloshed over the rim onto her sandaled foot, dripping between her toes.

"Yes! Use the drink! Brilliant." Mrs. Smoot shone with excitement.

"Excuse me, Mr. Smoot."

He paused and looked at her with interest. The woman at his side didn't look happy about the interruption.

"Yes?"

He smiled at her, and not in a gentlemanly fashion. Suddenly, she didn't feel sorry for what she was about to do.

"Your wife has a message for you. She knows you were sleeping with this woman while she took her last breaths."

Mr. Smoot's eyes widened. His date said, "Your wife?" And Sabrina dumped the Pink Squirrel over his head while everyone in the bar watched, including Ray. She took an instant to admire the ice cream slipping off his face, first exposing his eyes, then his nose, the pink liquid standing out against his black shirt.

Mrs. Smoot danced in glee, then glowed brighter and brighter until she disappeared. She'd moved on, and now it was time for Sabrina to do the same before people started asking questions she wasn't about to answer.

Dropping a few twenties on the bar, she meekly said "Sorry" in Ray's direction and hustled out of The Otter Club.

12

RAY ENTERED THE KITCHEN of his uncle's house, his current residence. Technically, it was his parents' house as of a few days ago. He flicked lights on in the dated dark-wood kitchen. One of the stove burners didn't work, and the oven door was so loose, it gaped open, letting out hot air anytime he tried to use it. An ancient white fridge covered in scratches stood out against the battered dark-walnut cupboards. The room even lacked a dishwasher since his uncle had rarely used more than the same six dishes. A similar seventies time warp spread through the rest of the house, complete with red shag carpeting in the den and dark wooden beams across the ceiling. His uncle could have renovated, but chose instead to keep buying up commercial properties, advising local business, and sponsoring all the Little League baseball teams. Ray could appreciate living frugally, but he itched to remodel, which he couldn't do until his parents stopped holding the property hostage.

While the decor was old, the emptiness was still new, like a vacant apartment that echoed with each step. He expected to see Uncle

Harry when he entered the study, sitting at his desk with a brandy and cigar, a stubborn ghost not ready to move on. But he knew better, right?

Wound up from a night at work, as he always was, he couldn't go straight to bed. His mind flipped through thoughts like a bad Power-Point presentation.

Was there a better place for the waitstaff to pick up drink orders?

Should he try different bar snacks?

Could he keep his supper club?

What had made Sabrina dump her drink on Mr. Smoot?

It kept going.

He needed a place to write all this down. He needed an office at home. Walking from room to room, he considered the best place to start—ignoring that it was two in the morning. Uncle Harry's study took up one corner of the home's large footprint, overlooking a wooded backyard that abutted another chunk of Jasper land they had left undeveloped and wild. Frequent visitors included deer, turkeys, and the occasional coyote. He thought he had spotted a fox scampering through one evening, but it was gone before he was sure. The room used the same dark wood as the kitchen, but in here it fit like a proper study, with bookshelves, a heavy desk, and comfortable leather seats in front of the large windows. It only needed a good purging rather than a complete redecorating.

Ray bounced a few times on the balls of his feet like a runner might do before a race to loosen his muscles. *Might as well start now, Ray.* He loaded his arms with books and moved them to the dining room, stacking them in irregular piles like the silhouette of a city skyline. Most of the books were old leather-bound encyclopedias, more for decoration than for reading, but some showed frequent wear and tear. A few were very old. When he had more time, he'd have to go through them—there might be something valuable.

In the office's built-in cabinets and the closet, he unearthed decades of family paperwork, most of which was old bills and tax returns that he no longer needed. He'd have a huge bonfire to get rid of it once he'd gone through it. For now, it joined the books from the library.

He saved the desk for last, emptying all the drawers into cardboard boxes until all that remained was a key and an old black journal, the journal he had found in the library of his family's home in New York. Flipping it open, it fell to the spot that had initially drawn him to Wisconsin. Near the spine, a jagged, tooth-shaped edge indicated where several pages had been torn out—twelve, if he had counted correctly. While in the same penmanship, the content of the pages wildly differed in tone. The early pages were upbeat and hopeful, with bold, firm handwriting and a bright future—the diary of an optimistic young man in love, his great-grandfather (or "Number One" as Ray liked to think of him, as he was the first Raymond Harold Jasper) and Uncle Harry's brother. The latter pages picked up more than a year later with him about to marry someone else. The handwriting was harsher, the letters cut and slashed at the page. The dark and cynical tone reflected a man accepting a life sentence of unhappiness. What had happened in the gap?

He ran his finger along the torn edge, as if touching the spot would cause the missing pages to miraculously appear, or at least give him a hint about where to search for them. His mom had warned that unearthing family secrets wouldn't give him what he wanted, but how do you know if you don't unearth them? A tarnished silver urn sitting on one of the cleared shelves caught the light of the desk lamp like a lighthouse, a warning that land was ahead. Danger, so proceed with caution.

He had been six the first time he had seen the urn in the library in New York at the will reading for Number One by Mr. Moore, the family's attorney. Nana, his widow, had worn a dark dress, setting off the creamy circle of pearls, the same pearls Lucy had worn around her neck at Uncle Harry's funeral. Nana perched on the edge of a leather chair with the family scattered around the room, her back stiff and her face stern. A fire crackled in the large fireplace. Ray remembered Nana's pink lips thinning as she pressed them tighter together until the color disappeared completely, the way everyone held their breath with each new item, and the sweat collecting under his small black suit.

Uncle Harry stood behind her, younger then, with only streaks of gray at his temples. After the expected bequests of land and money and family heirlooms, Number One had one more request that caught the family by surprise.

"I request that my ashes be returned to the Wisconsin Dells and buried with my first fiancé, located in the Spring Grove Cemetery under the name—"

"Is that all?" Nana said, interrupting Mr. Moore.

"I need to finish the reading," he said.

"Is that the final request, or is there more after that?"

"That is the last item."

"Then we're finished here. I'll take care of it. Thank you for your time, Mr. Moore." She picked up the documents from the desk in front of him. "Please send me all the copies you have."

"The firm usually keeps a copy, Mrs. Jasper."

"The firm needs to do what I pay them to do. I'm paying you to get me all the copies of Mr. Jasper's will. I'll expect them by the end of the day. Thank you."

She turned her back on the lawyer, letting him know the conversation was done. Mr. Moore looked around the room to see if anyone objected to this unusual request. When no one did, he left. Nana took the last page and tossed it in the fire, his parents glancing at each other but not speaking.

Nana moved the silver urn closer to a spray of white lilies that decorated the mantel.

"I can bring that home with me. I'll talk to Mr. Moore and make sure Raymond gets put where he wanted," Uncle Harry said.

"That won't be necessary. He's staying here," Nana said.

"That's not what he wanted, Etta."

Nana faced him, her eyes icy in the firelight.

"I don't care. That woman had his heart. I get what's left."

"You can't ignore the will."

"You wouldn't know where to put him." Nana pointed to where the page burned in the fire.

Harry held up a black notebook. "The answer is in here."

Nana smiled, but it was the kind devoid of humor. "Good luck with that."

Uncle Harry paged through the book, then held it out to Nana. "Where did the pages go?"

Nana crossed her arms. "They were gone before he moved here. If they exist, they are somewhere in your house."

"This isn't the end, Etta."

Nana smirked. "Possession is nine-tenths of the law. I have his ashes. I decide what happens. Go back to nowhere, Harry." She stood in front of the urn like a dragon guarding her treasure. Uncle Harry shook his head and left, followed shortly by the rest of the family. The urn had never left that spot until last year.

Ray had been in that same library last summer, reading through a contract, when a black book had fallen off a shelf. The black journal. He had intended to put it back in an empty slot, but when he bent to pick it up, it had lain open to the spot where the pages had been ripped out—the same spot Uncle Harry had shown Nana at the will reading. When he realized what it was, something clicked inside him. He recognized seeing it as a child, but he also saw too much of himself in the latter pages, a soul trapped by family expectations. He wanted a life like the one found in the earlier pages. He had hoped Uncle Harry could answer some of his questions or point him in the direction of someone who could, but they'd never gotten around to having those conversations.

When Ray had first arrived, Uncle Harry had been recovering from pneumonia. It became clear that his memory was also failing. He would forget to turn off the stove or where he put his wallet, only to find it in the liquor cabinet. On one particularly bad day, Ray had to explain who he was and why he was there. When Ray asked him about the missing pages, Uncle Harry couldn't remember anything. They had to be somewhere, right?

Now Ray looked around at the stacked books and boxes of paperwork. He'd have to go through everything page by page so he didn't accidentally toss the missing journal pages—assuming they hadn't been burned long ago along with the last page of Number One's will.

With the office purging done and no new ideas about where to look, the evening's earlier events drew his attention, like watching as Sabrina tossed her drink at Mr. Smoot—a horrible tipper and philanderer if ever there was one. She'd said something peculiar before releasing the Pink Squirrel—that it was for his wife. Why would she do that? Getting her to speak with him required every ounce of his charm, and he still wasn't sure she tolerated him.

Then there was Bobby. The high school boyfriend. Ray had disliked him immediately, like a driver who threw cigarette butts out the car window. Bobby probably did that, too, and there was no redemption from that kind of behavior.

His muscles ached from the long day and the late-night exertion, but the loneliness weighted his limbs exponentially. He didn't want to be alone, not like Uncle Harry—the confirmed bachelor. Not like his parents—married, but separate. He wanted someone to share his day with, someone he could bounce his ridiculous ideas off of, someone who warmed his bed and his heart. He wanted someone who embraced all his quirks and not just his bank account and family connections.

He traced the edge of the torn page, hoping it would give him some answers.

His phone rang—Lucy.

"Miss me?" he said.

"Have you forgotten how to answer a phone? You've turned savage already. Such a waste."

Ray could hear her smile through the phone. There wasn't much about New York he missed—only his sister and the ability to have any type of food delivered any time of day. He'd kill for some decent Thai food.

"Are you calling for a reason or just to mock me because you have nothing better to do on a Saturday night—or Sunday morning?" He opened a drawer and put in some pens, the key he had found, and the journal.

"I wanted to hear your voice. Are you up late or up early?"

"Late. I couldn't sleep after work. How about you?"

"Early."

"I'm going to ask again. Why are you calling?"

"Fine. I have to tell you something because I don't want you to hear it from someone else."

Ray sipped his brandy, taking a deep breath to prepare for whatever bomb Lucy planned to drop on him.

"Okay, hit me." Silence. Ray could hear Lucy tapping her finger on the table. "Just say it. I can take it."

"Mavis is getting married. To a sweaty old investment banker. I'm pretty sure he has a heart condition, and she's making him train for the New York City Marathon with her."

He took another gulp of brandy, letting it burn down his throat. Mavis. The last time he'd seen her, she had stolen his phone and had the gall to be angry when his lock screen wasn't her photo. She had been looking for information on his latest deals—hoping to pass it on to her father, a competitor. He should have known better.

Leaving her had been easy. He didn't want a life of one-upmanship, always worrying that those closest would take advantage of him. Mavis had had no intention of being his true partner. Well, at least Mavis had found someone who would give her what she wanted.

"You okay?" Lucy asked.

"I am. I wonder if the New York City Marathon could be considered a murder weapon?"

Lucy laughed, and Ray swirled the amber liquid around his glass. The color reminded him of something that he couldn't quite remember.

"I'm glad I don't have to fly out there and scrape you off the floor."

"I think I'll survive. I don't know why I attract women who only care about what I can do for them. Is 'sucker' stamped on my forehead?"

"You're too nice."

"You might be the only person who thinks that."

"I'm serious. Have you ever truly screwed anyone over—even in business?"

Ray sipped and thought about it.

"No, that isn't my style."

"Exactly, you want everyone involved to be happy."

"Doesn't everyone?"

"Hell no. I want to make as much money as possible, and I don't care how much it hurts the other side."

Ray rolled his eyes, knowing that wasn't entirely true. But it wasn't completely false, either. Lucy was much more ruthless than he had ever been. He'd liked everyone in the deal to feel like they had won. Lucy wanted to win and the other side to lose. She usually won.

"Thanks for telling me. I'm sure I would have seen it eventually, and now I won't be blindsided if Mom brings it up. And you know she will."

"She wants little Jasper babies to cuddle and spoil and carry on the family name."

"You have the family name and are better equipped for actually creating said progeny."

"Are you implying I'm a baby maker?"

"Obviously. Just not barefoot, as you are never without your stabby-heeled shoes."

"They make it easier to impale opponents," she said, then paused. "I have no intention of reproducing, so it's all on you."

"Do you think Mom would be satisfied with puppies? Puppies are adorable. I could make a place at the restaurant where guests could meet and play with them. Maybe I could partner with a local shelter?" His mind kicked into gear as it did when promising ideas percolated.

"On that note, I'm hanging up. Enjoy oblivion. Love you."

Lucy hung up, though Ray barely noticed. He liked this puppy idea. He'd reach out to the humane society tomorrow, but the idea could have legs . . . or paws. Guests would be distracted during the increasingly long waits, and maybe they could complete more adoptions. He jotted down a few notes to remember to talk to Chef Rick about it. He was good about telling Ray when his ideas went too far.

Now that he was off the phone, the house seemed emptier than before. He felt fine that Mavis had found a more appropriate husband than him, someone who would give her everything she wanted in exchange for her company. Unlike her, Ray didn't want a transactional marriage. He wanted someone who would make life interesting. He knew he would marry for love or never marry.

13

"**WHAT DID HE SAY** after you threw the Pink Squirrel at him?" said Sabrina's mom. She still wore her pajamas, a yellow cotton set covered with a tidy white robe that went to her knees. Slip-on socks like ballet slippers covered her feet so she didn't have to walk around barefoot like a heathen—or her daughter.

Her mom sipped the still-steaming coffee as she waited for Sabrina to continue her story.

In the light of the morning, Sabrina hated to admit that she had enjoyed helping Mrs. Smoot. Given how exhausted and overwhelmed she had been last night, she had expected to need gallons of coffee, but she'd bounced out of bed before Molly could start singing her favorite songs from the eighties to wake her up—Wham! being her personal favorite.

It was the same good feeling she'd had while fixing Mrs. Randolph's door.

"I didn't stick around to see what he would say. I threw forty dollars on the bar and left because I felt guilty about the mess. I can never go to The Otter Club again."

"That will make Ray quite sad. He asked about you as we left."

"What do you mean he asked about me? Why are you only telling me this now?"

Sabrina's stomach contracted. Had he seen her talking to Mrs. Smoot?

"He asked about Bobby and you. Is there something you're leaving out?"

"I should ask you that. Bobby was all flirty with me, then hurried off after a bunch of texts, but not before kissing me." Her mom made a face of disgust. "Yeah, I know."

Her mom looked guilty. "I probably should have mentioned it sooner, but I didn't want you to not come home or not take the job at the Real Dells Ducky Tours."

Sabrina's stomach plummeted. She didn't know the specifics yet, but she knew what her mom was about to tell her would be nothing but bad for her.

"Bobby and Erika got engaged at Christmas. Their wedding is this fall—right after the Goodbye Gala."

Shit.

The spiral started strangling her, like a boa constrictor encircling her bit by bit. She wanted it to stop, but once it began, she could rarely control it. It wasn't the general vague dread of interacting with people that got her. It was the immediate and all-consuming need to break down every possible what-if scenario leading up to an event, followed by the detailed analysis of every interaction, what it could possibly mean, how she'd embarrassed herself forever, and how everyone she had ever encountered would judge her.

It took up a lot of time. The coil tightened, and Sabrina remembered she had to be back at work in twenty hours.

Would Bobby tell Erika about their kiss?

Would she blurt it out when she saw Erika?

If Erika did find out, what would she do?

Would Sabrina lose her job?

Would Erika let her keep the job but hold it over her head?

Why would Ray think she dumped that drink?

Did he think about her?

Could she avoid Erika for the rest of the summer?

Why had she accepted that job? But she knew the answer to that one.

Erika would never believe that Sabrina hadn't known about the engagement. She would assume Sabrina wanted to win Bobby back for herself, when nothing could be further from the truth. Bobby hadn't ruined high school for her on his own, but he had been the sneeze on the shaky house of cards that was her life.

After the Goodbye Gala her senior year, no one had spoken to her, and she had eaten lunch alone in the guidance counselors' office. Not even a quick "hi" in the hallway. She might as well have been one of the ghosts only she could see. Even the teachers had sensed the change and called on her less. One less opportunity for everyone to judge her.

The only person who hadn't ignored her had been Erika. She'd delighted in talking at her. She'd liked to remind Sabrina that she and Bobby had started dating after the gala, implying that Sabrina had been the butt of some hilarious joke—as if Bobby Meltzer would really like her, the weirdo, the whack job, P. S.

That was when Sabrina had started leaving five-dollar bills in her favorite library books with notes that read "You're in for an amazing read. Enjoy a treat on me" or "This great read deserves a great snack to go with it." Knowing someone's day would brighten a little because of her had made her own days a little brighter, too. That's what she had been doing when Ray had tripped on her at the library. Leaving a few five-dollar bills had lifted her spirits, making it more than worth it. Kindness didn't have a price tag.

"You okay, honey?"

Her mom sipped her black coffee but kept her eyes on Sabrina.

"I guess. I have some e-mails that need answering."

She didn't, but she needed an excuse to leave the kitchen. Her mom would know there was more to her anxiety if she stuck around. At the top of the stairs, Molly waited, wearing a flowing ankle-length sleeveless teal gown, the type Ginger Rogers would wear while being twirled around a ballroom.

"Fancy," Sabrina said.

Molly twirled. "I saw it in a movie and wanted to see how it would look. Do you like?"

"Beautiful."

When Sabrina went into her room, Molly followed.

Sabrina changed out of her pajamas into a comfortable summer dress made of navy-blue cotton jersey, then sat on her bed staring into space as her predicament evolved from hypothetical to real.

"What if Erika finds out he kissed me? Then I'm out of a job. What am I going to do?"

"What-ifs get you nowhere, doll. The only way forward is with what is. Do you want me to follow her around and find out what she actually knows?" Molly sat next to her.

"No." She answered quickly, then thought about it. Maybe she should. Knowing the truth would help her prepare so she wasn't blindsided. "No, that wouldn't be right."

"You know your parents would help."

Sabrina flopped back on her bed.

"I'm not taking their retirement money. I chose to spend more than they'd saved for school. If I'd stayed in state, or not gone to grad school . . . If I'd done things differently . . ."

The regret burned. She wouldn't let her parents pay for anything more. She didn't have much, but she still had a little bit of pride left, hiding somewhere in her childhood bedroom where she now slept.

Molly shrugged and played with the ribbon around her waist. It was easy to forget she wasn't really there. Sabrina had to look closely to see the haze. It was more pronounced in newer ghosts, but Molly had been around for so long, she had more substance. Would she ever get so strong that someone who didn't have her family's curse could see her?

"I need to tell you something. It's good, I promise," Molly said.

Sabrina nodded.

"Ray likes you. I watched him at The Otter Club, and his eyes followed you like the fuzz on a bootlegger."

"How is that good?" But Sabrina's stomach unclenched long enough to let a butterfly escape. Traitor.

"Have some fun. A summer fling would do you good."

"Have you met me? I don't fling. Flings either fizzle or flourish, and neither is worth the stress."

Sabrina sat on her bed and opened her laptop, clicking on a spreadsheet. She entered her ten dollars for the library notes. Seeing so many big numbers in the red stung, erasing any of the uplift from her notes. She could only manufacture so much good. Eventually the universe had to help her out, right? Out of curiosity, she entered the income Ray had written on the napkin to see what would happen. One column switched from red to black, and the biggest number became almost manageable. But she wasn't accepting Ray's offer. She switched the numbers back and closed the spreadsheet, then searched through her bookmarked news sites, checking for available work like a toothpick in a woodpile. Then there it was, the toothpick—a job opening at a DC-based website.

Thank the universe. If she could line a job up by the end of the summer, that would get her out of here. Then it wouldn't matter what Erika thought.

She sent off her résumé with a prayer for an interview. She couldn't sit around all day. Sorting the change from her tip jar, she separated out the quarters, dumped a handful into her dress's pocket, and went outside for a walk.

14

THE NEXT DAY, SABRINA arrived at work early, sneaking into the mechanics' garage and leaving a box of donuts before anyone arrived. She checked over Norman, making sure he was clean, and got him first in line for tours. Once they opened at eight a.m., she'd head out with the first group and, hopefully, stay booked all day. The less time she spent at the dock, the less chance she'd run into Erika.

With the chill still lingering on this June morning, she wore a fluffy white fleece jacket over her regular white polo. She'd twisted her hair into two braids, which poked out the back of her yellow hat. After spending all day Sunday replaying Saturday night in her head, from Ray's delicious bartending to Bobby's awful kiss (and it became more awful as more time passed) to Mrs. Smoot's demands, Sabrina's anxiety simmered at a buzzy five, ready to crank up with the slightest heat.

Norman started with a gusty rumble and settled into a soothing chug. She eased the vehicle into gear, drove across the parking lot, and pulled into the empty chute. Each time someone emerged from the office, her shoulders tensed, then released when she realized it wasn't Erika, spiking her anxiety level to eight, then back to five. It drained her. She shouldn't even be worried. Erika rarely showed up before nine, and once the day was in full swing, Erika wouldn't be able to confront her.

Ten minutes to go, and Sabrina relaxed. The parking lot filled with more customers, and a few more ducks lined up behind Norman. She waved at Josh and Kyle, two college guys from Madison working for the summer. They were nice enough, if a bit young. They partied with the Tommy Bartlett water skiers, having Around the World bashes at their small houses, usually ending with missing clothes and memories, but they always made it to work on time, so who was she to judge?

"That's not the uniform." Erika had arrived. Shit. She stepped over the chain and boarded Norman. Sabrina took a step back as Erika charged up the aisle to the driver's seat where Sabrina stood. "Take it off."

Sabrina wanted to argue, to tell her she'd take it off once the tour started. It blended with the rest of her uniform, only lacking the little yellow duck. Never mind the red hoodies on Josh and Kyle—which matched the color their competitor used. Erika didn't even glance at them.

Sabrina couldn't form enough words to defend herself. She nodded and unzipped the fleece, stuffing it into the backpack she kept tucked under the hopper seat. When she stood back up, Erika was still there, studying her.

"You ran into Bobby on Saturday."

It wasn't a question.

"Yeah. At The Otter Club. Congratulations on the engagement."

"Like you didn't know before." She sniffed and crossed her arms over her chest, making sure her left hand featured prominently. Sabrina wasn't sure how she'd missed the strobe light on her finger before, but now it was unmistakable. It was the kind of ring you took off when you got weighed at the doctor.

"My mom didn't tell me until yesterday."

Erika's nostrils flared. What had she said wrong? She replayed the words and realized she'd just admitted that Bobby hadn't mentioned their engagement to her. Erika's eyes narrowed, then she tilted her head and smiled. Sabrina braced for whatever was about to come. She'd seen this look a million times in high school right before Erika would deliver her worst, like a lion right before it pounced on the lame gazelle that had been separated from the herd. Erika couldn't help herself—she was drawn to the weakness. A predator couldn't help it.

"I'm sure she didn't want to upset you. It's all anyone is talking about. Everyone's invited." Sabrina was not. Nor did she want to be, but that wasn't the point. "Bobby keeps begging me to elope because he can't wait for me to be his wife. He's so in love."

Yeah, sure he is.

"He's all yours," Sabrina said, sliding on her headset and pointing at the people ready to board.

Erika's eyes became slits, but she left without further comment.

What had Sabrina just done? Even a doomed gazelle might land a kick before its inevitable demise, but had Sabrina gotten a reprieve or pissed off the lion more?

Even after Erika left, the panic kept rising. She could do this. *Deep breaths. Focus on the next moment.* Her tension eased.

She started the speech, and instinct carried her through as the guests boarded and found their seats. Erika knew about Bobby kissing her. Sabrina knew that she knew. But had she guessed or had someone told her? She wouldn't put it past Bobby to blurt it out—he could be that dumb. If Erika thought she wanted Bobby back, she'd lose her job. At this point in the summer, all the well-paying jobs were taken, and Sabrina couldn't afford to work for minimum wage.

In Erika's mind, if you were a single woman (or man), you would want to steal Bobby away from her. She needed to not be single. She could pretend she was still dating Charles, but all Erika would need to do was google him to see happy pictures with his gorgeous lobbyist girlfriend (#NoStrawLeftBehind). She'd know Sabrina was lying. She needed someone real and someone local. All the guys who worked for Real Dells Ducky Tours were too young and way too single for her. She needed someone who might believably want to date her. Not someone she'd gone to high school with. Not one of the college guys who were there for the parties. She thought back to all the guys she knew even slightly. The list was short.

Ray.

15

Ray heard the crunch on the gravel parking lot. No one should be here this early in the day other than the cooks, who had already been prepping for hours. He set down his hammer and wiped the sweat off his face with his faded gray T-shirt, leaving the front damp and sticking to his skin.

Once he finished repairing the wood fence keeping his guests and their roaming children out of the river, he would really enjoy a well-earned shower. The pile of wood planks waiting to be nailed to the posts made him groan. Holding an eight-foot board steady while trying to hammer in four-inch nails tested his patience and can-do attitude. He wanted it done and didn't want to bother the kitchen crew, who had more important work to do. First he had to deal with this interrupter. He rounded the side of the supper club as he saw a woman pulling on the door handle.

"Sorry, we're closed. We open at four."

The woman jumped and turned to face him.

Sabrina.

He pushed his glasses up his sweaty nose and wished he could sniff his armpit without her noticing. Here was hoping he didn't offend too much.

"Oh." Sabrina's eyes widened as she stared at him.

"Sorry to startle you. I hope you aren't planning to throw any more drinks on my guests."

She tapped her legs and nodded a few times before bringing her gaze up to meet his. Thick lashes fringed her amber eyes—the color of the brandy he had been drinking the other night; that was why the color seemed so familiar. A person could get drunk staring at them, and he needed a drink. He took a step closer.

"No, not today." Her hands trembled as she smoothed back a stray curl that had fallen on her forehead. He didn't like that she was nervous around him.

"It's okay. Really. I hear he deserved it."

"He did." She clipped off the words as if she wished she could suck them back in. Her eyebrows wrinkled together, then she took a deep breath. "Can we talk? I tried calling, but no answer."

The words tumbled out of her, and it took Ray a moment to separate and sort them.

"I left the phone inside. I get work done faster that way. Can we talk while I finish fixing the fence? If you agree to help hold the boards, I'll buy the drinks."

"Deal." She smiled. She had a good smile, one that didn't get overused, which made it all the more valuable.

They walked around the side.

Sabrina paused, looking over the same view he stared at all day. Without a breeze, the air hung heavy over the glassy river, the leaves as still as a painting.

"It's peaceful."

"My view is your view." He liked the idea of her being here, even if it was more for the quiet than for him.

She breathed deeply, dragging her eyes to his. He cleared his throat, but before he could say anything, she looked to her right and shook her head the tiniest amount, almost undetectable, except her curls jostled from the small motion. There was nothing in the spot where she looked. Something was different about her, more than the usual, but it was none of his business until she wanted to tell him. Even then, it wouldn't change anything. Her eccentricities made her all the more interesting.

"If you could hold that end while I nail, that would make my life easier," Ray said, nodding toward the end of the board at her feet.

Sabrina did as he asked, and he hammered three nails in. Then he pounded the nails into her end. He reached for the next board.

"If you have another hammer, I can help. It'll go faster," Sabrina said.

"Gladly." He found an extra hammer in the toolbox and a handful of nails. She pocketed the nails, keeping three in her hand. Ray hammered the first nail in his end of the board. By the time he finished the third, Sabrina had her end nailed securely and was digging into her pocket for more nails, her actions confident. He picked up the next board and handed her one end so they could keep working.

"What did you want to talk about?" Ray asked.

He looked up from his hammering to see her blush. He wished he was closer so he could study the lovely pink hue of her skin. As she kept her eyes on the board in front of her, driving in a nail in one sure swing, she answered.

"You know that guy I was talking to at the bar? Bobby?"

Ray was not thrilled this conversation started with another man. He had hoped she would accept his job offer at the very least, or maybe ask him out. He didn't want to discuss that ass.

"Yeah." That was all he trusted himself to say.

"He's engaged to someone." Ray paused his hammering. "Not me," Sabrina continued.

He smiled. "I figured that out."

Sabrina let a small laugh out.

"You know the Hendricks family?" Ray nodded. "He's marrying their daughter, Erika. We all went to high school together. She didn't like me then, and that hasn't improved."

"You don't want her to know how he was all over you."

Sabrina cringed. Good. It made him want to cringe, too.

"That would be bad. I work for the Real Dells Ducky Tours. She's my boss."

Ray missed the nail completely and hit his thumb, dropped the hammer, and shook the injured hand. Sabrina winced in sympathy.

"You okay?" She grabbed his hand and turned it over, looking at the injury. The pain evaporated instantly, replaced by the touch of her soft hands. He sucked in his breath, worried that any movement from him would make her pull away. While she studied his reddened thumb, he studied her. A small line formed between her eyes, and her lips pressed together. So serious.

"No blood. That's good. Can you move it?" He bent his thumb, resisting the urge to wince. "It's probably not broken, but if it starts to swell a lot or you can't move it, go to the ER." She paused. "My mom was a nurse, and I have two older brothers. You pick up some stuff."

She released his hand, but the comforting sensation remained even when he opened and closed his hand a few times.

"I think I'll make it." He picked his hammer up from the ground, and she returned to her end of the board, much too far away from him. "So, why did you stop by?"

"It won't matter to Erika that I have no interest in Bobby. I need her to know I would not want to be with him." She paused. "I need a boyfriend."

Ray stopped working to stare at her. She swiped her hammer through the air near her head, as if shooing a bug with it. This conversation was improving exponentially. He motioned with his hand for her to continue; that way he wouldn't betray his eagerness.

"Would you be my fake boyfriend?" Sabrina continued. "It won't be real. Just put in some public appearances where people will see us. Go out to dinner. I can stop by the bar after work. Maybe you pick me up at the ducks. That sort of thing." The words poured out in one enormous wave, like that giant bucket at the waterpark. "It won't be for long, just until I get a new job and move home." *Home?* Ray had thought this was home. Where was she going? "I promise it won't take much of your time." Her words came faster and faster as she spoke, and she finished with a big gulp of air.

He had hoped to take her on a real date. But, maybe . . . It was an excuse to spend more time with her. He had leverage here. She wanted something from him. This was his sweet spot, identifying what someone wanted so he could get what he wanted, with everyone happy in the end.

He held the next board, and she continued.

"Will you?"

"Perhaps." He saw some of the tension ease from her shoulders. He liked being the cause of that. "But if I agree to do this, that means I can't date anyone else during our charade."

"Got a lot of prospects, do you?" She blurted the response, her eyes widening like she couldn't believe she'd said the words, either. He smiled. That was what he wanted to bring out of her—he wanted her to say what she meant without worrying about his feelings. He needed time to get to know her better. They hammered in the last board. The fence was done.

"You don't know who might be clamoring for all this sweatiness." He pulled at his shirt, and she smiled that special smile. This was going well. "As I was saying, this will require a bit of effort on my part. I think I should get something out of it." Her back tensed again. Damn. That didn't come out right. "To clarify, I want you to help me with the Goodbye Gala. I'll pay the amount we talked about. And I'll happily take you on fake dates and be the doting boyfriend for as long as you need me."

Sabrina bit her lip, and that frown line reappeared.

"I help you. You help me. We both get what we need," he said. "Deal?"

He held out his hand. As she thought, she closed her eyes and wiggled her fingers as if checking items off a list. Ray held his breath as he waited for her answer. Would she walk away? When she put her hand in his, he exhaled. *Yes.* Her grip was strong and warm, even compared to his own sweaty palms. He didn't want to let go.

"Deal," she said, and eased her hand out of his as he resisted the urge to hold on longer.

"So, when do you want to start?" he asked.

"The sooner the better. How about that drink?"

He pointed to the fence. "Now that this is done, we could go to one of the bars downtown. I hear the Showboat Saloon is where the locals hang."

Sabrina coughed and frowned over her right shoulder. Was there something there he couldn't see?

"Is that not a good choice?" Ray asked.

"No, it's cool." Sabrina paused. "They have good pizza."

"Meet you in an hour? I need to shower."

Sabrina coughed as if she were choking on something, but nodded. And blushed.

"Sure. I'll see you there," she said.

As she walked away, Ray leaned against the fence they had repaired. He knew they'd work well together on the gala, and all that extra time was what he needed to prove that the connection he felt between them was real. Getting to know Sabrina reminded him of the first time he had tasted truffles. With their robust and pungent flavor, truffles were an acquired taste, but with each new truffle experience, the more interesting they became, the more he discovered the nuanced and earthy notes. The truffle had always been perfect; it had been his taste buds that had to evolve. Sabrina was like that—he knew time would unveil fascinating and complex depths that most people never appreciated.

He couldn't wait.

:◠◠◡◠:

"YOU'RE NEVER GOING TO shut up about this, are you?" Sabrina asked Molly as she stepped into the shower. Between her nerves from asking Ray to be her faux beau and the summer heat, she was a sweaty mess.

Molly hummed with joy on the other side of the shower curtain.

"You had the meet-cute, you've had the casual run-ins, and now you're pretending to date. Shakespeare couldn't have written it better."

"I should never have let you watch 10 Things I Hate About You." Sabrina rinsed the soap off her face. "He's helping me so I don't lose my job, and I'm helping him because otherwise he wouldn't have helped me."

"He's paying you, don't forget that."

"Exactly. This is nothing but a business deal. More like *Pretty Woman*."

"You believe what you want, sugar, but this is fate pulling the strings. I almost died again when he said you should meet at the Showboat."

"I noticed. You weren't helping the situation. I almost hammered my own hand. He can't know about you."

Molly blew air out between her lips. "*Phhhht*, nonsense. Ray is not Bobby. He's going to be just fine when you tell him the truth. I can tell these things."

"How can you possibly tell?"

Sabrina stepped out of the shower and wrapped a large towel around herself. Molly followed her into her bedroom. "I can tell because I'm the wise best friend who always knows what's what."

"Not sure about the 'wise' part."

She wanted to ignore the little curl of excitement in her chest, but thinking about how Ray's T-shirt had clung to his chest only coiled it more tightly. She had no intention of dating Ray for real, but Molly's excitement was infectious. What would happen if they really started dating and summer ended? She would move back east, and he would stay here. The curl flattened, and her mood drooped with the reality of the situation. There was no reason to be excited.

"Just promise you'll chill." Sabrina held up her pinky, and Molly tapped it with her own finger.

This was business, and she was the Julia Roberts character in this scenario, minus the hooker part. Sabrina took a deep breath, slipped on a dress, and looked in the mirror. Focus on the money, pile it up, pay off her credit cards, take a chunk off her loans, and get out of the Dells. Stay on task.

Molly didn't notice Sabrina's sobering grip on reality and continued her dreaming. Sometimes Sabrina envied Molly. Not the dead part, but being able to watch the world unnoticed. She couldn't interact with anyone, and yet she still made the most of it. She found joy, she found happiness, she had found a life with Sabrina's family, relatively speaking. Despite the many years she'd been floating around the area, there was still an innocence about her. She never dwelled on the bad stuff, just the good, always rooting for the happy endings that Sabrina knew to be rare. If they weren't, Molly would have found her own.

Sabrina pulled out a few more outfits and laid them on the bed, holding each up to her chin as she narrowed down the options, all the while ignoring Molly's smug grin at Sabrina's efforts.

There was no secret meaning in the green sundress she finally chose. Or the lip gloss and mascara. She was going to a bar, so a little dressing up seemed warranted. It had nothing to do with Ray or his sparkly blue eyes and velvety voice or the way his forearm flexed when he used a hammer. Besides, if people were going to believe this charade, then she needed to look the part for a romantic date.

16

MOLLY USUALLY AVOIDED THE Showboat Saloon—or Ghost Molly's Showboat Saloon, as it said on the side of the building. The only thing they had right was that she had lived and worked here—and there was that one time she'd slammed a door as a spirit. It was just the once—but they still blamed her for haunting the place even though she was rarely there. Too many memories. The only places with permanent ghosts were the cemetery with Belle and the Monroe house. And Tabitha down at Stand Rock, but no one knew about her. She never spoke to Molly and only cared about keeping the dog that jumped from the cliff to Stand Rock safe.

It was hard to live in the now when the past surrounded her like it did here. But she wasn't missing Ray and Sabrina's first date, fake or not. Why couldn't Sabrina see it? It was so obvious how they were drawn to each other, like an invisible ribbon bound them closer and closer. The attraction between them was like gin to a bathtub or a child to a mud puddle. Inevitable and wonderful.

They sat at the bar across from her, beers and a half-eaten sausage pizza in front of them. Ray and Sabrina talked about what they needed to do for the Goodbye Gala, and Molly wandered through the bar, occupying herself until those two did something interesting. Mostly she remembered how the building had looked when she was alive.

White marble-topped tables had dotted the space the bar now occupied, a candy display had covered the north wall between the windows, and a soda fountain had taken up the east wall. It had smelled of chocolate and malt powder. During the day, she waited tables and sold candies to the ladies and children of the Wisconsin Dells, then at night, her job and the clientele changed. The lights dimmed and the doors were locked, but beneath the store, a labyrinth of small, poshly decorated rooms was filled with red velvet chairs and thick carpets to keep the noise down. Hidden Hiawatha's was the place to get something a bit stronger than the fizzy sodas and ice cream offered upstairs—a well-known secret among those who could still afford the expensive libations.

At the time, an alley behind the building contained two doors. One door went to the offices and apartments upstairs, including hers. The other door went to the candy shop's back room, where they dipped all the chocolates and stored supplies for the soda fountain on a heavy wooden shelf. People looking for the speakeasy would tap on that door and say the password, "Hiawatha," to get Benny the bouncer to open the door. Inside the storage room—like many places during prohibition, even houses—there was a hidden room. The heavy wooden shelf swung open to reveal a dark wooden staircase, which led down to the maze of rooms below.

Men stopped by on their way home from work or wandered in after their dinners and were joined by the occasional woman who flirted with the edge of polite society. They all came for the same thing: hooch. Mr. Oliver, her boss, had connections, and Molly never asked questions about where the cases of bottles came from, but she had put two and two together when Al Capone stopped by. He had been a good tipper.

On the night she met her love, she'd worn a black lace dress, drop-waisted and sleeveless, and had had a long black feather curved around the top of her head, setting off her blond curls. A new table had just sat down, and Molly skedaddled over to take their order, setting some dirty glasses onto her tray as she crossed the room, always looking for ways to make fewer trips.

"Welcome, what can I get . . . ?" But she never finished, stopped by the very handsome man in front of her. Tall with thick dark hair and a thin mustache on his lip. He wore a ritzy dark pin-striped suit, damp on the shoulders from the rain outside. He was joined by an older, rounder man who had similar blue eyes, Mr. Jasper. Her tray tilted, and the glasses tumbled to the floor, smashing into each other.

"Oh, my," she said.

Her heart fluttered as she bent to pick up the pieces. Hopefully Mr. Oliver hadn't heard.

"That is coming out of your pay, Molly." Mr. Oliver came from a back room where they hid the illegal booze, then stopped when he saw the customers. "Mr. Jasper. And Raymond, I didn't know you were back."

"Arrived this morning," Raymond said. "And please, let me pay for the glasses. I startled Miss . . ." He left it hanging, hoping she would fill it in.

"Cantor. Miss Cantor." Molly stretched out her hand, not caring that she was being a bit forward. "My flippers are always dropping things, so no need to pay for it."

"Miss Cantor. Lovely to meet you, and I'm terribly sorry I startled you. I insist on paying. Either take it now or I'll leave an exorbitantly large tip."

"You can do that anyway." Molly smiled larger, knowing it brought out her dimples.

"Molly," Mr. Oliver scolded her, but Raymond smiled. He had straight teeth that weren't yellow from cigarette smoking.

"Right away, Mr. Oliver."

Molly swept up the mess while Mr. Oliver fussed over the men.

"We need good brandy," Mr. Jasper said, "not that moonshine Oliver tries to pass off as potable. We're celebrating my son's graduation. Raymond is an educated man."

Raymond's bright-blue eyes met hers and she was lost. A moment passed before Mr. Oliver reminded her she had a job to do.

"Go on, now," he said.

She scurried to get the drinks, then served them, but for the rest of the evening, she took every opportunity to peek in his direction. Every single time, his gaze met hers. As promised, he left a large tip at the end of the night.

He came back alone the next night and sat at the same table, sipping a brandy.

The regular customers arrived, including the town drunk, Mr. Henson. Mr. Henson took turns visiting the different establishments that had worked out ways around prohibition. The drugstore served whiskey if you had a prescription from Dr. Schimms or bitters if you didn't. A few others served illegal booze made in their own stills, foul-tasting stuff that made the drugstore bitters taste refreshing.

As long as Mr. Henson got his drink, he was pleasant enough company, but tonight, he'd run out of money earlier than usual. Normally, Mr. Oliver would handle him, but he'd had to go home early because his mother-in-law had come to visit, and she didn't know about Hiawatha's. That left Molly and Benny to handle the customers. Though Benny was up the stairs and behind the shelf, she had a buzzer in case anyone got rowdy. When she had to cut Mr. Henson off after three shots, that was what he became.

"What do you mean I can't have any more?"

"I'm sorry, Mr. Henson. I can't give you drinks for free. Mr. Oliver keeps track. I'll give you one more, but then you have to go." Molly poured him one more shot of the cheap stuff, but he grabbed her wrist, his strong grasp grinding her bones together.

"Uppity bitch. Think you're too good to serve me."

He yanked the bottle from her hand, and she stumbled against the wall behind her, bumping a few more glasses to the ground. There went more of her paycheck. Now she was angry. But before she could push the button that would call Benny, Raymond jumped from his seat.

"That'll be all, Mr. Henson. Time to go."

Mr. Henson didn't agree. Using the bottle, he swung it at Raymond's head, but Raymond ducked and in one smooth motion grabbed the bottle and twisted Mr. Henson's arm behind his back. Molly pressed the buzzer.

"Out you go," Ray said.

Benny rumbled down the stairs, grabbed Mr. Henson by the back of his coat, and carried him up the stairs like a piece of luggage.

Now they were alone.

"Thank you, Mr. Jasper."

"Raymond. Please, call me Raymond, Miss Cantor."

Molly blushed. First names.

"Then call me Molly."

He nodded but didn't say anything, just watched her. Molly had to keep busy before something stupid tumbled out of her yap. She always said something dumb at the worst possible moment. She picked up the few remaining glasses, put the bottle away, and swept up the broken glass. With her work done, she could leave, but Raymond still sat at his table with his brandy.

"Time to scoot, sweetie," Molly said. He stood from his chair and handed her his glass along with too many bills. "This is too much."

"It's for the broken glasses."

"I can't accept this."

"It's not for you. It's for Mr. Oliver."

She rolled her eyes. "That's just semantics."

Raymond smiled. "Semantics. That's not a word I expect a waitress to know."

"There's more to me than booze and broken glasses."

"I bet there is." He paused. "Molly." Then paused again. "Molly."

He said her name like he was tasting a new food, letting the new sensation flood his mouth, the changing flavors rolling along his tongue and seeping into his other senses.

She put his glass behind the bar where she would wash it tomorrow. He still stood there.

"Can I get you something else, doll?"

He nodded a few times as if rallying his courage, then finally spoke. "I was hoping, Molly, that you would allow me to walk you home."

Her heart beat faster, and her cheeks heated. It was her turn to rally a response.

"Oh, well, sure. I'm all done."

"Don't you have a coat?"

"It's not far."

They walked up the stairs, and she said goodnight to Benny, who nodded at her. Raymond stepped out the door first, making sure Mr. Henson hadn't lingered. She closed the door behind them and walked five paces to the right, where she stopped in front of her apartment door and faced him in the dark alley.

"This is me."

Raymond laughed, rich and from his heart, the kind of laugh that warmed everyone around him.

"I had hoped our walk would take a bit more time."

"Then ask me on a proper date."

Was that too forward? While she would flirt with customers for better tips, she rarely did so when she meant it.

"A dame who knows her own mind." Raymond shuffled his feet. "Miss Molly, could I have the honor of escorting you on a proper date?"

Her smile spread slowly until it lit her entire face like a summer sunrise.

"Absolutely."

He stepped closer, careful not to touch her. It wouldn't have been proper as they barely knew each other. But they would. His sweet breath brushed her cheek, and she could smell the lemon in his soap.

"Until tomorrow, then." His voice was soft and smooth in her ear, weakening her knees enough that she had to grab the doorknob before they buckled completely. He stepped back and gave her space to open her door and go up to her apartment.

The next night, he returned. And the night after that. On her night off, he took her to the show. A few weeks later, they had a photograph taken at the H. H. Bennett Studio to celebrate their engagement. Nothing fancy, just the two of them being in love. They hadn't told his family yet. They wouldn't be keen on him being seen in public with a shopgirl and speakeasy waitress, even though his father had been more than happy to ogle her gams before Raymond had returned from Harvard.

After having their picture taken, they walked down the street toward her apartment. When they arrived at the door, he leaned in to kiss her cheek, and she stopped him.

"I have something for you. It's upstairs."

"I can wait down here." Raymond refused to go into her apartment. He insisted they do everything properly so his parents would have less ammunition against her.

She dashed up the steps and grabbed the paper-wrapped package off her dresser.

As he unwrapped it, she bounced on the balls of her feet. She'd had to dip into her savings to buy this, but it was worth it. Raymond looked at the green cloth-bound book with a gilt figure on the cover. Raymond looked up at her with awe.

"I don't have this one yet."

"I know. I asked your maid to make a list of the Oscar Wilde books on your shelf. The only one missing was *The Canterville Ghost.*"

"You shouldn't have. Mr. Oliver doesn't pay you enough for you to be spending it on silly things like this."

"You are more than worth it." Molly pointed to the title. "You can think of me whenever you see it. I can be your Cantor-ville ghost."

Raymond kissed her, long and slow, like he was memorizing the taste of her. Her hands found the back of his neck and pulled him closer. Raymond pulled back with a deep sigh.

"I want you to be my wife."

"Soon, my love. We need to tell your family, and then we can get married as quickly as you want. I'm yours forever."

He cupped her face with the book-free hand. "Tomorrow. We'll tell them tomorrow." He kissed her once more on the cheek. "I've never received a better gift. Thank you."

And then he was gone. She went to work the next day, and he never called or stopped by the store. Then nothing the next day, or the next. On the fourth day, his father came into the shop and said, "You won't see him again," and walked out.

Molly didn't want to remember what had happened next.

She blinked, and the past evaporated. Only the here and now mattered.

The bar had grown crowded, and a big group had situated themselves behind Sabrina and Ray—a bachelorette party, complete with a veiled and sashed bride. Sabrina wrote in a notebook on the bar in front of her, while Ray's body was turned to focus on her. Every once in a while, he would put his arm behind her to block the swaying drunk bachelorettes, keeping them from bumping into Sabrina. He never touched her, and Sabrina didn't seem to realize he was protecting her. A small, simple gesture, but those were the ones that added up.

Molly liked him even more. He didn't ask for credit. He only wanted Sabrina to be undisturbed as she worked. It was a small and thoughtful act that told Molly everything she needed to know about him. Ray didn't want to alter her or the way she chose to interact with the world, he wanted to give her the space she needed to be herself.

Now, how to get Sabrina to see that?

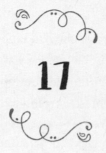

17

AFTER COMING UP WITH a general plan of attack for the Goodbye Gala, Ray and Sabrina had to wait until the next day, when they both had off work, to buy supplies. Sabrina had offered to get them on her own, but Ray insisted he come so he could pay. At least he didn't balk as she tossed more and more items in the cart.

Not much thrilled Sabrina like picking out new office supplies for a project—it topped her list of favorite pastimes—even better than taking a summer nap in a hammock. Each of the binders, tabs, and notebooks represented a possibility. Choosing the right ones could be the difference between success and failure, and if Sabrina could handle one thing, it was choosing wisely. Calling strangers for interviews or speaking with former high school classmates sent her into a spiral of negative thoughts and nausea, but creating a strategy and being in control each step of the way, that she loved.

Her hand reached for her preferred pen in green—it didn't smudge or blob, made a fine line, and sounded like a quill scratching across the paper. She paused and remembered the last time she'd used a green pen like this.

Her stomach had roiled as she had tapped the number using her favorite pen. It was stupid. She knew it was stupid. Just a phone call. Her thumb hovered over the Call button as air solidified in her throat, her heart pumped faster trying to dislodge it, and pressure built behind her eyes. Before it became too much, she turned off her phone and slid it under a stack of papers, as if hiding it meant she didn't need to make the call.

"Sabrina, a moment," her boss said over the cubicle wall.

She followed him into his office and perched in the chair across from his desk, her mouth dry.

"I need to let you go," he said.

"But my story . . ."

"Was due yesterday. I need people who make deadlines."

Sabrina nodded numbly. Another job gone, but deep down inside, where all her secrets lived, in the bitter memories that tainted her tongue when she remembered them, she was relieved not to have to make another phone call. It wasn't until she looked at her budget spreadsheets that she realized the truth. Without a job, she'd have to go home to the Dells.

Now she was there, staring at the Walmart pen selection. She grabbed a pack of blue pens.

Sabrina pulled the cart closer to her side and sighed at the lackluster selection of paper clips—all of them traditionally shaped and silver. Boring. She tossed a box into the cart.

"Here are sticky notes," Ray said, reaching for a pack.

"Stop. You can't grab just any sticky note." Ray froze, then pulled his arm back. "You need to carefully consider colors, what you'll be using them for, and how much variety you'll need. For example, we'll need five different colors, and a spare just in case another category presents itself. At least two packs of each."

Sabrina tapped her lip, then grabbed a multipack with five vibrant hues of blue, green, and pink, plus a two-pack of classic yellow.

"You're the boss," he said.

Sabrina smiled to herself. She tossed them into the cart and moved on to binders. She preferred a one-inch binder—neat, tidy, and its smaller size encouraged brevity—but for their purposes, a three-inch was more practical. Now, what color?

Behind her, a dad with two kids joined them in the aisle, interrupting her binder ruminations. His arms overflowed with toilet paper, diapers, and a hooded towel that was either a unicorn or narwhal—it was hard to tell out of the corner of her eye. The children touched and picked up everything as he let out a steady stream of anxious directions.

"Don't touch that. Emma, put that down. Careful, don't drop it. We aren't here for that, Gabe. We only need envelopes."

Sabrina moved the cart closer to the side so he would have more room. The smallest girl, whom Sabrina assumed was Emma, clutched a sparkly blue pencil bag to her chest. The girl had good taste.

"No, Emma. Put that back."

The dad tried to reach for it with his arm that had the diapers tucked under it, but he dropped the box, then he lost his grip on the rest of his items. An avalanche of essentials. The poor guy needed four more hands. Sabrina scooped her pens and sticky notes out of the cart and handed them to Ray.

"Please, take our cart," Sabrina said to the dad.

All three of them stared at her, just realizing there were other people in the aisle. The dad had silver specks sparkling in his short dark hair—it was possible they'd emerged in the last five minutes.

"Don't you need it?" the dad finally said, already looking at the cart as if it was an ice-cold Spotted Cow ale.

"I'll grab another." Sabrina picked up the diapers and towel—it was a unicorn—and set them in the cart before he could object, then headed toward the front to get another cart. It only took a few minutes, and Ray waited where she had left him, still holding all their items. Right behind him was Harry, studying the colored pencils and markers. He'd been popping up more lately, but not doing anything that could help her figure out what he needed. Just hanging out. As long as he didn't do anything, she could handle it. He still didn't seem able to communicate what he needed. Perhaps he knew he would get there and wanted to be close by when he could finally speak. How could she ask Ray about his uncle's possible unfinished business without explaining why? Would he even know what it might be?

"The dad said thank you. You disappeared, so he asked me to pass it on."

Sabrina looked at her feet as Ray set their items in the new cart. When she looked up, Harry was standing in the middle of the basket, smiling at her. She moved around the other side so she could pull it forward without having to walk through him.

How could she bring up Ray's uncle without it being weird?

"I never asked, did you know your uncle well?"

Ray tilted his head to the side at the question.

"Huh," he said. "We were getting there. He liked to tell stories." Harry nodded. "And he loved a juicy steak, but was too sick to enjoy one for most of my time here. I wish I had come sooner."

Ray's and Harry's eyes made the same sad expression. How had she not realized they were related?

"My mom said he was really sick in the end," Sabrina said.

"There were days he didn't know who I was."

Harry pointed to Ray and then crossed his arms in front of his chest.

"I'm sure he knew in his heart." Harry nodded in agreement. "He would tell you that if he could. Anything else you wished he'd say to you?"

Ray frowned and rubbed his cheek as Harry's attention span ran out and he walked through the dry-erase section into the next aisle.

"I had a few questions, but nothing too important. Thanks for asking about him. People don't anymore, like they've already forgotten. It's nice to talk about him."

Sabrina wasn't likely to forget him anytime soon. She shrugged.

"You don't like that, do you? When people notice when you've done something nice, like with that dad."

He studied her face like she was the Rosetta stone, and if he stared at it long enough, he'd finally comprehend all the sides. Good luck to him. Maybe then he could explain how she worked.

"That's not why I do it." Sabrina went back to selecting a binder.

"Then why?"

She pulled a white binder off the shelf and set it in the cart. Ray waited for her to answer, but she didn't have words for it. She didn't understand it herself. She gave the only answer she could. "I don't know. I'm sure my therapist would have plenty of opinions."

"You see a therapist?"

Oops. She hadn't meant to tell him that. Now he'd know she was crazy.

"Not here. Back in DC."

"Oh, I was hoping you had a recommendation. I've been meaning

to see one since I moved here, but I haven't made the time to research."
Ray saw a therapist? He seemed so stable. He continued. "Well, maybe
we can be each other's listening buddy until we both find someone."

Sabrina laughed at the idea of sharing the chaos inside herself
with him.

"If I gave you a glimpse inside my brain, you would never come
back the same."

Ray stepped closer and set a hand on her upper arm. "I want to
know how that brain of yours works. I want to know everything
about you."

Well, shit.

:ᘓᘓᘓᘓ:

RAY SET THE WALMART bags on the dining room table of his
house, the one room not dominated by dark wood paneling and
built-in shelving. A wide white wall would be the perfect backdrop
for project planning. Sabrina unpacked the items into orderly lines,
then stepped back to admire their haul. Ray covered a grin with his
hand.

"What?" Sabrina said.

He stepped closer to her, setting his hands on her shoulders, and
she didn't pull back. Progress.

"I've never seen anyone so happy about office supplies."

"I'm a simple girl," she said.

"That's not true." He leaned in. "There is so much more to you
than you let people see. I want to know it all."

Before Sabrina could dwell on what he meant, he leaned closer to
her face, his eyes already tracing the curve of her bottom lip, focusing
on his target. It seemed like the right time. They were getting along
so well. He could smell lavender, and only lavender. Was it perfume?

Shampoo? He leaned in even closer so their faces were inches apart. She sucked in her breath, and her shoulders tensed. Had he read her interest wrong? Oh God. How did he course correct?

Ray pulled her into a hug and patted her back awkwardly.

"Your help on this means a lot," he said, then stepped way back, giving her plenty of room.

She visibly breathed in, then out.

"Don't be too grateful." She picked up a pen, then set it back down. "Remember, you're paying me."

They both chuckled, letting the awkward moment waft out of the room.

"Ray, you here? I saw your car in the driveway," a voice said from the kitchen, followed by Chef Rick's face in the doorway.

Rick's grin when he saw Sabrina made Ray want to punch his face.

"Sabrina, this is Chef Rick. He runs the kitchen."

"Well, hi there. I knew your brothers in high school."

She took his offered hand and gave it a quick shake.

"Nice to meet you," Sabrina said.

Rick waited for more, but Ray knew better. He needed to get Rick away from Sabrina.

"Something I can help you with, Rick?"

Rick still faced Sabrina, who'd gone back to moving office supplies around the table.

"I wanted to go over specials. I had some new ideas. I didn't realize you would have company."

He waggled his eyebrows. Damn. He didn't want Sabrina to see Rick's stupid behavior and get the wrong idea. He could screw things up without Rick's help.

"I should head home," she said, picking up a stack of sticky notes and the binder. "I'll get started with some preliminary planning. I'll let you know if I have questions, then we can go over them in a few days." She was out the door before Ray or Rick could say goodbye.

"Preliminary planning? Is that what the kids are calling it these days?" Rick said.

Ray followed him into the kitchen. "Shut up, you idiot. There's nothing going on."

"I get the impression you wish it were otherwise."

"That obvious?" Ray said.

"That was the first time I ever thought you were going to rip my head off, and I only looked at her. She doesn't say much, does she?"

"She's shy around new people."

Ray beamed a little over the fact that he was no longer someone new to Sabrina. They had no problem talking. Her confidence in taking over the gala planning was a new side he got to see, one he didn't think many people knew about.

18

"**How have you not** walked down here?" Sabrina said, leading Ray down the sidewalks of Broadway Street, then Main Street to look at shops. She paused to drop some quarters in a parking meter, barely slowing her pace.

"It's all for the tourists, isn't it? Other than our date, I mean our meeting, at the Showboat, this is the first time."

People dotted the sidewalks, dipping into stores, then out again, sometimes with the addition of a mildly obscene T-shirt, an already dripping ice cream cone, or a replica *Game of Thrones* sword. Part bazaar, part tourist trap, this stretch of shops offered a little bit of everything.

"Where do you get your cow decor?"

"I have a guy," Ray said, enjoying their banter.

"Seriously, though, aren't you the landlord for most of these places? How come you haven't been down here?"

Ray stopped walking. Sabrina was right. Uncle Harry, and now his parents, did own most of it, but he'd never thought of it that way.

It was always numbers on paper in his mind, never a real place where people worked and shopped. He looked at the lively street with fresh eyes.

"This way," Sabrina said.

Sabrina veered onto a side street, went past a few storefronts, and ducked into the open doors of a mostly empty laundromat. One woman pulled laundry from a dryer while her small children pushed a rolling cart back and forth in front of the washers. Without pausing, Sabrina set small stacks of quarters on each machine, even popping coins into the gumball machines by the door, a special surprise for the next child to check them out.

Before he could ask questions, she was out the door.

"You know that woman will take all those quarters."

Sabrina shrugged. "Then she'll have laundry money for the next trip, too."

As they walked back to Main Street, Sabrina added a quarter to each parking meter they passed, whether it needed it or not.

"Do you take a roll of quarters and do this often?"

"I always get a few dollars in loose change as tips. Maybe people didn't have bills, or maybe they didn't like the tour. I save up the change and spread it around. It's not a big deal."

But it was a big deal. Sabrina sailed through life leaving a wake of kindness behind her.

"Here, take some." She handed him a small handful. As they passed a soda vending machine, she pointed at it. He added enough so that the next person would get a free drink.

"Do you ever stick around to watch?"

"Why?" she said.

Of course she didn't. She wouldn't want the attention. Sabrina lived by a different code than most people.

"So, what else do you do?" Ray asked.

"Nothing interesting," she said, evading the question. "What did you do before buying The Otter?"

Ray was already formulating his answer before he recognized her not-so-subtle deflection. Who could resist talking about themselves? Certainly not him.

"Real estate."

She snorted.

"What's wrong with real estate?"

"Has there ever been a Jasper that didn't want to own the world? My parents' house is one of the few properties that the Jaspers ever sold."

"Really? That is odd. Any idea why?"

"My great-grandmother bought it in the thirties. It's been passed down to the oldest daughter since."

"So it will be yours someday."

"Not if I can help it, though my mom's still holding out hope."

"Not many journalism jobs in the Dells?"

Sabrina pursed her lips as she thought.

"There aren't, but that's not really why. Journalism was a means to an end."

"You don't love it?" Ray asked.

She looked up at the sky. "I love the writing and the planning."

"I've noticed that one."

Sabrina smiled at Ray.

"Chasing a story isn't my strength—it's not even a weakness. It just isn't a skill I possess."

"You could stay here."

"This place isn't good for me." Sabrina put the last quarter in a candy machine. "You ready?"

She held out her hand to him like they'd done it dozens of times before, instead of for the first time. She looked down at his motionless hand.

"Don't make this weird," she said, and reached for him, leading him through the other pedestrians toward their destination at the end of the street.

It wasn't weird at all. Holding hands with Sabrina was wonderful.

:◠◟◝◞:

"WHY HERE?" SABRINA SAID, looking up at the bearded wizard with a purple hat and robe guarding the entrance to Wizard Quest, the most unique of the Dells' attractions—and that was in a town with an upside-down White House, a life-size Trojan horse, and the former home of the Wonder Spot. Part scavenger hunt, part puzzle, and all fantasy, Wizard Quest was a mash-up of *The Dark Crystal*, *The Lord of the Rings*, and *Willow*. The line snaked out the doors onto the sidewalk, where they joined the end.

"It's date night." Ray pulled her closer to his side. "I thought we were supposed to be seen in public."

"You think Erika and her friends rescue fictional imprisoned wizards on their night out?"

Ray spread his button-down to reveal a T-shirt emblazoned with a twenty-sided die under the words HOW I ROLL.

"Ohhh. That explains so much." His floppy waves moved in the hot summer breeze, and his thick-rimmed glasses framed his eyes, bringing out the blue and giving her heart a new excuse to race. She stepped back six inches. "Still play?" she managed to ask. Being close to him made it hard to think.

"Not since college. The Venn diagram for dungeon masters and real estate tycoons doesn't overlap as much as you'd think. Do you play?"

How did a person share that she never had any friends to play games with? She deflected. "I was more of a reader."

"Right, the library."

Her head snapped up, and she could tell Ray knew he had said too much.

"You checked the book," Sabrina accused.

He had the decency to look sheepish. "Curiosity got the better of me."

The line had barely moved, and they still stood on the sidewalk. No reason to be upset, it wasn't like that was a secret. Ray reached for her hand, and she let him. She was starting to like it a little too much.

"We'll be here all night," Sabrina said.

"I don't mind." Ray's lopsided grin brought out a boyish innocence. Looking at him too long heated her skin, reminding her that she didn't have much experience with dating. She'd had the two boyfriends, Bobby and Charles—neither relationship had lasted long or ended well. She didn't like the loss of control over her body's reactions or the constant underlying fear that they might discover her family's secret. Ray's presence distracted her enough that she might say something too revealing.

Was that a tiny dimple on his chin? Her eyes returned to the door wizard. *Stop looking, Sabrina.*

"You can't solve it alone, P. S." A chill ran down Sabrina's spine as she recognized the voice.

She shouldn't have been surprised that Erika still used her childhood nickname—she had given it to her, after all.

Sabrina had stood in front of her seventh-grade social studies class, the desks in five straight lines, with Erika and her minions front and center. The best seats in the house for what was about to happen. The teacher sat at the back of the room behind his desk, focused on his computer rather than on her. Sabrina was giving her presentation on local Native American myths when an old woman wearing a flowered housedress and surrounded by a hazy glow appeared in front of her.

"The stove is on! I left the stove on! It needs to be turned off," the woman said, clapping her hands in front of Sabrina's face.

Sabrina had known she would see ghosts one day. A person couldn't grow up in her house and be unaware of the family secret, but she hadn't expected it to happen during the middle of her presentation at school. Anyone would be surprised if a spirit appeared suddenly in front of them, shouting and clapping. Horror movies employed the jump-scare approach for a reason. So, of course, she screamed.

"There's a person, there's a person," Sabrina said, backing into the whiteboard, knocking off the erasers and dry-erase markers.

The class's laughter spurred Sabrina's panic, letting it loose like a leaf in a tornado. It seemed to last for hours, the shouting and clapping, Sabrina's hands shaking, and her classmates laughing, showing off their teeth. Air escaped her chest so she couldn't form words, and her chest burned with the lack of oxygen until stars appeared. At last, a second, slightly-less-hazy figure appeared—a vibrant blonde with bouncy curls, whom she recognized as Molly from the description her mom had told her, but it didn't stop her from screaming again.

"Sorry, sugar," Molly said.

She reached her arm around the old woman, and they poofed

away. Sabrina spun away from the class, covering her face to hide her tears. How could she spin this so everyone didn't think she was crazy? A spider? Low blood sugar? But the damage was already done.

"Psycho Sabrina is seeing things," Erika said. "What else do you see? Unicorns? Boys that like you?" Her minions all laughed, and from that day on, she was Psycho Sabrina.

Sabrina put a hand on her stomach as a wave of dread flooded her. This was why Ray and Sabrina were pretending to date, but she still wasn't convinced it would work, even though it had been her idea. She turned to Erika, who was flanked by two friends, each of them dressed in heels and short dresses, as if the Dells had fancy nightclubs instead of rustic saloons and dude-bro sports bars.

"Erika," Sabrina said.

Ray stepped close to her side, setting his hand on her back. The warmth spread through her body and relaxed her stomach.

"She's not alone," Ray said with a smile.

Erika's eyes narrowed. "You're the new Jasper."

"Ray. Nice to meet you." He reached out a hand to shake. Why did he have to be so polite? Erika eagerly shook it. He wasn't someone she could dismiss so easily.

"We met at the Goodbye Gala years ago. Your mother introduced us."

"Of course. Then nice to see you again."

Erika kept her eyes locked on Ray, then shifted to Sabrina at the last moment. "When did this start?" Erika asked.

Sabrina panicked. How had they not worked out their story in advance? Of course Erika would have questions.

Ray didn't miss a beat.

"Sabrina"—he said her name with a special emphasis—"saved

me during a waterpark melee. I repaid her with a drink, and here we are about to rescue the realm."

Erika squinted her eyes some more, but Ray moved on to phase two, deflection.

"You should stop by The Otter sometime. We can discuss some sort of partnership with the Real Dells Ducky Tours and The Otter Club, maybe a tour-and-dinner bundle." Erika scanned him like a piece of meat. "Bring your fiancé," Ray added.

"He'd only get in the way." Erika put her hand on Ray's arm, the one not holding Sabrina's hand and stroked it. Ew. "Have fun," she said as she stared at Sabrina, but her tone implied, *Die a painful death from a million spider bites.* She gave Ray another once-over and click-clacked away on her high heels, one of her friends bumping into her, causing her to stumble.

"Back off, Cindy." Cindy took two steps to the left. She was a bitch to her friends, too.

Sabrina looked up at Ray, who was reaching for a notebook.

"What was that?" she asked.

"What do you mean?"

"You're supposed to be dating me so she'll think I'm not a threat. Not letting her hit on you."

"She wasn't hitting on me." Ray freed his hand and wrote in his notebook. She missed his warm touch immediately, even though she was peeved at him. His hand had been like a battery, sending her the energy she needed to get through the exchange. Now that it was gone, she wanted to slump onto the floor.

"Are you writing that down as an idea?"

"Well, yeah. It could be good for both of us."

Sabrina gaped as he scribbled his notes. Fine, Ray was a nice guy.

But he wasn't supposed to be nice to her enemy. Even if business was business, and the Real Dells Ducky Tour partnership would be a good one, especially since some of the tours puttered past the supper club. Was it too much to ask for never-ending loyalty from a fake boyfriend?

"You okay?" Ray asked. Sabrina nodded. "When you proposed this whole fake-dating thing, I thought you might be overreacting. I get it now. That woman wants your blood. It must drive her nuts that you don't rise to her bait."

"What do you mean?" Sabrina asked.

"She may be nasty, but do you ever react? She wanted you to explode, and you played it cool."

Sabrina hadn't felt cool, but Ray had a point. Until she'd worked for her, Sabrina had never really done what Erika wanted her to do. She'd avoided her as much as possible. What else could she do? She couldn't fight back, and behaving like one of her sniveling minions wouldn't have improved things, so why bother? She'd always thought of Erika as having the control and the power, but by not doing what she wanted, maybe Sabrina had created her own.

"You really want to do this?" Sabrina pointed to the giant wizard above their head.

"I already have our tickets." He held up his phone to show her, and she smiled.

"Well, I don't think I can win against this much enthusiasm. There's a first time for everything."

"Wait, you've never done this? You're a Wizard Quest virgin, too?" Ray said.

"Don't ever say that again. Weren't you an important businessman who made big deals?" She couldn't help but smile at him. His charm offensive had finally cracked her. Like seeing a party under a park shelter with lawn games, food-covered tables, and smiling participants, she wanted to go join the fun. Ray made her want to be a part of the action. He was the anti-Erika.

"Aren't you a little bit excited?" Ray said.

She was now.

Inside, a faux tree grew out of the floor, with colorful fairies peeking out from behind branches at the people waiting in line. Dragons, trolls, and magical sparkles adorned items in the nearby gift shop. Ray's head swiveled, soaking it all up, and Sabrina found it difficult not to do the same. Grabbing the iPad from the waiting attendant, Ray listened to his detailed directions as if they were covert op instructions and the survival of the world depended on his memorizing every word. At last, he stormed through the huge double doors into the mystical land that awaited. Standing on a balcony, they overlooked a vine-covered castle and an elven forest below. The production quality was pretty great.

"So . . . we get to explore and then we start?" Sabrina asked.

"Yep."

"You aren't going to let me hold the iPad, are you?" Sabrina asked, pointing at the device that would guide them through the game once they began.

"Not a chance."

"All right, Wizard Ray, let's do this."

She grabbed his hand, trying not to focus on how warm it felt in hers, especially in contrast with the cool air-conditioning. As she started to walk, he gripped her hand more tightly so they wouldn't get separated among the other questers who crisscrossed in every direction. She could get used to all the hand-holding. She led him downstairs and turned toward the Water Realm, where fewer people roamed. The game was divided into four realms—Water, Air, Fire, and Earth. A winding maze with narrow corridors and long strips of pleather that were meant to be seaweed obscured hidden passageways and clues. As they turned corners and bumped into people, their bodies pressed into each other. It was warm, and he was so close she could smell his soap—oranges and woods. She piled her hair into a topknot to cool off.

A person turned the bend and ran into her, pushing her along Ray's body and into the wall behind them. Her hand went to his chest and his circled her waist as they tried to find stability in each other. She expected to feel the cotton of her shirt between her body and his hands, but it had risen up, so instead his hand met the bare skin of her waist. His touch seared her. They stood face to-face as the rude person shoved past them. She confirmed that, yes, that was a dimple on his chin and fought the urge to kiss it.

"Sorry," he said, and stepped back when there was room, leaving his hands on her waist for a moment longer. The air left her lungs in a whoosh. She needed room to breathe. She stumbled in the direction they hadn't tried. At last, they broke into a short hall that led into Fire, a dark section with red lights and rocky walls.

Bracing herself with one hand on the wall, she gulped air.

"You okay?" Ray asked, his hands hovering over her back as if he wasn't sure if he should touch her or not.

"Claustrophobic."

"I didn't know."

His hands fell to his sides.

"Neither did I," she lied. She couldn't tell him that being close to him spawned feelings she could never embrace. Keeping her distance was the only solution. Her family secret prevented her from really connecting with anyone, but for a little while, she had lost herself in their pretend date and the pleasure of his company. She liked Ray enough that she couldn't risk ever having to see the fear and disgust on his face when he found out the truth.

19

Eighteen boxes of papers. That was how many Ray had pulled out of the office. Just the office. An entire family's history in receipts, bills, and outdated user manuals. He'd moved it all to the back patio next to the enormous fire pit, along with a bottle of bourbon and a couple of cigars. One for him and one for Rick, who had prepared a charcuterie board of some foods they wanted to try at the restaurant. Next to Ray sat an empty banker's box for anything he might like to keep. The rest would go up in flames.

He opened the first box, pulled out a pile, and started going through it piece by piece—crumpling each paper and tossing it on the fire, watching it turn into a tiny ball of flame, then flake into dark ash as he tossed on another. He lit his cigar and continued his routine. Crumple, toss, puff. Crumple, toss, puff.

"We're going to be out here for weeks," Rick said, setting down the wooden tray covered in different cheeses and thinly sliced cured meats next to homemade crackers on the table between them.

Ray picked up a slice of summer sausage and chewed, taking a deep breath when some heat kicked in.

"Watch out for that one. It's chili-spiked. Eat some cheese," Rick said.

Ray broke off a hunk of crumbling aged cheddar that had come from a nearby dairy. When he bit into it, tiny crystals popped on his tongue.

"Five years?" he guessed.

"Six."

"It's good." The cheese coated his tongue and eased the worst of the heat. He took another handful of papers and continued his purge. "People liked the micro-relish-tray veggies you served this week. Are they too expensive to keep doing?"

Rick puffed his cigar. "Not unreasonable, but I'm not sure we want to use them all the time."

"Just weekends?"

Rick pulled a flake of loose tobacco off his lip and flicked it into the fire.

"I was thinking weekdays—give people a reason to come in on a Tuesday night." He pointed at Ray with his cigar, the end glowing a dull red. "Weeknights can always use a boost."

Ray nodded. He liked Rick, and he was a damn fine chef. They'd found a natural balance. He let Rick run the kitchen, and Ray got him whatever he needed and stayed out of his way. The system worked.

Ray went back to his paper demolition. An hour in and he'd made it through two boxes, found nothing of interest, and acquired three new paper cuts. For The Otter Club, he and Rick had decided that the hot pepper summer sausage was too risky, but the aged cheddar, soft goat cheese, Wisconsin honey, and garlic summer sausage were easy choices.

He flicked the remnants of his cigar into the fire and leaned back.

"Why would you waste your time on that?" Rick asked. He'd been watching Ray for a while. "Can't you pay someone to haul it away?"

"It's all personal information about our family."

"Then load it in a boat, douse it with gasoline, and turn it into a Viking funeral pyre."

"Why didn't I think of that very practical solution? I'm sure that would delight everyone living on the lake." Ray wrapped a piece of pancetta around a hunk of soft young sheep's milk cheese he couldn't remember the name of. "I need to go through it and make sure nothing important gets tossed."

"Now it makes sense. You're searching for clues." He had told Rick about his great-grandfather's journal. "I get you now, Encyclopedia Brown."

"Except I might never figure it out." And he only had until the gala.

Rick checked his watch. "Shit. I told the wife I'd get home before ten thirty. It's ten twenty-five. I gotta go."

"See you in the morning." Ray waved as Rick walked around the house to his car.

Alone, Ray could focus on the task at hand.

Crumple, toss, burn. Crumple, toss, burn. The repetition was therapeutic, allowing him to think about other matters, like Sabrina. There was something between them, and he knew she felt it, too. Something held her back, and it was more than a few mean middle school classmates—though Erika was a piece of work. He'd want to get as far from her as possible, too. Sabrina was a mass of contradictions. Rarely speaking to people, yet going out of her way to leave quarters in parking meters and laundry machines. Avoiding Erika, yet working for her company. Hating the Dells, yet living here. He'd filled in a few blanks, but not enough to color in the entire picture.

He could understand it. After all, he had escaped one real estate empire, and now he was fighting to keep the one in the Dells. He'd pushed away what his parents had offered him, yet he was spending hours going through old papers because he wanted to learn more about his family. When he looked at Sabrina, he saw a kindred spirit, someone he understood and who could understand him in return.

As he pondered, he kept going through the papers. Crumple, toss, burn. How was he going to prove to his parents that they should sell him the local properties? How could he be a good Jasper? What did that really mean?

He wasn't paying close attention, so his hands recognized the change before his brain registered the difference in paper. The paper he'd almost crumpled was a photo. A thin white border framed the black-and-white image, dinged-up and yellowed by time. There were two people: a dark-haired man who looked a lot like him wearing a three-piece suit and a woman with blond pin curls and a deep dimple in her right cheek wearing a dark dress with a white collar. The two beamed. This must be his great-grandfather and his mysterious love. It certainly wasn't Nana, who had dark hair and a perma-scowl.

In the light of the fire, he held the picture close to his face, studying it for more details. They gazed at each other with devoted expressions, like they'd go through death and back to spend another moment with each other. Whatever they'd had, that was what he wanted. But wanting love wasn't enough—obviously. Number One hadn't married this woman whom he'd so clearly loved. Where had she gone?

He turned the picture over. The date, 1931, was written in pen that had faded to a brownish orange.

It didn't help much, but it was another piece to the puzzle. He knew they had been together in 1931. He knew Number One had married Nana in 1933. What was this woman's name? Maybe he could find that out. Someone in this town must know who this woman was.

20

SABRINA CHECKED HER BINDER and surveyed the scene in front of her. Tents set up—check. Pillows and comfy blankets—check. Fancy appetizers—check. Brats and burgers (because it was still the Fourth of July)—check. Her butter cookies that Ray liked with red, white, and blue sprinkles—check. A unicorn cake—check. The cake had been a last-minute addition when Arabella had realized that glamping didn't involve unicorns, at least not in this dimension. Fireworks—unchecked, but they would be starting as soon as the sun went down, giving everyone plenty of time to eat and get comfortable.

Ray's bespectacled form emerged over the side of the hill, carrying a tray of food under a wrapped present.

"You found it okay?" Sabrina asked, peeking at the tray—delicious-looking cookies. "Mmmm, chocolate chip."

"Close, toffee and chocolate."

"Even better." She slid her hand under the plastic wrap and grabbed one, ignoring the urge to touch his arm or hold his hand.

"Better not let the birthday girl see you snitching her treats," Ray said.

"She has an entire cake. She won't miss a cookie."

Oscar ran up and hugged Sabrina around her legs.

"Hey there, Oscar. Are you excited for fireworks?" Sabrina asked.

"Daddy said they won't be too loud out here." Oscar looked up at Sabrina with his wide eyes and whispered to her, "Is Molly here?"

Sabrina couldn't help but glance at Ray to see if he'd heard. He was looking at the giant white tent. Sabrina shook her head.

"We'll talk later. This is my friend, Ray. Ray, this dashing young man is my nephew, Oscar."

"I remember seeing you at the waterpark when your aunt got hit in the face with the giant drink."

"She was cranky," Oscar said.

"I was very cranky," Sabrina said.

Oscar ran off to join the other kids, who swiped handfuls of chips and cookies from the table of food, with Arabella leading them wearing a long green dress that flowed behind her like a cape as she ran.

"Why are we out here when the fireworks are over there?" Ray asked, pointing back toward town.

"This is Mr. Garnham's farm. He's an old buddy of my dad's. They realized years ago that you can see all the fireworks displays set off by the different resorts from this little hill. Several average fireworks displays equal one fantastic one. We've been coming out here for years to watch them."

Sabrina walked Ray over to the tent, a huge white canvas dome where, inside, white and pink tulle looped around white lights, warming the interior. Covering the floor was a mountain of pillows and beanbag chairs draped in soft fuzzy blankets and faux furs. The opening was large enough that they could all watch the fireworks from the comfort of the pillows. Her parents, brothers, and their spouses were already nestled into a comfy corner. Ray greeted her parents, whom he knew, and she introduced him to everyone else.

"This is where we'll watch the fireworks. You can set your cookies over there." Sabrina pointed to a few long tables. "And presents go next to it."

"This is incredible," Ray said. "I knew you were the right person to help me with the gala, and this is the proof."

Before he walked off to the tables, he gave her a crooked smile, and Sabrina forgot to breathe for a moment.

"He looks nice," her brother Cal said. He and his husband, Brendan, stood and gave her hugs. "Is he ready for a Monroe family gathering?"

"We're just friends."

"You know what I mean. We aren't always subtle, especially with Arabella claiming she can see blurry outlines and Oscar obsessed with the idea. She's only trying to impress the other kids, but . . ."

Shit. Sabrina hadn't thought about that. When they were together, everyone treated the family business as completely normal. It was what had made the few short trips home each year between high school and now tolerable. Her family was a safe zone. She had been so excited to show Ray this secret part of the Dells that she'd forgotten the other secret, one he couldn't know anything about. She was getting too comfortable with him much too soon. She didn't know anything about him other than that he was from New York, had worked in real estate, and made a great fried cheese curds.

"It'll be fine," Sabrina said, ignoring the clawing sensation in her chest.

The table was loaded with burgers, brats, buns, bacon-wrapped water chestnuts, puff pastry swirls, her cookies, and a dozen other tasty treats next to a two-tiered white unicorn cake complete with a rainbow horn. They filled plates with food, Ray taking a small stack of her sprinkle cookies, and found a spot on the pillows. Sabrina made sure it was as far from the kids as possible. She might as well be proactive. From a speaker hidden somewhere in the clearing, Mr. Garnham's annual playlist of patriotic favorites started with a bang, causing Ray to jump.

"It's Mr. Garnham's version of the Dells pops. He used to drive his truck up here so he could play a mixtape on the car's radio. I'm glad to see he's embracing modern technology."

"This is all amazing. The New York fireworks were so crowded unless you knew someone with a roof view."

"I'm sure you did," Sabrina said.

Ray smiled, seeming a little embarrassed, and nudged his glasses on the bridge of his nose.

"I had the roof."

"Welcome to small-town life. Here, you have to know the guy with the hill," Sabrina said.

"I have so much to learn from you. You'll be my Midwestern Yoda."

"Just what every girl likes to hear: she's a small, wrinkled green dude who lives in a swamp."

Ray set down his plate and stared at her. What had she said? She scrolled back through the last few minutes, and nothing seemed overly embarrassing.

"What? Do I have something on my face?" She brushed at her cheeks.

"Not at all." He said the words softly.

They looked at each other, and Ray leaned in closer. Was he really trying to kiss her with her parents and brothers and twenty other people around them?

Sabrina didn't move back.

"There they go," Sabrina's dad said, followed by a loud *thwump* and *boom*. White sparkles erupted in a giant circle, followed by a red, white, and blue one. The hill occupants cheered. Ray and Sabrina joined in.

The moment gone, Ray and Sabrina finished their food as the sky erupted in brightly colored circles and fountains and even the occasional smiley face. Sitting side by side, Sabrina's knee bumped Ray's, but she didn't move farther away. If he didn't like it, he'd move, right? He didn't move, either.

"How many years have you been doing this?" Ray asked. His voice was low, but she could still feel it like a finger brushing down her spine.

"As long as I can remember. When we were little, my brothers and I did that, too." Sabrina pointed to where her mom lit sparklers for the little kids, who ran away, leaving a streak of fleeting light in their wake. "I would write my name in the air, trying to finish the A before the S disappeared."

"That sounds perfect." Ray paused. "Why do you want to leave here so much? Your family is amazing. You have traditions like this, good food, perfect summer weather, beautiful places to get away from crowds. I don't get it."

Sabrina flopped back onto the pillows, the fireworks like sprinkle-laden cupcakes exploding in the air in front of them. How should she answer Ray's reasonable question? Did she even know? Before she could answer, Ray lay down next to her but kept his gaze on the light show. No eye contact made it easier to talk.

"I get anxious around most people. I'm sure you've noticed," Sabrina said. Ray nodded. She appreciated that he didn't pretend he hadn't noticed. That was a plus for him. "Living in a town full of people who have known you since birth, well, it's a town full of people who will make small talk every time you see them. In a bigger city, you can be surrounded and totally alone. In DC, I could go days without speaking to anyone. I'm never at ease here."

Never mind that she couldn't have a normal life here.

"I can understand that. Though there comes a point, no matter where you live, when people start to pay attention to you."

"Is that part of the reason you came here?"

Ray put his hands behind his head.

"One of them. Real estate in New York is not for the weak. Everyone has an angle. My sister loves it, but I hated assuming everyone wanted something from me. It made dating tricky. Was a woman with me because she liked me or because of my success?"

"I'm not sure it's going to be much different here. Being a supper club owner puts you on par with the Queen of England, or at least some third cousin who's eighty-fifth in line to the throne."

"Being royal would feel like less of a hassle than heir to Jasper Holdings."

Ray glanced down at his hands, a frown drifting over his features that faded into the night like the fireworks. Sabrina touched his arm with a smile. There was something about him, an earnestness. He said what he meant, and he meant what he said.

"How about breakfast? At not-Denny's Denny's?" Ray asked, changing the topic.

"Not-Denny's Denny's?" Sabrina asked.

"You know, the diner that isn't the chain. The not-Denny's Denny's."

Sabrina laughed.

"No one calls it that. It's Denny's Diner."

"Their cinnamon rolls are heavenly." He rolled onto his side, bringing them a few inches closer. If she rolled onto her side, too, they would almost be touching. She stayed on her back. "Do you? Want to go to breakfast?" he asked again.

Sabrina liked listening to Ray talk. His low voice occasionally tumbled into a growl, especially when he spoke quietly. It sent relaxing tingles fluttering across her scalp, like a massage on her brain.

"Breakfast sounds great. Maybe dinner on Thursday, too? Two public dates in a week seems right."

Ray looked down at the blanket, running his fingers through the white fur.

"Yeah, that's what I was thinking, too." He raised his head again and nudged his glasses higher on his nose. "Maybe some mini golf after dinner?"

Mini golf wasn't a likely place for people in Erika's gossip chain to see them, but maybe he really liked mini golf. They deserved some fun, too.

"Great."

The *thwump-boom*s came faster. The finales were starting. Side by side, they watched as the sky lit up, and Sabrina wondered why she was suddenly so excited about mini golf.

:ᙅᙁᙆ:

SABRINA'S PLAN WAS WORKING. She'd seen Erika three more times at work since the encounter outside Wizard's Quest without one word to her, only glares from across the parking lot. A public breakfast at Denny's Diner would only help. All the coffee klatches would spread the news that they were there. By five p.m., the entire town would know what they'd eaten and how much sugar they'd used in their coffee.

She stepped into the crowded dining room, tables and chairs packed in tight, the walls and ceiling hung with dangling faux-tiques and quirky decorations, like Chewbacca riding a motorcycle on a tightrope. It was a lot to take in, but the smells of baking cinnamon rolls and frying bacon kept her from dashing back to the quiet in her car. Ray waved at her from a booth in the corner, a yellow legal pad laid out in front of him.

"I thought we could go over the list of everything we need," Ray said.

"You're going to use that?" She pointed at the notepad and pulled the binder out of her backpack. "I got started already." She nudged the notepad toward the edge of the table and laid out the binder, already separated into tabs with color-coded labels.

"Did you dismiss my legal pad?"

"Rookie, *you* asked for *my* help. I'm here."

A waitress set down two coffees, water, and an enormous cinnamon roll with extra icing on the side. Sabrina tore off a hunk and dipped it into the icing.

"Should I order another one for me?" Ray asked, but the laughter was clear in his voice.

"Sorry. I'm starving." Sabrina took another chunk.

"I think they have more. Did you know it's illegal to serve margarine in Wisconsin unless a customer requests it?"

"As it should be."

Sabrina's phone pinged, and a quick glance displayed an e-mail address she didn't recognize. She opened it and froze.

"Everything okay?" Ray asked.

All she could do was nod and hold up a finger, so he knew she needed a moment. The e-mail was short.

From: KalyndraS@theelephantroom.com

To: SabrinaAMonroe@gmail.com

Subject: Re: Job Opening

Dear Sabrina,

Thank you for sending your résumé. I'm intrigued by your varied work history. Are you available for a 3 pm interview on Friday, July 10? Please let me know at your earliest convenience.

Best,

Kalyndra Smith

Freedom, or at least the hope of it. It was like keys that had been dropped outside a prisoner's cell. She just had to grab it.

"Finally, something good." Sabrina set her phone to the side. She didn't want to be rude to Ray, not after everything he'd done to help her, so she'd respond later. "I've got an interview at the *Elephant Room*. I've been waiting weeks for something like this. They're a news site that writes about under-the-radar issues, like how with the rising ocean waters, buying real estate in central Virginia might be the brilliant investment that will make you millions. Or the best matching sites that will help you find compatible doomsday-bunker neighbors. The issues that no one talks about now, but might be huge news next year. They're ahead of their time." Or possibly crackpots, but who was Sabrina to judge? It was a job not in the Wisconsin Dells.

As she spoke, she tore off another hunk of cinnamon roll and stuffed it in her mouth, the cinnamon-and-sugar pastry tasting ten times better than it had a few minutes ago. This would be how she broke up her summer. Pre e-mail and post e-mail. She'd worry about doing the actual job later. For now, she'd savor the keys she finally held in her hand—it was up to her to use them.

"This job isn't here, is it?"

"God no. It's the lifeline I needed."

Ray fidgeted with his glasses, cleaning them on his T-shirt and holding them up to the grimy fluorescent lights hanging from the ceiling.

"We should get started," he said.

Sabrina kept talking over him, not noticing his flat tone. "They want to interview me on Friday. I'll call in sick to the ducks, buy a plane ticket, come back on a late flight. Then I can rest all day Saturday." After the stress of travel and an interview, she'd need the entire day to recharge. "It's just twenty-four hours. What could go wrong, right?"

Ray looked at her through his sparkling-clean glasses. "Congratulations. I'm sure you'll get the job."

Sabrina finally noticed that Ray had gone still, and his face didn't look right without the ever-present smile.

"Don't worry, I'll be here to help with the Goodbye Gala. This is just the first step back to my real life."

21

RAY PARKED HIS CAR next to the library and walked off in search of the H. H. Bennett Studio, dropping quarters into parking meters as he went. Tucked between a gift shop and an old-time photo studio, the kind popular in tourist destinations, was the place for actual old photos—the H. H. Bennett Studio—part store, part museum, and part historic site. Inside, you could buy prints of the famous photographer's most iconic pictures, like the dramatic lighting of Witches Gulch, or the man jumping from a cliff onto Stand Rock. Now only a dog was allowed to make that leap.

He went straight to the counter.

"Can I help you?" a woman asked.

Ray pulled out the picture of his great-grandfather and the mystery woman. "I found this photo in my family's documents. I don't know who the woman is, but the man is a relative. Is there anyone here that might be able to help?"

The woman smiled. "This is a good place to start. This photo was taken after H. H. Bennett died, but his family still ran this studio until twenty years ago, so there might be someone who has seen this woman in other photos. If you'd like, I can give the picture to our local historians."

"I'd rather hang on to it. Could we take a picture of it instead? Then if they think it's worth it, I'll bring it back."

They took some photos, Ray left his name and number, and then he was back on the pavement, squinting at the sun, the damp air making the summer heat seem hotter than it was.

Some days he wondered why he'd given himself this ridiculous task. Number One was gone. He would never know whether his ashes were left on the mantel, buried where he wanted them, or dumped into the ocean. Not everyone got what they wanted, just like he wanted Sabrina to stay in the Dells, but she had other plans. Life sucked that way. He knew she didn't like the Dells, but he was the opposite—he'd known he'd wanted to live here the first time he visited, thirteen years ago, when he was in graduate school.

As he attended his first Goodbye Gala, Ray hadn't wanted to go back to Harvard, with its constant competition and metaphorical (and often literal) pissing contests between classmates. Who had the best grades? Who had the biggest trust fund? Who blew the largest wad of money in a weekend? But all Jaspers went to Harvard for business school. All graduated at the top of the class. All added to the family's legacy.

It didn't matter whether he wanted it or not. It was what was done. At least, that was how the New York Jaspers did it. Eight months left, and he could say goodbye to all the bullshit.

Ray pulled at the bow tie around his neck.

"Stop, you'll make it come loose," Lucy said, tucking her arm around his as they surveyed the room. In the warm woodsy glow of the River Lodge, tables circled a small dance floor in front of a band playing everything from covers of disco songs to big band standards. His family stood out in their custom suits and couture gowns, but not as much as he had expected. After a few more cocktails, they'd all look the same anyway.

His family had made the journey to celebrate the Goodbye Gala. It was an October tradition for the Wisconsin Dells community, and this year his uncle Harry was being honored for his long-standing generosity and involvement, so the family had showed up in force to represent. It didn't matter that Uncle Harry was the last family member left in the Dells; the Jaspers always publicly supported one another. Ray had only seen Uncle Harry at a few events over the years, all in New York. This was the first time the family had come to him. That was how he knew it was a big deal.

Uncle Harry handed Ray's mother a flute of champagne.

"To family," he said, clinking glasses with her. His mom sipped and gave him the smile she reserved for society wives and perfume counter employees—the *I'm being polite because society dictates it, but come closer and I'll cut you with my diamond-encrusted fingers* smile. She reserved a different smile for when they were alone at home, one that would reach her eyes as she gave Ray all of her attention, absorbing the details of his school day or lacrosse game or debate match. She stepped away to set the mostly full flute on a tray of dirty dishes. Harry's eyes followed its journey.

"So, Claire, when are you going to bring the ashes? I have to imagine they're getting dusty on whichever shelf Raymond has been relegated to," Uncle Harry said.

"Harry." There was the smile again. "You know that's never going to happen. Nana was very explicit."

"So was Raymond."

"You wouldn't even know where to put them. Nana saw to that," his mother said.

"I know more than you think."

Their grins chilled the warm air on the dance floor.

"Possession is nine-tenths of the law." A smirk twitched at one corner of her mouth.

Harry scowled. "That's what Etta used to say, too."

"I know," his mother said.

"You can't ignore his will forever."

"But I can, unless you plan to unleash a herd of lawyers at us." Grabbing Ray's arm, she said, "Darling, find me something potable. Scotch—anything old enough to drive will do."

Ray headed toward the bar, ready to top off his drink, too. The crowd—a mix of teenagers, families, and retirees—blended into swirls, clusters of teens in brightly colored dresses sneaking drinks from the bar next to a circle of gray-haired men talking about how it used to be back in the day. Ray loved it. The evening had started with a dinner and a silent auction, followed by drinks and dancing. Soon, the music would stop and a few awards would be handed out, all in the name of community—coming together to celebrate the end of the busy summer season—the Goodbye Gala.

He sipped his Scotch and plotted where to head next. He should find his mom and deliver her drink. A small hallway cut around the side, one used by the waitstaff to move through the restaurant without weaving around the tables. It would spit him out close to where his parents had taken up court, near the west windows, where the sun had disappeared hours ago.

At the sight of his sister making a direct line for him— she looked serious— Ray dipped into the hallway, which was empty except for a young woman with her back to him. Dark curls covered the top of her head, intermingled with tiny sparkling rhinestones. A russet-orange dress skimmed her figure, with matching shoes peeking out the bottom. She spoke to herself—even though he couldn't see her face, he could hear her.

"I'm going out there. I'm ready. I want this." She pointed to the nothingness in front of her. "And you. Will. Not. Follow. I don't care what Mom says."

Ray stepped closer to speak, a clever reply already on his lips, anticipating her surprised expression when she realized he had overheard her. What would she look like? Brown eyes? Green? Maybe a dimple? They would laugh about it. He would buy her a drink, which would be followed by a dance.

Lucy interrupted his thoughts. "She's not your type."

He turned around.

"How could you know that?" Ray asked.

"Because she's seventeen, at most. And dating the local football hero. Like I said. Not your type."

Ugh, seventeen. He should have known better. There weren't a lot of guests in his age bracket here—most were away at college like him.

He looked over his shoulder for one last glance, and the girl was gone.

"Mom is asking about her drink," Lucy said.

"On my way."

"You'd better hurry. She's been cornered." Lucy pointed to the edge of the dance floor. His mom waved him over.

"Ray, there you are." His mom grabbed her Scotch with one hand and his elbow with the other, yanking him to her side with a grip so firm he'd have to make a scene to escape. His mother was a master of unspoken commands, and he understood this one perfectly. Two women stood across from them, one silver-haired with huge sparkling diamonds at her throat and ears, lighting up like Studio 54 as they caught the light, and a younger, blonder version, complete with icy eyes and a haughty stare. "This is Madam Hendricks and her lovely granddaughter Erika. She's a senior at the local high school."

His mother squeezed his elbow until he extended his hand, shaking Madam Hendricks's limp-fish offering and then taking Erika's hand. Her firm grip lingered longer than necessary until he met her eyes, which delivered an even more aggressive message. He'd need to avoid isolated dark corners for the rest of the night.

"What a lovely song for dancing," Madam Hendricks said, tilting her head toward Erika. Ray was not falling for that one.

His mom pinched him. Only years of training kept his reaction internal.

"Sorry to steal my mom away, but my father was asking for her. Excuse us." Ray guided his mom toward the opposite side of the room, hoping his dad was in that direction.

As soon as they were out of earshot, his mom hissed in his ear, "Took you long enough. What a ghastly family. Steer clear of that one."

That wouldn't be a problem. They found his dad enjoying a cigarette on the porch. His mom wrapped her arm around his back, grabbed his cigarette, took a long puff, then rubbed it out in a nearby ashtray. Ray settled into a nearby Adirondack chair.

White twinkly lights hung from every railing and roofline, lighting them up with a soft glow. His mom whispered in his dad's ear as they swayed to the music that was spilling through the open windows, smiling into each other's faces. He'd never seen them happier. His dad had removed his tuxedo jacket and loosened his tie. His mom kicked off her heels

"Imagine living here," his mother said, leaning her head on his dad's shoulder.

His dad rubbed her lower back. "Barbecues with neighbors, pontooning around the lake drinking beers."

"Shopping at Walmart." His mom giggled.

Ray smiled, taking their words a face value. That all sounded wonderful to him. Were his parents considering it? The idea of coming home to this town, eating at this supper club, and attending this dance every year felt right. Like the swirl of whipped cream on a mug of hot chocolate or the sound of a bat knocking a baseball out of the stadium. The Dells was his perfect combination.

Leaving his parents to enjoy their evening, Ray left the porch and strode around the corner of the supper club into the huge, irregularly shaped parking lot. It had been expanded over time in whichever direction proved easiest to remove trees and pave an acceptably flat surface, leaving little alleys of darkened privacy where the attending teens could park their cars. In one such alley, the dome light of a car illuminated the dark shadows where two figures were emerging. He was far enough away that he couldn't hear any specific words, but he recognized the tone. They were fighting. Angry and pleading sounds echoed off the trees. Emerging from the dark, a young man, his sport coat crumpled in one fist, rushed from the car, its overhead light now out. Ray stepped aside to let him pass, noticing his shirt was still untucked, his tie was nowhere to be seen, and the laces of his shoes trailed haplessly behind his racing feet. The young man avoided meeting Ray's glance.

Ray watched the dark space, and a few minutes later, a second silhouette appeared. The figure was wearing a long gown and tiptoeing across the gravel parking lot, careful with each step as if she walked on hot coals. With the darkness and the distance, he couldn't make out her state, only that she kept her arms wrapped tightly to her body. Briefly, she stepped into the light of one of the few street-lamps in the parking lot, and he could make out that her dress was a burnt orange. She wiped at her face with one free hand. It was the girl from earlier in the night.

He stepped down the path toward her, intending to offer her a ride or an escort.

"Ray, it's time." Lucy had found him.

"One minute, I need to check on something."

"They've already waited an extra ten minutes. Once the presentation is done, we can get out of here." Her voice indicated that this event had passed its expiration date hours ago. Ray glanced once more at the girl, then followed Lucy inside.

It had clicked when he'd seen her with Bobby at The Otter Club. Sabrina had been the girl in the burnt-orange dress. Same location, same people, thirteen years later. He still felt guilty about not helping her the night of the gala—and this time he wouldn't let family ex-pectations stop him, even if he was just helping fund her escape. If he had cared about what his parents wanted, his great-grandfather's ashes would still be on the shelf in New York, not in his study, and he wouldn't be running around town hoping to find someone who could help him. Stepping into the cool air of the library, he went straight to the reference desk. Ten minutes later he emerged back into the sunlight with a stack of books full of old newspaper photos and town historical information. He'd keep looking until he found the identity of Number One's mystery girl. This time he would make sure to do the right thing. Helping Sabrina get out of the Dells meant he wouldn't get his girl, but he'd be damned if Number One didn't finally get to be with his.

22

"ARE WE STILL ON for tomorrow night?" Sabrina asked, her ear-buds digging into her ear as she tried to get comfortable in her bed, adjusting the pillow to make a divot around her ear.

"I wouldn't dare miss out on plopping balls into holes," Ray said.

Sabrina snorted. "It might rain and the balls will get slippery."

"If you're gentle, the balls will go where you want them."

"As long as the holes don't have other balls in them."

Ray choked back a laugh. They'd been on the phone for an hour already—he was working on paperwork in his office at The Otter, and she was tucked deep under her covers. This was the second night in a row they ended their day talking to each other, wandering through topics like a toddler at a zoo, switching at any moment with no reason to whatever new topic that grabbed their interest.

"Books," Ray said.

"Absolutely. Anyone as introverted as me likes to read."

"I wasn't sure—you could be a huge gamer or deep into moody French cinema."

"What do you like?" Sabrina asked.

"A little of everything, but I get most excited about fantasy—epic swashbuckling adventures with dragons and elves and magic."

"Why am I not surprised, oh great dungeon master?"

"I suppose you read fancy important books about middle-aged angst in the suburbs."

"Not even close. Some nonfiction for work, but usually a story that removes me from the day-to-day. I love a book that lets me know I'm not alone."

"That's not much different from what I read."

"Tell me about one you liked. Maybe I'll read it."

Ray launched into a detailed description of a favorite fantasy series about a monster hunter and his charge. As he spoke, his smooth deep voice had the same effect on her as a weighted blanket. She was half asleep when he started saying her name.

"Sabrina? Sabrina?"

"Sorry. I drifted. Your voice . . ."

"My voice puts you to sleep?"

"Kind of, but it's a compliment. Listening to you talk . . . it's better than a massage. You should charge for that."

"Are you saying I massage your brain?" Ray asked, his voice noticeably deeper.

Sabrina chuckled.

"Not if you're going to get weird about it." She rolled onto her back. "But yeah, your voice is better than Xanax. Can you follow me around all day, whispering in my ear when I get stressed?"

"I've got nothing else to do," Ray said. In the background, she heard muffled speech, then Ray's muted voice speaking to someone else. "Sabrina, I've gotta go. They need me at the bar. I'm looking forward to tomorrow's hole filling."

Sabrina laughed. "Good night."

He paused, then said quietly, "Imagine I'm still talking to you. Sweet dreams."

The line was dead, but the bass of his voice tingled the back of her neck. Sabrina let it spread like ripples from a pebble dropped in a pond. By the time they reached her fingers and toes, she was asleep.

:ᴖ﹏ᴖ:

SABRINA DROPPED OFF A group of passengers and looped Norman around by the garage where she could park him and have her lunch in the shade of the trees so no one would bother her. She removed her crunchy peanut butter and honey croissant from the container and took her first bite, thinking about what she should pack for her interview trip.

"P. S. Come down."

Sabrina coughed on a bite of her sandwich. What did Erika want now?

"What do you need?"

"Come off the duck. I'm not shouting up at you."

For a brief moment, Sabrina fantasized about firing up Norman and running Erika over, but then she would lose her job and the police would get involved. On the upside, the state prison wasn't in the Dells. On the downside, she liked her freedom. No homicide today.

"One sec."

With no ladder near her, she'd have to drop five feet to the ground, then wheel over a ladder to get back in later. Erika knew all of this. She made Cinderella's stepmother seem like a compassionate employer.

Sabrina chose the side opposite from Erika so she couldn't witness Sabrina's awkward duck dismount. She sat on the edge with her feet dangling off the side and hopped into the soft dirt. Her feet sunk a few inches, and she toppled forward into mud. While she managed to avoid getting her body dirty, her hands and knees were caked in gunk. She peeled off a few dead leaves and twigs, scraping the worst with an old tissue from her pocket, then went to face Erika, who flicked through her phone with militant swipes, one hand on her hip as if Sabrina had been the one making this difficult.

"Hurry up next time. I have things to do."

Sabrina didn't bother to respond; there wasn't a point.

"I put you on the schedule for Saturday."

"Saturdays are my day off."

"I need you at work."

She spun around to leave, her hair fanning behind her like a helicopter of doom. Then she paused and turned back. "And clean yourself up. You're disgusting with all that mud."

Sabrina could only blink as Erika walked away. She wished she could believe that Erika didn't realize the malevolence of her behavior, but Sabrina was not naive. Every interaction Erika deigned to have with Sabrina was intentionally and carefully planned for maximum spite. Her therapist in DC had plenty of theories about Erika's home life and childhood, but Sabrina preferred to think she was just a vindictive hag.

By the time she washed off the mud, found someone to help her with the ladder, and climbed back into Norman, Sabrina was frazzled and so angry she couldn't finish her lunch. There was no way she could meet up with Ray tonight as they'd discussed.

Can't make tonight. Worst day ever. Have to work Saturday, too.

She waited a few seconds to see if he responded, but nothing. She flicked through the news on her phone. A UFO spotted over Reno, an exorcism in Alabama, and a YouTuber who died while live-streaming his ascent up Mount Fuji. That didn't help. She spent the last five minutes of her lunch belly breathing, with her anxiety skipping along at a zippy 6.5. Every muscle clenched. Dreams of a hot shower, Aleve, and absolute silence helped her rev up Norman and get on with the rest of her day. The only way out of it was through.

:⁙⟿⟿⟿⟿⟿⟿:

ONE MORE TOUR TO go and she could go home and crash. One more to go.

Sabrina eased Norman into the chute, shifted him into park, and opened the port-side chain so the passengers could get off. Once the final passenger unloaded, she closed that gate and opened the starboard-side one, finally raising her gaze to greet the new passengers, but there was only one.

Ray.

"What?" she said.

He handed her twenty slips of paper, twenty tickets. He'd bought out the entire boat. Twenty little flags of freedom.

"I could hug you!" Sabrina said.

"I accept your offer." He looked behind him where Erika had come out of her office to watch them. "Let's make it a good one," he whispered.

He wrapped her up like a warm blanket, and she wanted to cry with relief into his shoulder. All the tension she'd stored in her back muscles for the last six hours eased enough that she could probably touch her toes without pulling anything important.

"Um, do you want the tour?" Sabrina asked.

"I paid for a tour, I expect the entire tour."

Sabrina smiled and set her headset and battery pack on the seat behind her. She wouldn't be needing that. "Make sure to tip your tour guide," she said.

She flipped open the hopper seat next to hers and gave it a pat. "Your VIP seat, sir."

They both settled into their seats, and she pulled away.

"What are you doing here?"

"I got your text. I thought you'd like this better than a boat full of tourists."

"Duck."

Ray nodded. "Duck?"

"Norman gets crabby when you call him a boat."

"Norman? Do I need to worry about a jealous boyfriend?"

"It's an open relationship."

Ray laughed, and it warmed Sabrina from head to toe.

"I brought snacks, too." He held up a container of sliced cheese, thinly sliced summer sausage, and an unopened sleeve of Ritz crackers. "Did you know Wisconsin has the only Master Cheesemaker Program outside of Europe?"

"I did not, but it's good to know I have options if I need a new career."

Sabrina loved his random facts.

As they drove and snacked, she pointed out the more interesting sites, leaving out the egregious puns and singsongy tour guide voice. It was one friend pointing out cool stuff to another friend. All that was missing was an ice-cold beer.

"I can't believe you bought all the tickets," said Sabrina.

"I insisted on the group rate, too."

"Erika looked pissed."

"Is she the reason for the bad day?"

"Isn't she always? If the money weren't good . . ." Sabrina trailed off, not wanting to ruin their time talking about her problems. She pointed up to a building on a cliff. "There's The Otter Club."

"I wonder if I've seen you drive by."

"Most likely. I come through here several times a day. I'll honk next time."

"Do that. It'll become our thing, like when Carol Burnett would tug on her ear at the end of every show."

"Who's Carol Burnett?"

"You did not say that. I'm not that much older than you," Ray said.

A smile broke Sabrina's confused expression.

"I kid. I know who she is. Mom had the entire show on VHS back in the olden times."

Ray laughed.

The rest of the ride was relaxing. He asked questions about Norman, the river, and the job and was interested in the stories she didn't usually share with the groups—like the infamous parties of the Tommy Bartlett skiers and her favorite rock formation shaped like a piano.

Instead of returning to the dock, she brought the duck to the parking lot where they parked at the end of the day, and a mechanic rolled over a staircase so they could get down. Ray waited as she did her final checks and punched out, walking her to her car. Was he expecting that they would still go out like they originally planned? She was wiped out, just happier.

"I still need to get some sleep."

"Of course." He waited for some response she didn't know how to give.

"Thank you. You didn't have to do what you did, but I'm sure it made an impression on Erika."

"I didn't do it for Erika."

Sabrina swallowed. "Why did you?"

"You said you were having a bad day. I wanted to make it better."

"You did." She raised on her tiptoes and pressed her lips to his cheek. "Thank you, Ray Jasper."

:ᗞᒿᑎᕲᕙᘛ:

BEFORE CLIMBING INTO BED, Sabrina finished packing for her trip. She didn't need much: a change of clothes in case of catastrophe, her computer, its charger, her makeup kit with everything she'd need to touch up her hair and face, a toothbrush, and toothpaste. It all fit in her computer bag.

She'd picked up her book to read before bed when her phone pinged. It was Ray, and he'd sent an attachment.

Thought you'd like a bedtime story.

She pressed Play on the attached sound file to hear Ray reading *Where the Wild Things Are*, complete with voices. She put in her ear-buds, turned off her light, and listened to him rumble and growl as a wild thing, a sound she felt deep in her own chest. It overwhelmed her; she'd never met someone whose thoughtfulness so perfectly matched what she needed. Charles had occasionally brought her flowers, but he'd never once thought about whether she liked them—

and she didn't. They died so quickly, it was a waste of money. Sabrina preferred consistency. Like a bedtime story she could listen to every night.

When it finished, she listened to it again, then again, each time falling deeper into the story, relaxing into her bed, with Ray filling her head as she fell asleep.

23

It HAD BEEN ALMOST thirty-six hours since Sabrina had had any decent sleep—she wasn't counting the twenty minutes of drooling on the airplane. After calling in sick for work yesterday, she'd flown to Washington, DC, and had her interview at the *Elephant Room*—which went great-ish. Four other candidates had been there for the interview, too. After the interview, one delayed flight, and one re-routing through Denver, she had landed in Madison at five a.m. Enough time to get home, heavily caffeinate, take a brisk shower, and get to work.

As she muddled through the day, her mind fuzzy and vision blurry, the floor seemed to move while she stood still, almost as if she were drunk. She could think only of her bed, which she would flop on in less than two hours. Every muscle hummed with pent-up angst, and a dull pounding threatened to implode her head as she pulled into the chutes for her last tour—a twilight cruise. On a good day, she'd pepper her speech with sparkly vampire jokes, but today, she would go for the bare minimum. Hit the highlights, answer the questions, get back in record time. She didn't care if she got tips, and she'd already planned to skip the normal shakedown stop.

After the last passenger disembarked, she did a quick walk-through, picking up any stray trash. Harry sat in the last row humming to himself—at least he was behaving. Sabrina believed he understood more than he let on—which was a good sign that he would be able to verbalize what he wanted soon. The longer he stuck around, the more likely Ray would discover her secret.

"Come on, girls, let's get the booze cruise started!" Erika's voice hammered into Sabrina's head.

No, please. Don't let her mean my duck.

Erika boarded Norman, curled and primped like she was starring in *Real Housewives of the Dells*, followed by a small army of clones carrying penis-shaped balloons, a cooler, and tote bags of gluten-free, fat-free, taste-free vegan snacks. Erika wore a sparkly tiara and a snug-fitting white T-shirt that read BRIDE in clear rhinestones.

Her bachelorette party.

The girls piled on and spread out. One had a small portable speaker that blasted Ariana Grande, another livestreamed from her phone. There was only one reason for Erika to have the party on Sabrina's duck, and it had everything to do with tormenting her. Nothing said a good time like bullying an employee.

Was Sabrina in hell? Had her plane crashed last night and this whole day was part of her eternal torture? Would a person know if they had died and were in hell? Was there an orientation before the torture, or were you plopped right into it? Was there a last-chance feast with all your favorite foods that were a few days past their prime—three-day-old pizza left out on a coffee table in a frat house, melted ice cream, and well-done rib eye steaks?

That seemed preferable to what Sabrina was about to endure.

She waited by her captain's chair as Erika sauntered up the center aisle like she owned it, which she did. Sabrina's skin crawled as if she'd sat on an anthill.

"Isn't this lucky? You get to drive my party," Erika said. Her gaze scanned Sabrina from head to toe, analyzing every flaw and cataloging it for future use. She didn't have to look long—Sabrina looked like week-old leftovers. "You look like shit. You should have called in sick again." Erika emphasized the word "sick." She knew Sabrina had faked it. Like all things Erika, best to ignore the bait or get hooked.

"What do you want? From me. For the tour." The words weren't coming out quite right, but that only added to Erika's enjoyment. She knew she had all the power.

"We want the tour."

"Wouldn't you rather I putter around? I can go straight to Lake Delton and loop around the lake."

"Absolutely not. We want the full tour, with all your cute fun facts. Right, girls?"

Her squad let out a rallying cry of woo-hoos at varying pitches, flicking every nerve in Sabrina's already tense neck.

"Of course," Sabrina said. She didn't bother to smile or look pleased. She'd need all her self-control to not burst into tears or scream or jump overboard into oncoming traffic. A hospital stay sounded pleasant. What had her life come to that hell or a hospital-worthy injury was the better option?

Everything about this screamed disaster. She slipped on her headset and started up Norman.

She could do this.

She could do this.

I think I can.

I think I can.

I think I can.

With a deep breath, Sabrina turned the key, eased away from the dock, and launched into her script.

"Welcome aboard Norman, a World War Two duck . . ."

She kept talking even though none of the women paid attention, except Erika, who sat in the first row on the starboard side, where Sabrina could see her in her peripheral vision as she sipped a Skinny-girl margarita from a penis-tipped straw poking out of a foot-long penis-shaped cup. These ladies were all about the class.

"We can't hear you," Erika said.

Of course they couldn't hear her, clone number four had the Blue-tooth speaker turned up to eleven. The voice of God would have trouble competing with that racket, but she had to try. She reached to the headset controls latched to her belt and turned up the volume as high as it would go. She could see the clones scowl at the back of her head in the large mirror she used to keep an eye on her passengers.

As they drove past a series of stone statues, Sabrina continued. "So I guess what I'm trying to say is don't take these statues for granite." She paused. Most tour guests let out an appreciative groan, but the girls kept drinking and Erika kept staring. Was this really her plan for her own bachelorette party? "If you don't like that joke, well, it's going to be a long trip."

Erika's evil grin lit up her face like a jack-o'-lantern carved by Satan.

Sabrina continued reciting her lines, the partiers kept dancing and drinking—no one was sitting—and Erika kept staring. Harry seemed to enjoy the dancing, bobbing his head along to the mind-numbing pop music. Any other group and she would be laughing and eager to tell her mom and Molly about it, but today it caused every muscle in her body to contract while nausea threatened to become all-too-real vomit. Call it common sense, call it a sixth sense, but Sabrina knew she wasn't getting out of today unscathed.

As they approached the Wisconsin River, she said her next lines in a monotonous voice. "There it is, the Pacific Ocean. It's much smaller in person. As we go in, it can be bumpy, so with your left hand, grab the seat in front of you and with your right hand . . . plug your nose."

As she drove the duck into the water, her foot pressed on the gas pedal harder than normal, causing the dancers to stumble, and a few fell into seats, spilling drinks onto their bedazzled clothes.

Her lips quirked for a second, enjoying a little bit of payback. Maybe she wasn't entirely devoid of power.

"Erika." A minion had approached their queen. "You have to try this chip. The bag says it's only one and half calories per chip, so I could eat, like, one hundred of them and it would only be, like"—she paused much too long for the third-grade math required—"under two hundred calories."

"You're lucky your daddy has money, Cindy."

Cindy smiled, then furrowed her brow, working out whether or not Erika's comment was a compliment or an insult. Her smile returned. She'd worked it out wrong.

Erika finally grew bored and joined the party, dancing with her friends and doing shots of flavored vodka in colors that would make a three-year-old girl squee. One of the concoctions even had glitter in it. Sabrina gave up on the tour completely and drove the duck. This wasn't horrible. Maybe it would be okay. She'd outlasted Erika by not sinking to her level, like Ray had said. Maybe he was right and she had more control than she thought.

Sabrina smoothly transitioned the duck out of the Wisconsin

River, over Highway 12, and into Lake Delton with barely a jostle as she pulled up the wheels and started the boat's motor.

If it weren't for the music hammering into her head, it might have been pleasant. The boat sliced through the lake water, the air was warm but not humid, and the sun hovered above the trees, turning the light from bright orange to a muted rose. Maybe it would all be okay. She allowed herself to relax and coasted around the shore, ogling the large homes that had popped up in the last ten years. Speedboats and pontoons crisscrossed the lake around them, sending waves to collide with the side of the duck.

Then it all went wrong.

The music quieted, and Erika climbed onto the folded hopper seat next to her—she had to crouch a bit to avoid hitting her head on the canopy above her, adding instability to her tipsiness.

"Erika, you shouldn't stand there. You could lose your balance."

A wave hit the side of the duck, and Erika wobbled on her heeled sandal, then she found her balance. Sabrina's heartbeat picked up its pace and a hot flash passed over her body, beads of sweat formed on her forehead and down her spine.

"I don't need you to tell me what I should do." She stood straight, looking down at her subjects, who reverently stared up at her. At that moment, perhaps now that he was no longer distracted with the dancing and music, Harry popped up in front of Sabrina, his head coming out of the duck's dashboard like an enormous bobblehead, and he started shouting at her.

"*Vrend cay. Vrend cay.*"

At the same time, Erika began her speech. Sabrina wiggled her fingers as the ends went numb from gripping the steering wheel too tightly.

"Ladies, thank you all for coming to this special day to celebrate my wedding to my longtime fiancé, Rob." When had she started calling Bobby Rob? "As you all know, we've been together since high school, after he had a tragically bad relationship." Erika looked right at Sabrina. "What you might not know is that tragic girlfriend is here. Right, P. S.?"

Oh God, what was she doing? The entire plan became clear. Sabrina gulped some air, but it was gone. The air was gone. She gulped again and found it. *Breathe in. Breathe out.* Erika was using this event to publicly humiliate Sabrina in front of her friends—because years of middle school and high school torture weren't enough.

Focus on the job. Ignore her. Breathe in. Breathe out.

"Rob admitted to me that a few weeks ago, he saw Sabrina at The Otter Club, and she was all over him. Desperate to reconnect with her only real boyfriend . . ." Not true—but Erika didn't know about Charles. ". . . even if he only dated her because I told him to."

Was that real? Or was Erika reinventing history to make this even worse? Sabrina wiped the sweat from her forehead. Harry shouted at her, his arms sticking out of the duck's dashboard as if he wanted to grab the steering wheel and turn it. Had Bobby dating her really been a trick? And she had played right into it. Telling him she loved him, alone in a car in a dark parking lot, windows steamed. The Goodbye Gala. Everyone knew. Sabrina wanted to throw up or cry or maybe scream. She could feel the tidal wave coming at her, and deep breathing wasn't going to save her. Time was limited before the wave pulled her under.

Focus on five things she could see. Water. Sky. Clouds. Houses. Harry.

Focus on four things she could feel. Steering wheel. Norman. Sweat. Her heart thundering.

Breathe in.

Breathe out.

It wasn't working.

"Stop it," Sabrina said to Harry, trying to whisper. If she could stop one thing, maybe she could pull back from the oncoming attack, but Erika had the ears of a bat.

"What did you say?" Erika said, narrowing her eyes. She swayed a little as waves from a passing boat bumped the prow.

"Nothing."

"That's right, P. S. You. Don't talk. To me." Her thinly veiled speech now turned to blatant vitriol directed at her. "Rob told me you kissed him." The clones gasped in shock, though Sabrina was sure they already knew and this was part of a carefully planned takedown. One of them in the back held her camera high to catch all the action live. "How dare you try to steal my fiancé? As if you could."

Sabrina opened her mouth to defend herself, but couldn't speak. She could have hard evidence that Bobby had initiated the horrible kiss and Erika would still choose not to believe her. He must have felt rejected by her and decided this was the best way to save his own ass. How was she going to get out of this with her job intact? She needed the money so she could get away from this town, these people.

Tears collected along her lashes. Sabrina wouldn't last much longer.

Then it happened fast, and she wasn't even sure who did it. Harry grabbed hold of the wheel at the same time that Sabrina—reacting on instinct—jerked it to the left to avoid a large incoming wave from a passing boat. Maybe it was Harry's added muscle, maybe it was all her, but either way, the boat made a hard left turn. Erika lost her balance and tumbled overboard into the evening waters. The splash came after a painful-sounding smack, arcing water over the sides of the duck in dainty, sparkling missiles. A chorus of shrieks erupted from the clones, a caterwauling that echoed over the lake.

A surge of satisfaction blossomed, then instinct kicked in. Sabrina killed the motor, grabbed the emergency floatation device—a flat white square with handles and a rope attached—and leaned over the hopper seat to see where Erika went in. Her head had already emerged from the water, tiara askew atop her flattened curls. Harry was nowhere to be seen.

She tossed the floatie to Erika and pulled her toward the back of the duck, where Sabrina heaved the silent and fuming bachelorette onto the deck. The rest of the party had fizzled, with the silence being worse than the loud music. Now all that pounded in her head was the vein at her temple and the thoughts about how bad it was going to get when they returned to the chutes. Only the pleasure of seeing Erika bedraggled buoyed her enough to keep driving.

24

THE RIDE BACK TO the Real Dells Ducky Tour's offices had been silent save for a few whispers, but with each minute, the inevitable end neared. Sabrina hung on second by second, doing her best to keep the waves of panic from pulling her under. She'd been through this before. She would survive.

Three things she could smell. Diesel. A dead fish. Spilled margarita.

Two things she could hear. Norman's engine. Her heartbeat.

Get through this second. Now get through this second.

Her job was gone. She'd deal with that reality tomorrow.

Just get through this next second.

With trembling hands, she steered Norman into the chute. Waiting on the pier was Erika's mom, her back stiff and her coral lips pursed. Behind her was Ray. Why was he here? She'd had enough witnesses to her humiliation.

As the clones filed off, leaving a mess of empty bottles and partially eaten marijuana edibles, Erika waited for Mrs. Hendricks to board. Sabrina avoided Ray's gaze, though he tried to catch her attention by waving his arms, as if she could miss him on the empty platform. Swallowing became nearly impossible, all the moisture in her body exited through her pores, pumping in time to the frantic pace of her heart. Her chest rose and fell as if she'd sprinted up a steep hill through a foot of snow.

She'd never pay off her debt. She'd never move out of her parents' house. She'd never leave the Dells. She was trapped in a box with all the oxygen sucked out of it, leaving her mind unable to engage with the recent events. Her body moved separately from her brain—finding some autopilot commands she hadn't programmed.

Her hands shook as she patted Norman's steering wheel in a silent goodbye. He had been a reliable duck, and she knew this was their last moment together. Bending over to load her water bottle into her backpack, Sabrina double-checked that she'd gathered everything, even shoving a pack of S'NUG'erdoodles, snickerdoodle cookies containing weed, into a pocket. Hoisting the pack on her back, she stood to face her fate. Mrs. Hendricks stood at the end of the aisle in a slim, fitted sheath dress and expensive heels, more appropriate for elite society than a small town in the middle of Wisconsin. The pale-yellow dress matched her immovable shoulder-length bob. She crossed her arms and blocked the exit.

"Sabrina."

"Mrs. Hendricks," Sabrina said, the words sticking in her mouth so she had to force them, like shoving a beanbag chair through a pet door. It could be done, but it took effort. Erika stood slightly behind her mother, grinning.

"We hired you with respect for your family's long history in our city, but clearly that trust was misplaced. I cannot continue to employ someone incapable of doing their job. Erika warned me that you would be a disaster, and I'm sad to see she was right. You have risked the life of my daughter."

Sabrina had known this would happen, yet now that it had, she couldn't help but be shocked, the surrealism of her very worst fears becoming reality. Most of her fears only ever played out in her head, real enough to her, but no one else. This time, people really would talk about her, eager for Erika's firsthand account of her public humiliation, made even worse by Ray's presence.

"I'm horrified by what Erika said has happened, but I'd like to hear your side as well."

Sabrina could apologize and beg. Maybe she'd even keep her job until Erika contrived the next impossible scenario—another Kobayashi Maru test. She opened her mouth, but then Sabrina realized, no matter what she did, she would lose. Erika's lips twitched upward. She'd get to see Sabrina either grovel for her job or be humiliatingly fired. Win-win.

The only thing Sabrina could control was how she left this boat. In a whimper or a roar. She'd lived her life whimpering along, slinking in the shadows to avoid being noticed. She wanted to let loose a rant that would make Dixie Carter on *Designing Women* sit back in her chair and shout a "Hallelujah." She wanted to reveal all the horrible things Erika had said and done to her. About how Bobby kissed her and groped her thigh, about how Erika was angry because Sabrina didn't try to win her approval. She wanted to say it all.

She could want all day long, but she was staring down the biggest wave of panic yet, and she had to leave. Now. She pushed herself between the Hendricks women and jogged toward her car, her backpack bouncing against her shoulders and her bra threatening to burst at the seams from the unexpected demand on its durability under pressure.

"Wait up," Ray said from behind her. She could hear his steps matching her pace, but she couldn't stop or she'd slump to the ground. She needed to make it to a car and the safety it represented. Right now, all that kept her going was momentum.

She unlocked her car door and tossed her keys to Ray, pointing to the driver's seat. "Get in."

He did. He didn't ask questions or make any effort to convince her to get in his car instead. He just opened the driver's-side door and had the car started by the time she was buckled.

"What—"

"Nope, no talking yet. Shark mode. Keep moving or I'm done. Head to the state park on River Road." She hoped he knew where it was. She needed to be away from people, Ray excluded. She didn't want to answer questions.

There was only one place she could go right now. Her spot. Now that she was in the car, away from Erika, wave upon wave slammed into her. She thought about telling him to go to the hospital, because surely she was about to die. She opened her mouth to breathe, and the air wouldn't come in. A ten. She choked on the emptiness tearing at her lungs, the pain of it finally unleashing the tears. In great gasping sobs that shook her body, she managed to suck in enough air to stay alive for that moment, and then it was gone again.

Her breathing wouldn't regulate, and the tears wouldn't stop. The moment wouldn't end. Like a record player skipping on the same scratch, it couldn't get past the flaw, only becoming more and more irritating and oppressive with each new skip. Right now, this moment was a two-inch gouge in the middle of "Rockstar" by Nickelback, a nightmare she couldn't escape.

Her body had flicked a switch, each part powering down in turn, going dark, until all that was left was the vibrating panic coursing through her like an electrical wire. She just wanted it over. She knew huge portions of her life were shattering around her—her future, her career—but she couldn't regain any control. What was the point of it all when she couldn't participate in her own life when she needed to the most?

It hadn't been this bad in a long time. As they rolled past looming waterslides and roller coasters that cast twisty shadows on the road, she was reminded that she'd never get to leave this place now. All during high school, she'd used her free time, which was plentiful, to study. She had earned scholarships, disappointed her mom with her plans to leave, then taken out too many loans in order to stay gone. Without her duck income, her debt spreadsheets would be completely red. Her only hope of ever paying it all off was to continue living rent-free with her parents and find a job to at least cover the minimum payments on her credit cards and student loans. She couldn't see past all the roadblocks.

She'd never get that job. She'd never pay off her debt. She'd never leave her parents' house. Every day would be a constant reminder of her failure. Her humiliating childhood had evolved into her humiliating adulthood.

And those same thoughts looped and looped and looped.

What must Ray think? She was dragging him to the middle of nowhere, where he'd be trapped with her for who knew how long. He pulled into the parking lot and stopped the car. She tried to pull herself together and found she could breathe now. *Focus on that.*

Breathe in.

Breathe out.

Belly out.

Belly in.

Repeat.

Better.

Now get out of the car.

She grabbed her backpack and a blanket from the back seat and opened the door. Ray followed her as she disappeared down a path between the trees where the undergrowth thinned.

"Is this where you murder me?" Ray said, jogging to keep up. The promise of her destination kept her moving forward, like the allure of a hot bath after a day playing in the snow. She managed a wan smile over her shoulder and wiped away some of the tears, but a steady stream replaced them. They had to run out on their own now.

After ten minutes of walking, she broke off into the trees. There was still enough of a path from where other visitors like herself had sought out a special spot off the trail.

"Since murder is off the table, where are we going?"

"My spot." Her voice was rough, but it felt good to speak—she had made it to the down slope.

There was a pause before Ray spoke. "Sorry. I didn't mean to intrude. I . . ."

Sabrina squeezed his hand to reassure him that he was welcome. His hand was cool and dry against her overheated skin.

She broke through the underbrush to a small grassy patch that was surrounded by tall pines to the right and left. Directly in front of them was a rocky drop-off that met the dark Wisconsin River forty feet below. Along the river, sandstone cliffs carved by water and wind resembled a messy stack of pancakes. Dark green pines sticking out at odd angles topped the cliffs, with a few growing out from the side. The river wound its way around a corner, like a smaller version of the Grand Canyon. They had made it in time. The sun was just starting to touch the tips of the trees.

"Wow," Ray said, then he stopped at her side and absorbed the view. The rushing water echoed up the sides of the cliffs, drowning out any sounds that might carry. Ray gently took the blanket from her hand and spread it on the ground. They both sat.

The worst of the episode was over. The isolation helped calm her. Her hands still trembled, and Ray reached out to hold them. That helped, too. He moored her in the rocky waters inside her head.

The sun was almost completely behind the trees before she could speak.

"I've been coming here since high school." She took another deep breath so the words didn't wash out of her mouth in a rush. "Even though this is state land. We aren't supposed to come out here, so not many people find this spot. It's a safety thing. But you can't beat the view."

She dug out one of the edibles and ate half, hoping it might help calm her. "You're probably wondering what happened."

"I'm curious."

He smiled at her, that boyish expression that was all genuine warmth. In the growing dusk, some of his features were obscured, but she couldn't miss that comforting grin. She took another shaky breath. They came easier now.

"On the upside, I'll have a lot more time to work on the gala. On the downside, I'm no longer employed as a prestigious Real Dells Ducky Tour guide." Another deep breath, and she rubbed her arms. The sweating had stopped, so chills would be close behind. "I stole the hat, and I'm not giving it back."

"I got that part. What led up to it?"

Sabrina tried to explain the long history between Erika and herself, dating back to grade school, but leaving out the parts about seeing ghosts. She would never share that part of herself again. The sky turned orange, then red, then blue and purple. The light faded into darkness, with stars breaking up the monotony of the night sky, flickering in time to the fireflies.

"Why has Erika singled you out? I can't imagine you doing anything to warrant years of bullying."

"Can't a person be horrible because they were made that way?" Sabrina said, but thought back and sighed. "I've thought a lot about it, and my best guess is Cammy. She came to our school in fourth grade. New students were rare, let alone interesting ones like her, with a Scottish accent and light-blond hair, braided and finished with plaid ribbons. Her parents had moved here because her mother was the architect for a new waterpark. Erika expected them to be friends, but Cammy chose me instead. We ate lunch together, sat under a tree during recess to read, and had sleepovers every weekend. When Cammy's mom finished the job, they moved on to the next one."

"You lost a friend and gained Erika's hatred."

She leaned her head on his shoulder. The exhaustion had crept up on her, making it hard to even hold up her head. She'd done a lot of talking. She shivered. "It has been a day," she said.

He put his arm around her, rubbing her shoulder. She shivered again, and Ray moved her between his legs where he could wrap his arms around her until her back flooded with heat. She was warm and safe.

"I guess this means we don't have to fake date anymore," Sabrina said, but she regretted the words immediately because she didn't want it to end.

"I was never fake dating, Sabrina." Ray's voice was soft, close to her ear. "The reason I stopped by today was to see if you needed a ride home after a night of no sleep."

She sat up straight so she could turn around and look at him.

With his face so near, she could feel his breath. It smelled of winter-green mints, the kind you buy at the cash register at not-Denny's Denny's. He continued.

"I understood you wanted to pretend, so I respected that, but those dates were real to me. The only difference is there would have been more kissing."

Her eyes dropped to his lips, so close to her own. His jaw and chin were dusted with a dark stubble. Would she feel it if she touched her lips to his? As soon as the thought skittered across her mind, she knew she had to find out the answer. She turned in his arms and leaned toward him, but he held her shoulders so she couldn't get closer. He didn't want her to kiss him. The rejection stung.

She retreated, but his arms kept her still. She couldn't get closer, but she couldn't get away.

"Sabrina." His voice was like velvet on her cheek. "I want to be clear about something." His hands slid down her arms and curled around her hands. Part of her wanted to pull away, but she didn't. "I want to kiss you. I really want to kiss you. But I don't know if you'd regret it. I can't imagine the emotions that have coursed through you in the last few hours, and I don't want there to be any confusion about what you're feeling and why."

He squeezed her hand, and she squeezed back.

"Is that okay?" he asked.

She nodded.

He was asking if it was okay that he give her space to make smart choices she wouldn't regret, though she was fairly certain she wouldn't regret kissing him, no matter what the circumstances. He pulled her to his side again, and she let herself bask in his warmth. Being this close to him caused her heart to thump for different reasons.

She giggled.

"Everything okay?" Ray had pushed her back a bit so he could look at her.

She focused on him, giving him a serious look so he knew she was being serious. She didn't want to get distracted by the pretty stars that streaked across the sky. There were so many of them, all twirling and swirling around the earth.

Oh.

"I think the edible has kicked in."

Ray chuckled. "Understood. Carry on, then."

They lay down on the blanket, with her head in the crook of his arm to keep her warm, though she really wasn't paying attention to that.

"Sabrina," a woman's voice said. It sounded familiar. "Sabrina, blink if you hear me."

She blinked and looked to where the voice hovered. Molly stood not far away.

"Molly." Sabrina blurted the name out loud.

"What?" Ray asked. "What did you say?"

Shit. She may be high, but Sabrina knew she shouldn't have said Molly's name out loud.

"Just thinking about the cookie. You know, Molly. Mary Jane. The S'NUG'erdoodles are definitely working."

Even high, she knew she sounded like an idiot. Ray laughed it off and pulled her closer, though he did look around the clearing.

"Goodness gracious," Molly said. "You're flying. Do not tell your mother. She's heard about what happened and is worried. You aren't answering your phone, and she asked me to find you. I'll let her know you're with Ray and tell her not to worry."

"Mmm, wonderful," Sabrina said. And nuzzled closer to Ray. He smelled good. She did want to kiss him. He made her heart pop, pop, pop. Pop like fireworks. Pop like popcorn. Pop like Pop Rocks.

Right now, it was hard to remember why she shouldn't.

She should head home and sleep. Tomorrow she'd have a lot to deal with, and there was a good chance she wouldn't want to move. But she was too comfortable and too happy to move. If every day could be like this moment, maybe she could stay in the Dells. Close to her family. Close to Ray.

25

KISSING SABRINA WAS ALL Ray could think about. They had almost kissed before he'd stopped them because it was the right thing
to do. Her face had been so close he could smell the cinnamon from
the edible. Sometimes doing the right thing sucked.

After driving her home, he had walked her to the door and
handed her off to her bemused mom, who had invited him in for tea.
He'd declined when Sabrina had snort-laughed at him. If things went
the way he hoped, there would be plenty of opportunities for late-
night tea with her parents.

It was only eight in the morning, and The Otter Club's kitchen
staff was already in prep mode for the night, simmering stocks,
chopping vegetables, and prepping steaks. Today he was working on
a new creation—Wisconsin risotto made with Spotted Cow beer, a
two-year cheddar from a local dairy, and crispy-fried bratwurst
made in-house by Chef Rick. He'd been playing with the recipe for
a while, struggling with the right balance of beer and cheddar. Too
much beer overshadowed everything. Too little and what was the

point? He'd finally found the right mix using chicken stock to dilute the malty ale. The cheddar was even trickier—too much and it became clumpy and gooey. He needed to mix it with Parmesan and Colby cheese so it melted smoothly. Today was the final run-through. At the last minute, he diced a brat and crisped it in a frying pan. He ladled a serving into a bowl and added a small mound of brat to the center.

Before tasting, he checked his phone. No Sabrina. Only two messages from Erika Hendricks about a partnership with the Real Dells Ducky Tours. He ignored them.

Should he contact Sabrina? They had a lot of work to do on the Goodbye Gala, and now that her schedule had opened, he wanted to take advantage of her time. Plus, he wanted to see her again. Hold her again. Smell her hair again. He held the phone near a window to make sure a weak signal wasn't preventing messages from arriving, even though he knew there was a strong Wi-Fi connection through his entire supper club.

"You have it bad," Rick said.

"I have what bad?"

Rick gave him a look, but let it pass for now.

"You gonna let me try it?" Rick pointed at the risotto, and Ray slid the bowl across the stainless-steel counter. Rick scooped up a bite, making sure to get some of the bratwurst. Ray did the same with a fresh spoon. As they chewed, they breathed through their noses, letting the air mingle with the flavors in their mouths before swallowing.

"Not bad. It's missing something, but it's close. You nailed the texture, creamy and not overcooked."

Rick could be stingy with compliments, so Ray tried not to look too proud.

"You're right that something's missing. What about a little sauer-kraut?"

Rick took another bite and waved his spoon at Ray. "Yes. But homemade. Don't you dare put the canned stuff on this."

Ray jotted down the idea in his notebook and took another bite, checking his phone as he chewed.

"You going to tell me who it is?"

Ray sighed, and Rick went back to his prep work.

"Sabrina Monroe."

Rick kept his eyes on the rib eye steaks he was slicing off a side of beef. Which was odd. Rick always looked at you when you had a conversation, and he didn't need to watch his hands while cutting. He could be blindfolded and wouldn't get a nick.

"What aren't you telling me?"

"I went to school with her older brothers. We hung out some-times."

"And?"

"I don't really *know* anything. When it came to their sister, they were protective. She didn't have it easy—a lot of bullying."

"Some things haven't really changed," Ray said.

"There are stories. Rumors—so you never really know what's true and what's malicious and what's local lore. It's a strange small town with people to match."

He went back to cutting.

"Are you going to tell me what these rumors are?"

Rick shrugged, then looked Ray in the eye. "A former dishwasher swears that Sabrina's mom gave her a message from her dead grand-mother shortly after they buried her. Like, said things that only a family member would know. That's just one story. There are a bunch more. Mrs. Monroe was caught breaking into a person's house. When asked why she was there, she said the curling iron was left on by the woman who had just died. And it had been. How could she have known that? It isn't bad, it's just odd."

"Are you saying they can talk to dead people? Like *The Sixth Sense*?"

Rick held up his hands.

"I'm not saying anything about your new girlfriend."

It couldn't be true, could it? Ray should have been more sur-prised, but if people thought there was something odd about her, that would explain a lot. Holmesian fallacy and all that. He was more surprised by the pleasure he derived from Rick labeling Sabrina as his girlfriend. He needed more information, while proceeding with caution. He didn't want to scare her away. If any of the stories were true—and the more he learned about her, the more likely they were—she needed to trust him. Perhaps the way forward was to get to know her family better.

Looking at his risotto, an idea formed.

:ⓒ ⅉ ⸱ ͻ:

RAY PARKED IN FRONT of the Monroe home. He hadn't seen much of it last night, but in the daylight it was cheery and welcoming, with colorful flowers hanging on the porch and a garden gnome smiling at him from under a bush, unlike the cat that glared through the neighbor's screen door, pawing at the thin barrier.

Grabbing his insulated bag, he headed to the same door where he had delivered Sabrina the night before. He knocked, and after a mo-ment, Sabrina's mom answered.

"Ray, what a surprise. Sabrina's still upstairs." Mrs. Monroe looked over her shoulder and gave a little nod, as if she were answering someone, but he saw and heard no one. "She'll be down in a few minutes, I'm sure." She stepped back from the door while holding it open. "Come in. Can I get you some tea? Coffee? Water?"

"I'd love a coffee, Mrs. Monroe."

"Please, call me Jenny." She smiled warmly.

Sabrina had her mother's bright skin and smile, though she was more selective with it. Maybe that was why he loved seeing it so much. It was rare and special when it appeared. Jenny pointed to the table as she went to the coffeepot and poured him a cup. He sat.

"Sugar? Cream?"

"Black. I like my coffee strong enough to lift a tank."

Jenny laughed as her husband joined them.

"Who is making my girl laugh?"

Ray stood to shake his hand.

"Good to see you, Ray. What brings you over on a Sunday morning?"

"I've been working on perfecting a Wisconsin-style risotto, and I brought some for tasting. I trust your experienced palates."

Doug rubbed his hands together in anticipation.

Ray unzipped the cooler and pulled out a glass container with a blue plastic lid, along with a handful of spoons, enough for everyone. The heat still radiated off the bowl.

"If you're willing, grab a spoon and dig in. Make sure to get some of the brat."

Jenny and Doug had each taken a spoonful and were chewing thoughtfully when Sabrina slid into the kitchen on her socks across the hardwood floors. She wore colorful cotton pajama pants covered in dragons and an oversize T-shirt displaying the words WELL BEHAVED WOMEN SELDOM MAKE HISTORY. His heart gave a quiet lurch.

Nerdy was his kryptonite. He'd really never stood a chance with Sabrina.

"What are you doing here?" Her hair drooped in a charming haphazard ponytail.

"Don't be so rude, honey. He brought us snacks," Jenny said, pointing to the risotto on the table. Doug scooped another bite.

"Cheesus. It's tasty."

Sabrina cringed. "Really, Dad?" She pulled her hair into a more secure knot atop her head, though a few tendrils escaped, framing her face.

"Thanks, Doug," Ray said.

"I'm a man who appreciates his cheese." He patted his belly. "Are you considering this for The Otter Club?"

"Oh no. Chef Rick would kill me if I tinkered with his menu." Ray took a spoonful. "This is my hobby—part of my Wisconsin assimilation. Did you know Wisconsin makes more cheese than any other state?"

Doug rubbed his hands together. "Son, who do you think you're talking to? Did you know over ninety percent of Wisconsin milk is used to make more than six hundred different types of cheese?"

Ray grinned—clearly he'd found a kindred spirit.

"I did not, but now I have a goal to try them all," Ray said.

"Get in here, Sabrina." Doug grabbed her arm, steered her to the table, pulled out a chair, and nudged her to sit next to Ray. She rolled her eyes but did as he encouraged her to do. "Eat."

Sabrina scooped a spoonful and chewed. Then scooped a bigger bite. "Really good, but it's missing something. The back of my tongue wants in on the action and it's left hanging. Something tangy, maybe?"

Ray liked that Sabrina could tell it needed something extra and that she wasn't hesitating to share her opinion. "Like a little sauerkraut?" he said.

"Yes." Sabrina and Doug said it at the same time.

Doug continued. "We need to talk. I can take you to a few places that do some amazing things with kraut, and we've got to take you to the Hideout."

"I'd love that. What's the Hideout?"

Doug ignored his question. "Sabrina can give me your number, and I'll get something on the books."

Jenny grabbed Doug's arm. "Honey, I need your help in the living room." As excuses went, it was a classic. Ray looked down to hide his smile as Jenny led Doug from the room.

Sabrina chewed another bite. "I've never had a beer-brat risotto before. Clever."

"Thanks. It's been tough to crack."

She tapped her fingers on the table and studied him. "What are you doing here?"

Dark circles shadowed her eyes, more pronounced against her paler-than-normal skin. Was she sick?

"I wanted to talk about the gala and how you wanted to proceed." He moved the dish from side to side. "And I wanted to see how you were doing after yesterday."

Sabrina closed her eyes and drew circles on the table with her fingers. He couldn't guess what she might be thinking. Was she upset? Sad? Happy that he came? Did she still want to kiss him? He wished he could read her moods at a glance.

"I'm . . . not great. I was sleeping when you arrived, still overwhelmed at the moment."

"Not the best time, then?"

Sabrina shook her head.

"I need a day or so to adjust to my new circumstances, if that's okay."

Ray set his hand on top of hers, and Sabrina stared at it, then looked up at him.

"Of course that's okay. We can discuss when you're ready."

Sabrina tilted her head in question. Why was she so confused?

"About the gala, right?" she said.

"And other things." Ray smiled at her and squeezed her hand.

Sabrina pulled her hand away and used it to tighten her topknot. Did she really need to do that, or was it a pretense to get her hand away? Her body leaned away from him.

"About last night," Sabrina said. Ray leaned back in his chair. That was never a good start to a sentence. "If I said or did anything that gave you the wrong idea about me . . ." She left the words hanging. What did she think she did last night? And what did she think he thought she did? How had this conversation gone so sideways?

"You didn't do anything . . ." He didn't know how to finish that. "You were going through a lot. I'm glad I could be there for you."

Sabrina smiled and relaxed.

"Good. One less thing to overanalyze." She yawned. Ray took that as his cue and stood.

"I'll let you get back to sleep. Text me when you're ready to talk gala."

He leaned in to hug her, but she didn't reciprocate. Ray caught himself and gave her a pat on the shoulder instead. He grabbed his bowl and left before he could misread another situation.

MOLLY AND JENNY WATCHED Ray drive away as Sabrina tiptoed to the stairs.

"Not so fast. A few minutes, please," Jenny said.

Sabrina froze with her foot on the bottom step.

"Can we talk later? Bed." She pointed up the stairs.

"You can make it." Jenny pointed at the couch, and Sabrina shuffled over to it and nestled into the corner, pulling a blanket up to her shoulders. It reminded Molly of Sabrina's teenage years, when she'd curl up on the couch like that and they'd watch movies together.

Jenny sat next to her, and Molly settled into her chair by the window. "Tell me."

"It was bad. Real bad. It was a setup from the beginning. I don't know why I ever took that job."

"Because it's the best paying job in the Dells for seasonal work, most of it cash," her mom said, repeating the response Sabrina had used to convince herself that working at the Real Dells Ducky Tours was a good idea.

Sabrina nodded. "There's a million should-haves and could-haves, but this was always going to end in disaster."

"There really are other decent paying jobs."

"That's not what I mean, Mom. This whole summer. Coming home. It was always going to be a mess. I can't live here like you. I can't do this." Tears welled in her eyes, and Jenny pulled Sabrina in for a hug and rubbed her back. Molly wished she could comfort Sabrina like that.

"If I had any money, I'd leave right now."

"I know. You've had it harder than anyone. But I'm not sure leaving is the answer you think it is. Besides your school loans, you are a Monroe, and while you won't see ghosts in other places, that doesn't change who you are or what you've experienced. It won't magically make you different. You are who you are, no matter the location. Some responsibilities are too big to escape."

"Not helping." Sabrina sat back, her expression faded and droopy, like a wet newspaper draped over a scraggly bush—add the slightest pressure and it would fall to pieces.

Jenny kissed her forehead. "We can talk more later. Go rest. I'll check on you in a few hours. Bring you a grilled cheese?"

Sabrina nodded and drifted upstairs, her stocking feet sliding on the wood floors.

When they heard her door shut, Jenny turned to Molly.

"You said they almost kissed?"

"So close. I wanted to shove them together, but he was a complete gentleman."

"And today in the kitchen?" Jenny asked.

Of course Molly had watched the entire exchange. They needed to look out for her.

"Those two are going to screw this up on their own. Back in my day, he would have proposed and this would all be settled by now. None of this consent business."

"It is actually a good thing, Molly." Jenny smiled. "Especially for Sabrina, because once she's committed, she'll be all in. Ray is doing the right thing."

"That doesn't mean they aren't going to bungle it."

"Agreed. How about some great food and better company?"

Molly smiled. "That would help, but shouldn't we be more subtle? She's going to know what we're up to."

"I don't care as long as it works," Jenny said.

Molly knew it would take more than tasty vittles, but it was the small things and little moments that made a relationship. For all her love of romantic movies, none of them would work if there weren't dozens of little glances, hand touches, tiny smiles, shared sundaes, slow walks, late-night phone calls, and inside jokes. Ray and Sabrina needed time together to make the kind of tiny moments that added up.

26

RAY CHECKED THE ADDRESS he'd gotten from Sabrina's dad to make sure his phone's map was taking him to the right place. He turned down a dirt road lined with pines, the early-evening sun barely making it through the branches. After a quarter mile, a log cabin appeared around a bend, with a handful of cars in the parking lot and a lake sparkling behind it.

If it weren't for the dumpster tucked behind a fence, Ray would think he'd stumbled across someone's vacation cottage. Triple-checking his phone, he got out of his car and headed to the door, but he stopped when he heard his name.

"Ray." Doug trotted across the lot, his shirt pulling across his belly and one arm waving. "I meant to get here earlier, but at least you didn't get to the door yet."

Doug slowed to a walk and led Ray to the porch, where there was a screen door in front of a normal wooden door, as if it were a typical house. Small flower pots containing red and white flowers lined the railing. Doug didn't go through the door like Ray expected, but stopped at a small window to the left of the door and rapped twice, paused, then rapped two more times.

The window slid open, but a curtain still blocked Ray from seeing into the building.

"Password," a voice said.

"Blind pig," Doug said.

The window closed and the door opened. Doug looked over his shoulder and waggled his eyebrows at Ray, who was utterly baffled. Where was Doug taking him?

Inside, a young hostess greeted them. "Good evening, Mr. Monroe. I'll show you to your table. The ladies are already here."

Ladies?

Sure enough, at a white tablecloth–covered table overlooking the beautiful lake and sunset sat Jenny and Sabrina. Sabrina looked just as surprised to see him.

"Hey, you. I didn't know you'd be here. Your dad only said he was taking me to his favorite restaurant. Which, Doug, I'm a little disappointed isn't The Otter Club." Ray gently punched Doug's shoulder. The dining room was small, with ten tables, a door leading to a cozy bar, and another door into the kitchen. "Where are we?"

Doug looked pleased, and Sabrina rolled her eyes.

"It doesn't really have a name," she said, "but everyone calls it the Hideout. It's a private supper club that used to be mob-owned back in the day. Local lore says Al Capone used to come here, but every place north of Madison claims that. Each member has their own password to get in. It's a bit silly, and Dad loves to bring people here. Great food. There isn't a menu, only a few daily specials. You might get some molecular gastronomy or classic French food or meatloaf and mashed potatoes, but it's always amazing."

"Today they have family-style broasted chicken. The best in the state," Doug said.

"Broasted?"

"Fried, but under pressure. I don't really know what magic happens, but it's extra juicy and crunchy."

Ray studied the room with fresh eyes. A waitress brought out a mountain of golden chicken to a neighboring table, while another group sipped cocktails. A third, who were already eating, sat at a table covered with a platter of chicken and large bowls of mashed potatoes, green beans, corn, and few other things he couldn't identify from where he was sitting. What an interesting idea. Not many places could make it work, but a private club with limited seating . . . it had potential. He leaned back in his chair as a waitress emerged from the kitchen. He wanted to get a peek under the hood, hang out where the action took place. That was the best part of owning a restaurant. The Otter Club ignited a part of him that had suffocated in real estate, with its combination of creativity and business, food and customers.

He finally had work that invigorated him, and he couldn't lose it.

:ᘓᓀᘙᓀᘗ:

SABRINA HAD KICKED HER mom's leg under the restaurant table when her dad had arrived with Ray. This wasn't an accident. Her mom and Molly had been plotting with the subtlety of a marching band in a monastery, but she didn't want their interference. As she replayed the other day in her mind, she obsessed less about the events on the duck and more about her time with Ray. What did he think of her meltdown? Did he realize she hadn't intended to say Molly's name? She should never have eaten an edible in the middle of a panic attack.

Sabrina appreciated that he had dressed nicely to go out with her dad in dark pressed pants, a tucked-in blue button-down shirt, and his glasses. She was developing a serious attachment for his glasses and the way they slid down his nose and had to be scooched back up. Sometimes a lock of hair would curl onto his forehead and bob for a minute or two before he swooped it back.

All through dinner Ray watched the action around him carefully and asked questions about the restaurant. As they sipped after-dinner drinks—he had a port and she slurped down a brandy alexander—her parents stood to leave.

"We're going to head back," Sabrina's mom said. Sabrina moved to stand, gulping her ice cream drink faster. "No, sweetie, you stay. I'm sure Ray will be happy to give you a ride home. And don't worry, the bill's taken care of, so feel free to order more if you want."

Then they were gone, and an ice cream headache flashed across her forehead.

"Sorry," Sabrina said.

Ray smiled. "I don't mind at all. It's a perfect way to end this meal." He swirled his glass. "I hope you don't mind being stuck with me."

"Not at all. It's nice to see you now that I'm feeling more like myself."

"Glad to hear it."

This was so awkward. She wanted to get back to how they'd been before he'd seen her dissolve into a useless puddle.

"Do you want to talk about the gala?" she asked.

"I guess. Though it seems a shame to waste that view on work talk."

They both turned to look out the window, where the sun had set and the light from the restaurant twinkled on the water like shattered glass on blacktop. Sabrina sipped more of her drink, then cringed as it reignited her ice cream headache. She needed to say something else, anything to break the silence.

"My parents aren't very subtle," Sabrina said as she wiped the condensation from the cocktail glass onto the white tablecloth with her fingertips.

Ray sipped his port, then set it down, placing his hand next to her own, close enough that their pinkies grazed each other, pinging her brain to react. Should she move her hand away? Entwine her pinkie with his? Pretend to faint so she didn't have to decide?

His blue eyes focused on hers, making it impossible for her to look away. "Subtlety is for people who don't know what they want."

He made the decision for her by moving his hand over hers.

Any remaining brain freeze from the brandy alexander evaporated in the heat sizzling through her entire body. Why was she resisting him? If touching hands caused this reaction, what would happen when they actually kissed? Or more?

Sabrina used her free hand to take another sip of her drink, needing the liquid courage and cool relief. She shivered as the cold ice cream did its job, except for the heat that still pulsed from where their hands connected. A smile began to form at the corners of her mouth.

"No, not that table." An entirely different chill ran from her head down her spine. Erika and Bobby had entered the restaurant. "We'll sit there." Erika pointed to a table in front of the window that would block Sabrina and Ray's view. As they walked by their table, Erika stopped.

"Hello, Ray. Did you get my e-mails?"

Ray cleared his throat and shot a glance at Sabrina before looking up at Erika.

What e-mails? She pulled her hand away from his.

"I did. I'm looking them over and will have some edits for you next week."

"I look forward to it."

Erika pulled Bobby along behind her, but Sabrina didn't care where they sat anymore.

"You're e-mailing her?"

Under what circumstances would he have anything to do with Erika after what he'd witnessed at the ducks? Did he care so little for her feelings?

"It's for work. We're negotiating a deal for duck rides and dinner," Ray said.

Sabrina stared at him for a moment, then nodded, before setting her drink down and walking out of the restaurant, ready to call a ride. Shit, no service. She turned to go back into the restaurant to use their phone and bumped into Ray's chest, her forehead knocking into his chin.

"Hey," he said, grasping her upper arms so she didn't topple over. "It's just work."

Her entire head felt like it was on fire, and she wasn't sure if she'd ever been so angry.

"It's never just work with her. How could you ever speak to her again after seeing what she did to me, how that affected me?"

"I will have to work with them. It's a small community, and they're local business owners. I can't just burn bridges on a whim."

"I'm a whim? How can the same man who sends me bedtime stories and delivers risotto work with the woman who destroyed my life?" She held her hands up. "I can't with this right now."

Sabrina walked down the dirt road toward town.

"It's ten miles back to town. You can't walk."

"It wouldn't be the first time."

"Let me give you a ride home. I promised your parents I would."

Sabrina stopped and walked to his car. "Fine, but I'm not talking to you, and you will not talk to me. Understood?"

He nodded.

She got in his car, crossed her arms, and kept to her word.

21

"I DON'T GET IT. I didn't think she could get that angry. It's just business," Ray said. "Sometimes we have to interact with people we'd rather not."

He fed hunks of cabbage into the food processor, shredding it for homemade sauerkraut, while Rick simmered a sauce for tonight's special.

"Dude, you're smart. You went to Harvard, right?" Ray nodded, already seeing where this was going. "How are you so dumb?"

"But . . ."

"No. Don't even go there. It's a matter of loyalty. You can't expect Sabrina to trust you if you're working with Erika and Bobby."

"It's just Erika."

Rick pointed his knife at him, but the action was unnecessary. Ray had known it was wrong the second Erika had mentioned the e-mail and the guilt settled into his stomach. His mom had always emphasized the importance of opportunities and keeping options open no matter how distasteful. But this wasn't New York, and Sabrina wasn't an heiress. He had hurt her, and he needed to make it right.

"Point taken."

"Ask yourself what is more important. A good relationship and maybe more with Sabrina or a mediocre business opportunity with Erika? You need to apologize, and you better make it good."

"I don't even know what I am to her, though. Are we work partners? Are we friends? Are we into each other? I thought we were all three, but now I don't know."

"She wouldn't be this pissed if it wasn't all three. When do you see her next?" Rick asked.

"She's coming over to the house tomorrow to work on the gala."

"Then let's talk about what you're going to do."

:·ᥫᩭ·:

SABRINA ARRIVED EXACTLY ON time, walked into his house, past where he stood by the kitchen island, and went directly to the dining room where her supplies resided—all without acknowledging him. When she entered the room, she paused, then looked over her shoulder to where he'd waited in the doorway for exactly this moment.

"I am so, so sorry." He joined her in the dining room, stepping in front of her so that the sticky notes he'd used to spell out YOU WERE RIGHT were behind him.

"I'm listening," Sabrina said.

Ray took a deep breath as he realized this was the first true apology he'd ever given—not that he hadn't done plenty of stupid stuff that he should have apologized for, but people usually let him off the hook. Not Sabrina. She expected more of him. That wasn't quite right. More like he expected more of himself because of her. He wanted to be more like her. Thoughtful and compassionate. Kind and generous.

"I shouldn't have even considered working with Erika. While I don't know a fraction of the hurt she has caused you, I've seen enough. Any excuse I give is irrelevant. I care about you, Sabrina. I had hoped our pretend dates would become real ones, but I understand if that's out of the question. You're my friend, and I didn't think about how working with her would hurt you. I hope you can forgive me."

Sabrina reached for his hand, but her expression didn't give anything away. What if she didn't accept his apology? What if she didn't want anything to do with him? He'd have to finish planning the gala on his own, and it wouldn't be good, then he'd lose his chance to retain the Jasper properties. The thought of Sabrina gone from his life because he had hurt her too deeply for her to forgive was like a bowling ball to the chest, slamming the wind out of his lungs and cracking a few ribs. The pain would linger much longer than he'd expect.

She looked into his eyes, and he nearly drowned in hers, the rich amber drawing him to her.

"I appreciate this. Thank you. My reaction was . . . a lot, but you need to know more of the story." She leaned against the dining room table, her hip nudging it a few centimeters.

"I didn't have a lot of friends in school. Erika herself branded me the school's outcast in fifth grade, the school wacko in eighth, but it went next-level in high school. At the beginning of senior year, to everyone's surprise—especially mine—Bobby asked me out. Fast-forward a month and I'm buying a dress for the Goodbye Gala."

"Two thousand seven, right?" Ray asked. Sabrina tilted her head. "I was there that year, too. Uncle Harry got an award that year."

"I missed that part. You'll see why soon." Sabrina rubbed her hands on her shorts, then took a deep breath, but Ray already had an idea where this was headed. His blood heated, urging him to find Bobby and flatten his face. "Bobby was my first boyfriend, and I was 'in love.'" Sabrina made air quotes with her fingers. "He made me laugh. He gave me attention. I finally understood all those high school movies where the awkward girl gets the popular guy. You were there, so you know the gala is like a town-wide prom in every respect." She paused meaningfully. "I had decided that would be the night that Bobby and I . . ."

"No." Ray winced. "You don't need to say it. It's like a bad after-school special."

"It gets worse. I'll spare you the details." Ray appreciated that, matching her version of events with what he remembered of that night. "We were in the parking lot, in his Bronco, fumbling to get our fancy clothes back on in the confined space." Sabrina paused and swallowed. "Then there was a . . . weird sound in the car. It freaked him out, so he got out of the car, and I followed . . . Bobby grabbed his keys, locked the car, and went inside. My shoes and phone were still locked inside, so I waited by my parents' car until they came out. He drove Erika home that night."

"He left you outside? Alone?" Something was missing in the story, because even for Bobby that seemed pretty weak. If he filled in the blanks about what he knew, Ray could see how a teenage boy might get freaked. But no matter what happened in that car, even if a ten-foot werewolf was outside the door, Bobby had failed Gentleman 101—always respect your lady.

"That's about right."

"What a dick. And then he hooked up with Erika?"

"Definitely. It's all anyone could talk about at school on Monday. They've been together ever since."

He pulled her into a hug. "I'm sorry that happened to you. I can't believe you agreed to help me with the gala."

"I had some good times there, too, but that was the night I realized I had to leave if I ever wanted a normal life."

Ray wished more than ever that he had gone after her in the parking lot. He pulled her tighter, willing his warmth back through time to that heartbroken Sabrina. He would never abandon her again.

She turned to the wall and pointed at it. "This is a tragic waste of sticky notes. Once they've been stuck to something, they're never quite the same."

"I promise, I will buy you all the sticky notes you could use in any color you want."

:୧୨ ୨ ୬:

"DON'T MAKE PROMISES YOU don't intend to keep," Sabrina said to Ray, but the tension drained out of her as if a plug had been removed, and it was washed away. He had apologized and meant it—sticky notes never lied. She had told him her story, at least the parts she could. The real story, he could never know about.

That night, the Goodbye Gala had sparkled with thousands of twinkling white lights intertwined with birch branches and maple leaves of every hue. She stood in an empty hallway off the main room at the River Lodge. Tonight would make up for all the years of being excluded from every other teen rite of passage. Tonight she would be a normal girl at a fancy dance with her boyfriend. She was nervous but ready. She'd told Bobby she'd meet him outside at ten—it was nine fifty-five. Excitement and nerves churned in her stomach, but nothing would change her mind.

"I know what you're going to do. Don't." Molly had appeared in front of her in a glamorous sequined gown, like she'd been dipped in gold, her bold red lips the only dash of color.

Sabrina stopped her pacing.

"I'm going out there. I'm ready. I want this." She pointed at Molly. "And you. Will. Not. Follow. I don't care what Mom says."

Before Molly could respond, she headed to the door. Molly's mother-hen antics had solidified her resolve. Tonight was the night.

"Sabrina . . ." Molly followed.

"I mean it, Molly. Stay away."

Between one moment and the next, Molly disappeared. Sabrina pushed open the doors to find Bobby waiting for her, a rose from one of the centerpieces in his hand, his arm bent to escort her to his car.

It didn't take long for the windows of Bobby's Ford Bronco to fog up. He'd come prepared with the back seats down and piles of blankets. In the limited space, they managed to get out of their finery, kicking her shoes under one of the seats and draping her dress over a headrest so it wouldn't wrinkle.

All in all, the whole process didn't take long. Sabrina was surprised everyone made such a fuss. Lying on top of the blankets, Sabrina and Bobby slipped back into their underwear, Bobby's lanky limbs spread wide, taking up most of the space and leaving Sabrina to curl awkwardly to avoid the wheel bump.

Should they be talking? Kissing? Was Bobby snoring?

"Your mom is getting worried," Molly's voice interrupted Sabrina's rambling thoughts. She had popped into the driver's seat. "She wants you back in the dance."

Sabrina yelped.

"Is everything okay?" Bobby asked.

"I thought I saw something." She scowled at Molly over Bobby's head.

"She's noticed you and Bobby have been missing for a while. You should use your little phone." Molly held her hand to her ear.

Sabrina tried to wave her away while Bobby kissed her forehead and pulled her back down by his side.

"Call her. Call her!" Molly shouted.

Ugh. Molly was worse than the most annoying sibling.

"Call her. Call her. Call her."

"Shut up. I will," Sabrina said.

"What?" Bobby sat up, and Sabrina realized what she had said.

"My mom is worrying. I should text her."

"Then why did you say shut up?"

Sabrina couldn't come up with an excuse fast enough, at least not anything that would sound plausible.

"You don't need to lie to me. You're always doing slightly weird things. Tell me what it is. You can trust me."

She wanted to believe him. Sabrina had wanted to tell him the truth. Maybe it was time. As she considered what sharing her secret with him would be like, an entire future unrolled in her imagination. Dating through college as they both went to UW–Madison. Engaged their senior year. Married sixteen months later—the ideal amount of time to plan a wedding. Move into a house near her parents— something they could fix up before they had a baby. She'd help her mom with the family business as Bobby took more responsibility at the waterparks. Maybe she'd be a writer and tell stories. It was all starting right now. She took a deep breath.

"This will sound unbelievable, but I was talking to someone you can't see. It's a ghost."

"It? I am not an 'it,'" Molly said.

"Not now, Molly," Sabrina said. Bobby leaned away from her and sat up, then pulled on his undershirt. "Like right now. Molly is here. She's been around for a while. You know, the Showboat Saloon ghost? That's her." Molly humphed. She didn't appreciate that as her claim to fame. Sabrina talked faster as Bobby pulled on his pants. "Most ghosts only stick around until they wrap up their unfinished business. That's what my family does. We help them with their unfinished business."

Sabrina reached for him, and Bobby shoved her away, his eyes wide. He yanked on his tuxedo shirt. Maybe Sabrina should be getting dressed, too. She pulled her dress over her head. Bobby finally found his voice.

"Jesus! I thought you had Tourette's. You think there's a ghost here now?"

"Molly," Sabrina said with her head stuck behind layers of tulle. She yanked it down and could feel a few of the pins fall from her hair.

Bobby's eyes wildly searched the darkness, as if that would help and Molly would suddenly appear.

"He doesn't believe you," Molly said.

"Shh, Molly." Sabrina reached for Bobby's hand, but he yanked it away. "It's okay."

"Do you want me to move something to prove I'm here?" Molly said.

"Bobby, Molly wants to know if you want proof she's here?"

He nodded, though he didn't seem sure about it.

Molly put her hand near the ignition where the keys dangled. "Later, gator," Molly said, and turned the ignition. The Bronco roared to life in the quiet, then Molly poofed.

"Fuck me." Bobby shoved his feet into his shoes and jumped out of the car. Sabrina followed, holding her unzipped dress around her. The October ground chilled her feet as she stepped on damp leaves and twigs in the gravel parking lot.

"It's okay. She's gone now. There's nothing to be afraid of."

Sabrina reached toward him to reassure him that it wasn't a big deal.

"Get away from me, you freak. Everyone said I was nuts for dating you. I don't know how you did that or what you're playing at, but you really are psycho."

He turned off the car, took the keys, locked it, and went back into the dance, leaving her in the dark, alone and without her phone. It was four miles back to her house. Without any shoes. Those were still in the car. She shivered as the damp cold wrapped around her bare shoulders, the gravel cutting into her feet. She couldn't go back into the dance. Bobby was sure to tell everyone what happened. Maybe her parents' car was unlocked.

Too shell-shocked to process what had just happened, she found their car. Shit. It was locked. She slid down the side of it and waited until her parents came out a few hours later.

"Sabrina." Ray whispered her name, sending tingles cascading down her body like a waterfall, bringing her back to the present. She closed her eyes to savor the sensation of his nearness.

When she opened them, Ray stood inches away. The scent of his soap—oranges and something woodsy—wiped her mind clear, a blissful sensation. His finger traced the line of her jaw, stealing the air from her lungs. She swayed closer to him, setting her hands on his chest, where she could feel the thump-thump of his heart matching her own. This was happening. She hadn't fully believed she wanted this, but now? Now it was all she wanted. Her mind scrambled to memorize every scent, touch, sensation, so she could replay them over and over.

Their lips brushed, gentle and eager, Ray pausing only to set his glasses on the table. All that existed for her was where their bodies touched. She wrapped her arms around his back and pulled him closer. For now, she wouldn't worry about money or embarrassing secrets or why she hadn't heard back about the interview or whether she was ever going to move out of her childhood bedroom. Her only thought was the mesmerizingly slow way Ray's soft lips moved on hers, tasting one corner of her mouth and then the other. Her breathing turned to quiet gasps, growing quicker, neither one wanting to break the kiss. Her hands explored his back, tracing a line between his shoulder blades to his belt loops. His arms wrapped fully around her body, their legs overlapping each other so his hips pressed into hers, but he was still too far away. He walked her back against the sticky note-covered wall. She pulled him against her while his kisses maintained their slow exploration, his mouth lingering where her earlobe met her neck. Then down to her collarbone, shooting heat to her core. She sighed as he found her lips again, more fevered than before. At least his control was starting to crumble like hers.

His hands skimmed her sides, settling on her hips.

With each touch, with each kiss, Sabrina wanted more. To feel a connection . . . it had been too long. A cold thought interrupted her heated bliss. What if it wasn't Ray she wanted? What if she was so desperate for anything, she wasn't thinking clearly? She was setting herself up for heartbreak. What happened when she did manage to leave the Dells?

Sabrina pushed Ray away lightly, and he instantly stepped back, his lids and breathing heavy. Sabrina regretted it immediately, but she needed to think long term.

"Sorry," Ray managed in a rough voice. God, that voice.

"Not an apology situation." Sabrina stepped around him, sticky notes falling to the ground behind her. She needed to not see him when she spoke. Ray was dangerously attractive—she lost brain cells looking at him, and she needed every single one. "But . . ."

Sabrina set her hands on the dining room table.

"No buts. Please not buts." He appeared at her side but didn't touch her.

She longed to trust him, but she knew herself too well. She knew any summer romance would inevitably end with more scars. Love never worked out for her once a man really knew her. She kept her eyes on the table, glad for the cooling air that had returned her good sense. What was she thinking? Work and love never mixed, doubly true in the Dells.

"But . . ." Sabrina sorted the already tidy office supplies until her eyes betrayed her and found his face. He had put his glasses back on, and they magnified his uncertainty. The same uncertainty she felt every day. *What does this person think of me? Will they like me? Am I enough?* Inside her head, a brain cell massacre ensued. As she spoke, she knew it was a bad decision, but logic had lost. "We have a lot of work ahead of us. We should focus on that . . . rather than other distracting activities."

She couldn't do it. She couldn't say what her brain knew she needed to say—that they should keep it platonic. That they shouldn't get involved because it wasn't going to go anywhere. But the relief on his face was a perfect reflection of what she felt. If it was such a bad decision, then why was she so tempted? Why did it feel so right?

"Okay." Ray nodded his head, and a slow smile grew. "Okay. We should do some work. I'll leave you to it in here, and I'll be in my office. The walls should help keep us on task." He placed a soft kiss on her forehead and entered his office, turning to shut the door with a grin.

The walls weren't going to be the problem.

28

Ray stayed in his office for hours so Sabrina could have space. She had decided something, and he didn't want to accidentally change her mind. There had been a moment when regret had flashed in her eyes, like the hangover after a rousing party, but then it was gone.

He'd had plenty of mistaken kisses in his past, when regret had hit almost as soon as lips touched. But this was the opposite. Kissing her had been as necessary as breathing. No one ever regretted breathing, but now that he'd experienced such rarefied air, he needed it again.

His phone vibrated on the desk. It was a number he didn't recognize.

"Hi, Ray. This is Susan from the H. H. Bennett Studio."

He dug out some paper and a pen, eager for the new information. Would he finally have some answers about the mystery woman?

"Hey, did you discover who the woman in the photo was?"

"Not entirely. We don't know her name, but we found her in another photo taken at the candy store with the shop's owner, Mr. Oliver. Our best guess is she was a relative or maybe an employee? I can text you a picture of it. I'm sorry we don't have more information."

"That's helpful."

They ended the call, and a few moments later the text arrived. It was a bit blurry, but the blond curls and dimpled smile were unmistakable. Standing behind the candy counter, she was short, at least compared to Mr. Oliver with his handlebar mustache and center-parted hair. Looking at their faces, Ray decided there was no way they were related. It was likely she was an employee. He needed to think about where else he could get information.

To occupy his mind and hands, he organized his desk drawers, which had already become clogged with paper clips, pens, and paperwork from the restaurant. He dumped out a small box that had become a catch-all and sorted out staples, paper clips, and pins into neat piles. Leftover was the mystery key he had found when he had cleaned the office of Uncle Harry's things. He still wasn't sure what it unlocked. He studied it more closely, holding it in the sunlight from the window behind him. When he'd first found it, he'd thought it was for the drawers on the desk, but it didn't fit in those locks. There were numbers on it, but he wasn't sure where it would go. He slid it onto his key chain so he'd remember to look around the house when he had time.

:·ᢍ·:

THE LIGHT IN THE room had changed from direct sunlight to ambient daylight when Ray came in with a cup of coffee and a small cheese plate for Sabrina.

"I thought you might be hungry," Ray said, holding the plate toward her. A rainbow of little squares made up her kaleidoscope of plans, each one precisely placed in one of the orderly columns covering the wall his apology message had previously decorated. "That's a lot of sticky notes."

"I don't tell you how to do your job," Sabrina said, taking the plate. "Thank you." She had shoved the table to one side and sat on small pillows scavenged from other rooms. A much fuller binder sat in front of her, along with a mountain of blank stickies waiting to be employed. She would study her binder, write on a sticky note, then place it on the wall in a place that made sense to her.

Occasionally, he caught her waving her hands, or talking under her breath. These little movements intrigued him. She could be having a conversation with herself, plotting out the best course of action and nixing paths that wouldn't be useful. But it reminded him too much of the way his mother would interact with him when she was busy and he peppered her with questions, shooing him away with her hand when he became too distracting.

He couldn't prove it, and he didn't know how to ask, but he was almost convinced Sabrina was reacting to someone in the same way. Rick's rumors appeared true. Someone he couldn't see. He stared harder at the pile of paperwork where Sabrina was waving her hand the most, and looked for a troublesome insect—the more rational answer—or a ripple in the air that might indicate there was something more to the scene. Neither was there.

"You could judge me, because compared to you, I have no clue how to run anything. Were you a general in a previous life?" Ray said.

She rolled her eyes at him. He loved that. Over the last month, he'd noticed Sabrina wasn't comfortable with most people, keeping her mouth shut and her head down. She would only talk freely with her family—and now with him. His heart beamed to be included in such exclusive company.

"Look, if we're going to get this done, then we need detailed plans, then contingency plans for when things go wrong. This is a flow chart. Each color is a category: food, entertainment, auction, etc. . . . The stickies underneath are different things we need, people we can ask for auction donations, places we can hire, and so on. If a lead doesn't work, we toss the sticky in here." She held up a plastic bin that already had a few crumpled stickies decorating the bottom like colorful dead bugs. "Hopefully, we won't run out of options. I've organized them in order of importance, so we won't ever stall on what to do. And each sticky has an R or an S on who should do that one."

"Amazing. I already feel like the gala will be a huge success. I can't believe you did all this in an afternoon, but you're missing one."

He picked up a sticky and a Sharpie.

"Is that the right color for the category?" Sabrina asked. "That's very important. And Sharpie color matters, too. I didn't want to over-complicate my explanation since it really only matters to me, but everything has a color. Tell me what it is and I'll do it."

Sabrina reached for the marker and Sharpie, and he turned away and quickly wrote, making sure to put a large S next to it, so it was clear who needed to accomplish the task. Before he turned back, he stuck the note on his forehead and turned to face her.

As she read the note, the wrinkles on her brow smoothed and a huge smile replaced the frown. She sat up on her knees and put her hands on his face.

"I think you might be better at this organization thing than I thought. You're a natural."

Leaning in, she pressed her lips to his. Ray pulled her back so she was lying on top of him, their legs entwined. Sabrina paused.

"The binder?"

He looked over her shoulder. "Out of the way."

He pulled her back to him, the feel of every inch of her zinging through his body and his breath already becoming shallow. This was their second kiss, and it was like they were picking up right where they'd stopped. When would he stop counting their kisses? At ten? One hundred? One thousand? And how did he separate them when one kiss rolled into another, taking short detours down a neck or onto an earlobe or across a brow? All he knew was that there would never be enough. He would always want that next kiss, and then the next, and then the next.

As his hands roamed the curves of her hip and waist, her hips rolled into his, causing them both to sigh.

She pulled back again, breathless this time.

What would it be like without layers of fabric between them, skin on skin? The thought of what her naked body would look like nearly undid him. He rolled her over so he could press more firmly into her hips, propping up his weight with his elbows next to her head, his hands deep in her thick, wavy hair. She gripped his T-shirt, twisting the fabric in her hands. He could feel the line approaching, where matters would move from question marks to the inevitable, and he had no intention of making love to Sabrina. Not yet. Not when he knew she didn't trust him completely.

He slowed the kiss, then broke it, leaving one last kiss at the corner of her mouth. Glossy eyes looked up at him. He hoped his return look conveyed all the desire that hers did.

"Perhaps now is not the best time to continue this."

Sabrina breathed deeply, then let out a sigh, followed by a wide-eyed expression, but she didn't flee this time. She slid away on her pillow, then stood, smoothing her hair and shirt. "Now stay over there with your adorable sticky note, or we'll never get anything done."

She crunched a cracker from the snack plate and returned her attention to the wall, but her lips were still swollen and her cheeks still pink from their kisses. He didn't trust himself to be any closer. He turned his attention to the rainbow wall.

"Now that we have a plan, time to get to work," he said. "Where do we start?"

29

MOLLY WAS WAITING ON Sabrina's bed when she walked in. The ghost was wearing fuzzy pink-and-white-striped pajamas, her hair was in two ponytails, and she had a fluffy stuffed rabbit clutched in her hands. Could she feel the bunny, or not? Sabrina had never asked Molly about that. Guilt blossomed. She needed to be a better friend. It's not like she had any to spare.

"Hi, Molly."

"Someone had a good day." Molly beamed at her.

Sabrina's skin flushed. "I don't know what you mean."

"Those pink cheeks say otherwise."

"Were you watching?" Sabrina frowned.

"I left before it got interesting. I do have snooping ethics."

"Not many of them." Sabrina smiled at her, then toppled backward onto her bed next to Molly, whose legs disappeared into the bed as it bounced from Sabrina's weight. She grabbed a pillow and covered her face with it.

"Talk to me, sugar."

Sabrina moved the pillow to see Molly's face, the face she'd told so many of her secrets to over the years. Molly knew everything.

"I made a bad decision today. I shouldn't have kissed him back. I should have emphasized that I'm not staying, nothing can happen, and it doesn't matter how adorable he is or how sweet or how blissfully weak my knees get when he kisses me. They feel impossible, which makes everything possible. That doesn't even make sense when I say it out loud, but I can't explain it any better."

Molly tucked her knees under her chin. "You explained it perfectly. I know exactly what you mean. I don't see why you think that's a mistake, honey. That's the opposite. That's what it's supposed to feel like when it's right."

Sabrina sat up.

"It can't be right. He's a lifer—I can see the roots growing out of him and winding their way into the soil. I can't be with someone here, not without them knowing everything about our family. I won't do that. Never mind that his dead uncle follows me around until we can figure out what message I need to give him. How am I going to explain that to Ray?"

"Ray isn't like Bobby. He's not going to abandon you."

"You can't know what it was like. One blip and Bobby ditched me. I don't know if it was because seeing ghosts was too weird or because he had gotten what he wanted that night or because it was really a prank devised by him and Erika. I'll never know the truth—you can't know how that feels."

Molly's eyes flashed, and her edges became almost solid rather than their usual subtle blur. "I know better than anyone. Why do you think I'm still here, Sabrina?"

Sabrina blinked. She didn't know, not really. She'd known Molly her entire life and had never asked about it. It had always seemed rude, but now it seemed rude to not have asked.

"You're right. I'm sorry." She paused. "But why are you still here?"

"Because the man I loved disappeared and I never heard from him again. Unlike now, I didn't have Google to find out what happened. I didn't know if he died, left town, or just didn't want to talk to me anymore. His family wouldn't give me any information because they didn't approve of me. Before I could get any answers, I got sick and died."

She said it so matter-of-factly.

"I found out later that he at least knew that I died, and he either really loved me or felt a lot of guilt about abandoning me." Her lips twitched up at a memory she wasn't going to share, making her dimples deepen. "But I don't know why he left. Everyone who might have known is dead, too. I'll never know the one thing I need to know more than anything. I'll never see his face again. So I'm here."

Sabrina's heart broke for her friend.

"I'll find an answer for you, Molly. I have access to information through my journalism contacts. Who was he? We'll start there and see what we can find. Someone has to know something."

Molly's smile turned sad. "Sweetie, we've tried too many times already. Each time I get my hopes up only to have them crushed. It's been too long. He's long dead, and the answers died with him."

Molly set her hand on Sabrina's shoulder, leaving a chilly handprint, which Sabrina covered with her other hand.

"Now," Molly said, crossing her legs and hugging her stuffed rabbit. "Back to this nonsense about mistakes. Tell Ray about me."

"There's no point."

"You like him. He likes you. You both like the kissing. What more of a point do you need?"

Sabrina smiled, then it melted into a frown.

"Because when he kisses me, I don't ever want it to stop." Sabrina stood up and started to change into her pajamas. "I need to stop this before it goes too far."

"You're going to leave him, and he's not going to know the real reason. You'll break his heart." The words had more force than usual. "You're about to let someone wonderful out of your life, someone that doesn't come along for everyone."

Sabrina busied herself by picking up her dirty clothes and setting them in the empty hamper. Her mom must have done her laundry again. That should be a perk of being home, but it was just one more thing that made her feel like a failure. She was twenty-nine; her mom shouldn't be washing her underwear. She needed to change the subject.

"Can you feel that rabbit?" Sabrina asked, not bothering with any subtlety.

Molly's smile faded into pursed lips, and a small crease formed between her eyebrows—her thinking face.

"It's been so long since I've touched something. I think I feel it, but I've always had a good imagination, so I fill in the blanks for the senses I don't have. Sometimes I can even smell your mom's cookies."

"I hope so. They smell good," Sabrina said. She straightened the empty jug on her dresser where her tip money used to go. She'd deposited all of it earlier in the day. "I'm sorry I've never asked more questions about what life is like for you. Can we call it life? Afterlife? Is that a better word?"

"Afterlife works. It's not something breathers think about, so why would you ask?"

"Did you call me a breather?"

"That's what Belle says." Molly chuckled softly.

"How is she?"

"The same." Molly laughed. "Cranky and bitter and so nosy."

Sabrina grabbed her computer and notebook and returned to her bed. Molly took that as her cue to leave and poofed away.

Sabrina opened her laptop and logged in to her bank account, where for the first time in much too long there was money. All those tips from a few months of work had added up to more than she'd expected. She could pay off one of her credit cards and some of the other. With a few clicks, she made the payments, and a huge weight evaporated. Alone in her room, she enjoyed this tiny success, knowing she had a lot more work before she got out of debt, but she'd found some footholds to make the climb easier.

Her phone dinged. A message from Ray. No, not a message, a recording. She pressed Play. It was the first chapter of *Stardust* by Neil Gaiman, his voice bringing to life the words she'd read a dozen times. Another message pinged.

Chapter two tomorrow.

Something to anticipate. While she listened, she opened her notebook, and the number for the local therapist she still hadn't called fell onto her lap. She ran her finger over the digits, the paper wrinkled from shifting around in her notebook all summer, then shoved it back between the pages. Maybe it was time to book an appointment. For the first time, with Ray's voice for company, the idea of staying in her hometown didn't cause immediate panic.

30

RAY DRILLED THE LAST screw into the sign and stepped back to admire his work.

THE PUPS CLUB

Painted to match the woodsy exterior of The Otter Club in dark green and creamy white, the sign and the building it was attached to both blended in with the existing ambience—all that marked it as new was the absence of weathered paint and dried bird droppings. A new chain-link fence surrounded the refurbished shed, which now had electricity, a window air conditioner, running water, and several small pens.

The Pups Club marked the launch of his new partnership with the Dells Humane Society. Starting on Fridays and Saturdays (they'd add more days if the program proved successful), two volunteers would bring a few ready-to-adopt dogs. Customers could cuddle and play with the adoptable dogs while waiting for their tables under the supervision of the volunteers, who could also provide information for adoption—even for tourists. A well-marked donation box allowed a different way for customers to get involved. The dogs would get some much-needed attention and maybe a forever family, the humane society would get free publicity and money, and Ray would have a perfect distraction for his customers.

A van pulled up next to the building—his first pups.

"Hey." Gabby hopped out of the passenger side. She was the volunteer coordinator he'd worked with to create the program. "It looks great. While Jake gets the dogs out, why don't you show me around?"

He led her through the gate into the small grassy area where new toys waited next to buckets of water for floppy tongues. Small chalkboards hung on the fence where each dog's information would be displayed next to the donation box and pamphlets with additional information about adoption and available animals waiting for their forever families. A small hand-washing station reminded guests to wash their hands before and after playing with the dogs. Inside, four large crates—complete with blankets, more water, and food bowls—would provide a respite spot for the dogs. In the corner, a standing shower could be used to hose off dirty dogs or fill empty water bowls. Snacks for humans and dogs sat on shelves above a desk where the volunteers could fill out paperwork or take a break.

"If you can think of anything else you or the dogs will need, let me know. As a perk, I want to provide the volunteers with dinner—anything on the menu. Just text me when you want it, and I'll bring it out. That should make it easier to fill these spots."

Gabby smiled. "This looks fantastic. I'm sure I'll have some ideas after tonight, but we have everything to get started."

Jake came through the door with a huge white-and-brown Saint Bernard mixed breed that came right up to Ray and sat on his feet.

His body was only slightly smaller than a purebred Saint Bernard's, with thick fur, black eyes and ears, and a large wet nose that left strands of drool on Ray's pants.

"This is Frank. He thinks he's five pounds rather than ninety. Given the chance, he will find a way to sit on your lap." She scratched behind his ears. "If I didn't live in an apartment, this guy would come home with me."

Gabby took the leash and led Frank into one of the crates, where he sniffed the blankets, sampled the water, and deemed it up to his standards by curling up with a sigh.

Jake brought in the other two, a sleek lab-hound mix with a coat like a Holstein cow named Moo, and a small Maltese named Izzy who was mostly white with a few gray patches and had a perpetually surprised expression on her sweet face. While all three were in their crates, the doors stayed open in case they wanted to explore. Moo and Frank seemed content to rest, while Izzy stood at Jake's feet until he bent down and picked her up, then went about his work with her tucked under his arm.

Gabby and Jake settled into their new surroundings, writing on the chalkboards and displaying the flyers.

"Ray, you here?" The sound of the gate clinking followed Sabrina's voice. As Ray exited the shed, he was nudged to the side as Frank beat him out the door. Sabrina closed the gate behind her and knelt to greet him. "Who is this beautiful"—she tilted her head to check his underside—"boy?"

Frank's tail swished as he nuzzled closer, causing Sabrina to sit back on her heels. He took that as an invitation and sat down in her lap as if it were his throne. "Oof."

"That's Frank."

Frank licked her face, further confirming his excellent taste.

"Come here, boy, that's my girlfriend you're squashing. I need her in one piece." Frank licked Sabrina's face again. "I see how it is." Ray pulled out a piece of dried beef from his pocket and held it out. "Frank, come." Frank trotted over and gently took the treat from Ray's hand, but managed to leave behind a trail of slobber. "Good boy." Ray scratched his head and down his back while Sabrina got to her feet and looked around.

The other dogs emerged to inspect the action and sniffed Sabrina's legs before exploring the rest of the outside area. Moo found a bone and settled into a shady spot.

"This is incredible. I'd come here just to play with them," Sabrina said.

"That's the hope." Ray reached for her hand. "Can you stay for a while?"

She shook her head. "I'm picking up the signs and hanging them around town. If I finish early, I can come back."

"I suppose I have to let you do the job I hired you to do. But wouldn't you rather play with these guys?"

"Obviously." Sabrina looked distracted, her gaze focused on a corner of the fenced area. Whatever it was, all three dogs were looking, too.

Izzy approached the spot slowly, then started wagging her tail as if greeting a favorite person. Moo joined in, adding an excited hop. Frank hung back but didn't look alarmed, just curious. Ray couldn't see anything, but it seemed like Sabrina could.

"I should go," she said. Rising onto the balls of her feet, she kissed him on the cheek and went to her car. As she drove away, the dogs returned to their previous activities, with Frank sniffing Ray's pocket for more treats.

Gabby stood in the doorway. "That was weird," she said.

"So it wasn't just me?"

"Nope. Maybe they saw a rodent we couldn't. Or heard a critter coming from that direction." She shrugged and went back inside, Izzy following her like a shadow.

He wasn't imagining things. The dogs were onto something—and he knew in his heart that Sabrina knew what it was. Ray hoped to earn her trust so she would know there were no secrets she could have that would change his feelings for her.

:·✿·:

DRIVING OUT OF THE Otter Club parking lot, Sabrina looked over at her passenger.

"Now we know dogs can sense you," Sabrina said to Harry, who thankfully had followed her into the car. Harry nodded and smiled. "And you like that?" He nodded more vigorously.

For more than two months, Harry had been haunting her and only her, never bothering her mom or Molly. There had to be a way to help him.

"Fine, it's time we figured this out. You seem to understand me. Right?"

Harry nodded, though it was a little wobbly. Did he only understand some of what she said, like they were speaking different languages?

"Okay. We can do this. It's a process of elimination." Harry looked at her. She was going to go with the most obvious choice and pray that she was wrong. "Do you need Ray to know something? Ray, your nephew?"

Harry smiled and nodded vigorously.

Shit. There was no misinterpreting that response.

Harry nodded some more and looked out the window as they drove across the bridge by the Kilbourn Dam.

Harry pointed at the steering wheel, using his hand to make a twisting gesture. Sabrina looked where he pointed, but there was nothing. She looked up just in time to stop her car before hitting the one in front of her. She should focus on getting home alive first, or they might both have unfinished business.

Harry harrumphed.

"I know. It's frustrating for me, too. But we'll get there."

She pulled into her parents' driveway, picked up her purse and keys, then got out of the car. Harry followed her, pointing at her purse, and she stopped, holding her open palms in front of her with her purse looped over her forearm.

"What?"

Harry pointed at her hand with the keys dangling off a finger and made the same motion, turning his wrist. Like he was turning a key.

"Is it a key? Ray needs to find a key? At his house?"

Harry nodded. She could find a key. She was already spending time at Ray's to work on the gala, so it would be simple to poke around. She could do this without having to reveal anything about her family's secrets or that Harry told her what to find.

"Now we're making progress. Where do I look?"

Harry frowned as her mom stepped out of the house and toward them.

"Hey, Sabrina. Harry." She nodded at the ghost. "It's good to see you." He smiled.

"We need to find a key," Sabrina said, eager to hand the challenge over to her mom.

Her mom tipped her head to the side. "*You* need to find the key.

249

This one is yours. Harry has only come to you, not me. There has to be a reason."

Sabrina frowned. "But, Mom . . ."

"Don't even try that," her mom said, then directed her next question to Harry. "What does the key open?"

Harry used his hands to draw a square in the air, and her mom smiled immediately.

"I know that one. It's a box. A safe-deposit box?"

Harry nodded and smiled.

"How could you get that so fast?" Sabrina said.

"This is not my first secret safe-deposit box. It happens more than you'd think." She patted Sabrina's shoulder. "I'm off to book club. We're discussing *Station Eleven*. I'm bringing hand sanitizer for everyone." She held up a gift bag that swung from the weight of the bottles inside.

"Just what those ladies need, to be terrified of all the germs."

"I know." Her mom grinned. "I picked it. Now go find that key so Harry can move along."

Sabrina checked the time on her phone. "I've got to pick up the posters and start hanging them. We'll go to Ray's when I'm done."

Harry did a little sashay.

He might not be able to speak, but he moved just fine.

31

R*AY LOVED THE POST-DINNER* crowd at the bar. Full and happy, guests leisurely enjoyed after-dinner drinks with good company. Gone was the urgency to order their first cocktail and gobble their food—satiation mellowed everyone. He recognized some faces at the bar and made sure to give those repeat visitors a bit more attention for their loyalty. While Ray was grateful for the tourist business, the locals would keep him in business with their frequent meals and recommendations. Word of mouth was still the best way to succeed in any business.

The huge open windows allowed a balmy summer night's breeze to cool the air, while screens kept light-addicted bugs out. Under the chatter and background music, night birds hooted and leaves rustled as warm light bounced off the surrounding birch trees. He and the other bartender washed the glasses, cleaning up from three hours of old-fashioneds and ice cream drinks. It had become a routine. Make drinks, wipe the bar, wash glasses. He always looked three steps ahead so no customer had to wait with dirty glasses in front of them. That was why he noticed right away when his night took a bad turn.

Bobby and Erika appeared at the end of his bar. Her thin, bare arm wrapped around his left bicep to show off her enormous sparkling ring, which caught the light from every angle, making it impossible to miss. He had met women just like her, forgettable and shallow. It made him sick to think he had considered partnering with her.

He debated letting the other bartender deal with them, but if they were going to be difficult, he didn't want Sarah to have to manage it.

After quickly swiping the counter in front of them, he tossed two napkins down in the damp cloth's wake.

"What can I get you?"

"A Scotch on the—" Bobby started to say, but Erika dug her nails into his arm. "Make it a beer. Spotted Cow. She'll have a glass of chardonnay."

He'd made the switch smoothly. Most people wouldn't have noticed that she literally had her claws in him—at least now he knew who was in control.

"I'm going to need a credit card, Bobby. Last time you were here, you walked without paying." Erika scowled at Bobby and squeezed his arm again. Like a puppet, he pulled out his wallet and handed over a card. Ray poured their drinks and hoped that was it.

"It's been a few weeks since I sent the contract. Is there a problem?" Erika said.

"I've decided to go in a different direction."

Erika narrowed her eyes. "You're making a mistake." She said the words quietly as he set her drink in front of her.

"No, it's chardonnay." He held up the bottle.

"Not the wine. Sabrina." She hissed her name. "She's crazy."

Erika leaned in, letting her sleeveless shirt gape so he could count the polka dots on her bra. Was that intentional? With Bobby right next to her?

"Don't worry about me," he said.

Erika narrowed her eyes while Bobby sipped his beer and looked anywhere but at the two of them. He could respect Erika's drive. She knew what she wanted and went for it. But Bobby's spine flopped like an overcooked spaghetti noodle.

"I know you think you need to be nice to everyone, but you don't have to be with Sabrina."

"I'm sorry," Ray said, and Erika relaxed at his apparent acquiescence. "There's been a misunderstanding. I don't care what you think. I determine who I associate with. If anyone is too good for anyone else, it's Sabrina who is too good for all of us."

Erika's nostrils flared. "I didn't want to have to do this, but I suppose some evidence is needed. Bobby. Tell him about the gala."

Ray didn't need to hear Bobby's version of events. He knew enough from that night. With Bobby and Erika in front of him, all he could think about were the million different ways they had made Sabrina's life miserable. They could have left her alone through school. Erika didn't have to say nasty things. Bobby didn't have to treat her as if she were disposable. Ray's teeth clenched, and the muscle in his jaw twitched with the effort of maintaining control.

All he felt was anger. Anger at himself for being so slow. Anger at Bobby for being an enormous dickwad. Anger at Erika for being a cruel snob. He smacked Bobby's card on the counter.

"You need to leave."

"But . . ." Bobby pointed at his drink.

Ray slammed the glass he had been drying on the counter, causing the two of them to flinch. "Never come back here. You're banned."

Their visit had had the opposite effect from what they'd intended. There was no way he would ever give up on Sabrina. He'd find another way to make The Otter Club a success.

"I need to check something in the office," Ray said to Sarah, the other bartender. She nodded that she had heard him as she poured a glass of wine for a customer.

In his office, he dug out the partnership papers for The Otter Club. He hadn't read them since he and Uncle Harry had signed them. Perhaps there was a loophole. A provision that would allow him to keep control or buy out his parents' half.

As he read the document, he found the relevant passage. Upon Harry's death, the ownership would be treated like all his other assets and go to the heir designated in his will. Still struggling with his anger, Ray couldn't rally his emotions to return back to the bar. With the major rush over, Sarah could handle it on her own. He'd take the night to wallow in his disappointment.

32

"WHERE SHOULD WE LOOK?" Sabrina said.

Harry and Sabrina stood in Ray's dark kitchen. She'd let herself in with the house key he'd given her in case she needed to work when he wasn't there—this was the first time she'd used it. Dirty dishes sat by the sink, and the floor could use a sweeping. She considered tidying up but wasn't sure she wanted Ray to know she was there when he wasn't.

Harry didn't hesitate, leading her to Ray's office and his desk. He pointed at the top drawer. When they didn't find it there, she searched the rest of the desk. "Make a noise if you see it."

But nothing. Only a lot of paperwork, pens, and an old journal.

"Where else could it be?"

Harry held his arms wide.

"Anywhere?" she asked.

He nodded, then waved for her to follow him. He stopped in front of the door to the half bathroom under the stairs.

"You think it's in the bathroom? Trust me, Harry, there is no way anything is hidden in there. There's no room, only a sink and a toilet."

Harry walked in through the door and came back out, waving for her to follow him inside.

"If you insist." She reached for the door handle when she heard the door from the garage to the kitchen open. Shit. Ray was home.

"Sabrina, you here?" Ray said.

Harry poofed, as if Ray could see him. Coward.

"Yeah, I had to check something. I didn't expect you," Sabrina said.

She found him in the kitchen, his shirtsleeves rolled over his forearms, his body tense. Was it her? Should she not have used the key?

"Everything okay? Would you rather I not be here when you're not?" She held up her key. "I can give it back."

Ray's shoulders eased when he looked up at her, then collected her into his arms. Brandy and lime mixed with his usual soap scent.

"No, I want you to use that anytime. I . . . Work . . ." He struggled to find the right words. "I'm mostly angry at myself for being a moron, but finding you here . . ." He cupped her face. "My night got so much better."

Ray set his glasses on the counter. His lips covered hers, softly at first, then faster, as if kissing her would give him what he desperately needed. He backed her against the kitchen island, parting her lips with his tongue, tasting deeper. Sabrina's entire body responded, and she pulled him closer, nipping at his full bottom lip. He lifted her onto the counter, setting her at the perfect height to wrap her legs around his waist.

"Jesus, Sabrina," he gasped, his hands finding the edge of her shirt and sliding it up, leaving her warm everywhere his hands touched.

Rational thought gone, Sabrina yanked at his shirt, needing to touch more, see more of his skin. He stopped kissing her long enough to pull it over his head and toss it over his shoulder. She set both her hands on his taut chest, his pulse racing under her fingers. Her stomach curled with the realization of where this was heading. Her hands froze in their caressing, and Ray slid his hands along her arms until they lay over hers, not noticing her reaction yet. She released her legs from around him.

"Sorry," she said, and tried to slide off the counter, but Ray kept her there.

"No need to apologize." His words were ragged, and he leaned his head in the crook of her neck, his breath warm on her skin. "I didn't plan this, either."

Now that they weren't feeding the fire, embarrassment flooded Sabrina, horrified at what they were about to do. What had she been thinking?

"I've got to go." She slid off the counter, but Ray gently grabbed her arm before she was out of reach.

"What is it? Did I do something?"

He thought it was him and not her broken brain. She wouldn't have thought that a shirtless, toned man could look vulnerable, but he did.

"Not at all. It's me."

He let go of her arm. "I don't know what that means."

Ray found his shirt and put it on, then returned his glasses to their rightful place. She didn't want to talk about this, but it wasn't fair to leave Ray believing he'd done something wrong. How could she explain?

"I . . ." She rubbed her hands together as she stared at the floor.

He rubbed her shoulders and looked her in the eyes. "Sabrina, there is nothing you could say that would upset me."

"I haven't done . . . this." She waved her hand between them. "Much."

"Date?" God, he was going to make her say it.

"I've only had sex once," Sabrina said, the words dropping between them like bricks.

"You mean with one person." She could see Ray doing the math in his head, and she saw the moment he got there. "But you dated that guy in college . . . right?"

"Grad school, but we never got around to it. By the time I was ready, he'd moved on and forgotten to tell me."

Ray rubbed his forehead. Why wasn't he saying anything? This wasn't even the weirdest thing about her. Did he want more information? Less? Should she leave? She couldn't take the silence, not from him.

"I'll be back tomorrow for work," she said.

Ray shook his head. "No."

"No? You don't want me to come back to work?"

Her heart broke that he could so easily dismiss her because she wasn't willing to hop into bed.

"No, don't leave at all." His arms engulfed her in a tight hug. "I had no idea. I'm so sorry."

Sabrina savored the hug for a moment, then pushed back. "I don't want your pity. Being intimate is a big deal for me, and given that I'm not especially outgoing, I haven't met a lot of good candidates. I choose to believe it's because I have high standards rather than lack of prospects. But I also understand if that changes things on your end."

Ray's eyes flashed icy hot. "Do you really think that matters in the least to me? That I'm upset because you aren't ready to have sex at the same time as I am?"

"You wouldn't be the first."

"You're a smart woman, capable of making your own choices, but before me, you had really shitty taste in men. I'm angry that you haven't been treated like you deserve. I'm frustrated that I can't make everything perfect for you. But most of all, I'm here for you, no matter what. I'm in no rush, because I'm not going anywhere. I'm ready when you are."

Tears collected in Sabrina's eyes, but she refused to let them fall, worried Ray might misinterpret them as something other than the relief they represented. How did he always say the perfect thing?

:ᴄ໓ᴘᵔᴐ:

RAY WIPED THE SWEAT from his face using the damp T-shirt he'd taken off an hour ago. At least forty degrees hotter than the rest of the house, the attic sweltered in the August heat, but it was the last spot he needed to purge. He ignored the antique furniture the family had exiled after it went out of style and carried the cardboard boxes into his much cooler office.

Most of the boxes contained stained and dusty drapes or chipped Santa ornaments. Those he set aside to reassess in case any of it was worth salvaging. A few contained photos in tarnished silver frames, a black-and-white history of his family at major local events, like the opening of the Kilbourn Dam, the groundbreaking at Noah's Ark, or marveling at the Wonder Spot. Versions of his eyes and dark hair stared back at him, yet none of them looked happy, not like Number One in the photo with the mysterious blond woman or the more recent snapshots of Uncle Harry and his antics. He lined them up on a shelf, his family history in linear formation, a serious group, lacking in joy. Was it the dearth of modern photography and its ability to capture spontaneous emotions or a deeper familial absence of emotion? All he knew was he didn't want to be like them.

His computer pinged.

A FaceTime call from his parents. Goodie. He clicked Accept.

"Hi, Mom, Dad."

His dad waved. As usual, Mom would do the talking.

"Darling, where are your clothes?"

Behind his parents' heads, Lucy appeared holding a glass of Scotch. "You shouldn't have answered, little bro."

His mom waved her away with a scowl.

"I was working in the attic. It was hot."

"Couldn't someone from your restaurant do that for you?"

"No, Mom. I wanted to do it."

"How is our club going? Did you make the deal we discussed?"

Ray bristled. Even with the respite of spending time with Sabrina last night, irritation and frustration over Erika and Bobby's visit lingered. Despite wishing it so, he hadn't woken up with a perfect solution to cutting his parents out of the partnership. He didn't appreciate his mom reminding him of it.

"My restaurant is going great, and I decided to go in another direction." He took a deep breath. "We found a good balance between keeping what works and improving the weak spots. If everything stays on track, I'd say we're in great shape as we move into the fall. I'm already making a list of improvements for the winter. You'll be happy to know the gala is on track to be the best one yet."

"Very well." Her lack of interest could not be clearer. "Your father and I are having a Labor Day party at the Montauk house. You need to be there. We're inviting the Lancasters and Timmermans. I think you went to school with their daughters. You'll stay the weekend . . ."

"I'm not going," Ray said.

"Of course you are. You said everything's great at work, so it should be no problem to get away. I've already told everyone you're coming."

"Then you can tell them I'm not. This is another matchmaking scheme, and I'm dating someone here."

"Not that Hendricks girl."

"No. Her name is Sabrina. You don't know her." His mom opened her mouth to say something. "Or her family. They're locals. Her mom was a nurse, and her dad sells insurance."

His mom pursed her lips. "She's after your money. Don't give her anything."

"Oh my God, Mom. Not everyone in the world is after our family jewels." Lucy snorted in the background. He loved his sister. "If anything, Sabrina will be the one who has to be convinced about my family."

"Fine. Bring her to Montauk. I'd like to meet her."

"There is no way I'm subjecting her to one of your parties."

"Then we'll come there for Labor Day. We can have a barbecue in your backyard and meet Sabrina. Invite her family, too."

Discovering Death at his door would cause less dread than the idea of his parents mingling with Sabrina and her family. He'd prefer a meteor crashing into earth or a zombie apocalypse.

"What about Montauk? Your party?"

"I hadn't sent out invitations. There's no point if you're not coming. It's done. We'll be there that Friday. Have rooms ready. Kisses."

She hung up, and Ray buried his hands in his hair. It felt like he'd been smacked with a two-by-four. Lucy had tried to warn him. He couldn't expose Sabrina or the Monroes to his parents. One look at his domineering mother and Sabrina would never believe that they could make it work.

His parents were going to be here in three weeks. He had to tell her so she had time to prepare. He knew enough about Sabrina that getting comfortable with the idea of a new situation helped lessen her anxiety. If she could plan, she could avoid potential problems. Most important, she needed to trust that he'd keep her safe from any danger, even his parents.

33

"**YOU DO GOOD WORK,**" Ray said as he handed Sabrina a glass of cider, a champagne-style one from Door County with a cream-colored label. They stood in front of the wall at his house, covered in perfectly aligned and color-coded notes, and the table was even more littered, but most of the notes had small check marks.

They'd done it, or near enough. Phase one was complete. They'd booked a band, started soliciting auction items, and invented a signature cocktail—the Dells Old-Fashioned, made with a local cherry brandy, craft orange bitters, and a cinnamon-infused simple syrup. Plenty could still go wrong. Ads needed to be run, auction items collected and organized, RSVPs tallied, and dozens of other tasks. Sabrina glanced at her clipboard. She wouldn't flip to the next page yet, still basking in this first phase's accomplishment. All was in order and ahead of schedule. She sipped the cider, blissful that the only bubbles popping in her head were the ones from carbonation.

"Not too shabby." She smiled at Ray. "And I love the addition of 'Dine with a Dog.'"

"It was Gabby's idea. We'll put those tables on the porch so there's less noise and more places to go if the dogs get overwhelmed or antsy. It should raise a few grand for the humane society."

"She needs an extra thank-you, because it spawned themes for the rest of the tables, too. We have the food bank, the friends of the library, and the school district's Angel Fund. This money will really make a difference."

Sabrina sipped her cider again, closing her eyes to savor the moment. With a deep breath, she opened them and flipped to the next page on her clipboard, a fresh list with zero check marks, then turned to the wall to the right where she had added a whole new rainbow of sticky-note tasks.

Ray studied Sabrina's face.

"How come people don't see it?" Ray asked.

Sabrina raised her eyebrows. "See what?"

"You."

"People aren't supposed to see me. I like it that way."

"They're missing it. Missing how the little things matter." He looked at the ceiling. "All those little things add up to big things. You make a difference here, and you make me want to make a difference, too. You don't want anything from me, but I want to give you everything."

Sabrina could sense him ramping up to a big declaration. She stepped back, and he noticed.

"See, that's what I'm talking about. You've done so much to help me, and you don't even want to listen to what that means."

"It's not that I don't want anything. I do want my money."

They both smiled.

"You've more than earned it." He rubbed his hands on his pants, then set them on her shoulders. "Why is this so hard?"

"Spit it out, Ray."

"I love you." Sabrina's mouth dropped open. "I know. Stick with me. Since meeting you, I feel connected to you, to this town. Being with you is like an impossible dream, but you've shown me you make things possible. My life makes more sense because of you. I understand who I want to be. I love you, Sabrina."

Sabrina's mind couldn't digest what he'd said. He loved her for her. And she wasn't panicking, she wasn't anxious.

"You did ask me to spit it out. Now would be the traditional time to say something, anything, in return."

"I want to." She covered her mouth with her hand.

He took his hands off her shoulders.

"You don't need to say 'I love you' back, you know. I'm not looking for that, but a sign you aren't going to have nightmares about this moment would be helpful."

Tears collected at the corners of her eyes. He had said all the perfect things to her, things she'd dreamed of. She struggled to find the words for the flood of feelings inside of her.

"I don't care . . . I don't care."

Ray stepped back.

"No, that didn't come out right." Sabrina wiped at the tears. "I don't care that you're seeing me cry. I don't care that you saw me lose my job—anymore. I don't care if I dribble cider down my chin and you laugh."

Ray shook his head in confusion. "I'm not sure that's better."

Now she grabbed his shoulders.

"I care about *everything*, Ray. I retread each step of my day every night and parse out every tiny thing that other people might be judging me for. I know it's stupid, but I do. Every day is one long list of embarrassing memories that I'm convinced people silently judge me for. I get stuck on a loop, replaying every transgression, and it gets worse with each revolution. But with you"—she set her hands on his beautiful face—"I don't do that. I don't do that because I know you aren't judging me and you won't make fun of me. You make me feel safe, like I could tell you my deepest, darkest secrets and you would love me even more."

He pulled her in tight, his soft lips near her ear.

"There is nothing you can do or say that would make me not love you."

Tears dripped onto his shirt, and she didn't care. He only held her tighter. At last she had found dry land where the waves couldn't reach her. Not an isolated desert, but a tropical beach with plush lounge chairs and beachside piña colada delivery.

"I guess I can tell you about where I hide all the bodies," Sabrina said, pulling back enough to see his face. Ray's eyes shone more than normal.

"Absolutely. Then I can start using the same place to hide mine."

"A couple who slays together stays together?" She took his hands.

"Something like that," Ray said.

"I love you, too. I've never said that before to anyone but family. I wasn't sure I ever would."

He wrapped his arms around her, and as she heard her own heart thunder in her chest, she knew she'd finally found that person she'd been waiting for, but under the happiness, one wiggling worm of doubt jiggled, disrupting the moment. She might love Ray, but she hadn't been completely honest with him. For this to stand a chance, she needed him to know the truth about her.

SABRINA HUMMED AS SHE tidied up the gala's headquarters in Ray's dining room. He'd had to run to The Otter Club to finish up some work, and she planned to join him later. Should she be freaking out? Ray loved her. She loved him.

Her phone rang, and she answered it without checking the caller ID, assuming it was Ray.

"Hey, you," she said.

"Sabrina, it's Kalyndra Smith. I'm so happy you answered."

Sabrina dropped her binder on the table and sat down beside it.

"Hi, Kalyndra. It's good to hear from you."

Was this a good call or a bad call? Was she about to get the job? Surely they wouldn't call to tell her she wasn't getting it, but that didn't answer her question on whether this was a good call or a bad call.

"We've completed interviews, and I'm thrilled to say the job is yours. We hope you can start in the next few weeks, and as we discussed during the interview, you can work remotely, but we'd like you to make it to the office at least once a week for staff meetings. Some people on our staff do commute longer distances if you'd like to discuss with them how they make that work."

She had gotten the job.

Sabrina took a deep breath. Here was her path back to the life she wanted. But Ray had just told her he loved her. All at once, she remembered getting stomachaches as she worked up the courage to call strangers about political stories. Spending hours online tracking down minor facts to avoid making more phone calls and suffocating under the mountain of debt that her sure-to-be-paltry salary wasn't going to touch, even after the money she had earned this summer.

And Ray loved her.

Still not sure if it was a good call or a bad call.

Kalyndra kept talking.

"I'm e-mailing the offer. Sorry to say the salary and benefits aren't negotiable. It's what we pay all our starting staff writers."

Starting staff writer. Five years hopping from newsroom to newsroom and she was still a starting staff writer.

Ray loved her.

"Sabrina?"

She shook her head.

"Sorry. I wasn't prepared for this call. Thank you so much. Can I have a few days to think about it?"

"Of course, but I do need an answer soon. We need bodies. The news never sleeps and all that."

Bodies. That was what she was. One body of many who were willing to work for low wages in a dying industry. There were people who were making a huge difference, but when she was being honest with herself, she knew she wasn't one of them. If she went to work at the *Elephant Room*, she'd be taking a spot from someone else, someone who might be great at the job. Someone who might make a difference.

Good call or bad call . . .

She'd waited almost two months for this, and now home didn't seem so bad anymore. A large part was Ray, sure. But also, something more had changed. For the first time, she knew she had made a difference here. She was helping organize the Goodbye Gala. Life was more predictable in the Dells, and that was good for her. People watched out for one another. Even the ghosts weren't causing much mayhem—though Molly did seem to still enjoy interfering in her life as much as possible, and she liked it that way.

Now that she'd been back for a while, she realized how much she had missed Molly while she'd lived somewhere else, even more so than her parents or brothers because Molly was a best friend and sister all wrapped into one. She never felt lonely anymore. She didn't have a booming social life, but she did have people. Her people.

And she wasn't tied to her phone like before. She didn't care what the daily drama was. The daily dissection of which talking head said what and the following overblown discourse—she didn't miss that at all. She had made a difference in this tiny corner of the world by helping.

She read the offer and laughed, then closed the e-mail.

Ray loved her.

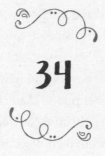

34

"**WHERE DID ALL THIS** come from?" Sabrina asked, setting the heavy cardboard box on one of the tables in the bar area of The Otter Club. The box clinked when she set it down. As she took each item out, she wiped it down with a clean cloth and stacked it on a chair. Ray set his box down on a neighboring table, dropped his keys next to it, and did the same.

"I've been cleaning out my uncle's house. I thought it might be fun to use some of it to decorate The Otter."

"And remind people your family has been here forever."

"Something like that," he said with wide-eyed innocence that melted into a devious smile.

"Subtle." Sabrina breathed in. She still needed to tell him about her decision, find a way to help Harry, and tell Ray about her secret, but every time she thought about having the conversation, it was like standing center stage in front of a dark crowded theater under hot spotlights wearing nothing but her underwear. She wasn't ready yet. "So, I finally heard back about my interview."

Ray met her gaze, his blue eyes blank, trying not to betray what he thought before he knew her decision. Sabrina appreciated that he was taking his emotional cue from her.

"And?" Ray said.

"I got the job if I want it."

"Congrats." He raised his eyebrows, almost as if he hoped they could pull up the sides of his mouth to match. He couldn't quite hide his disappointment that she might be leaving to take the job. "If you want it?"

"I asked for a few days to think. I'm turning it down." Ray's fake smile eased into a genuine one. "The Dells fits me better than it used to."

He set down the frame and swept her up in his arms.

"That's the answer I hoped for." Her feet dangled a few inches above the ground. "What are you going to do? I could find plenty of work for you here."

"I don't think working together all the time would be smart. I'm not sure, but it will come to me at the right time. Something with office supplies, though."

His soft lips pressed into hers like they were sealing a pact, a vow that would keep them together. She loved his lips and how they made every muscle in her body relax and tighten at the same time. Taking the breath from her body, yet giving her all the air she needed to breathe.

"We're never going to finish if you keep kissing me like that." She gave him a gentle shove. "Back to work so we can finish today."

He stole one more kiss and returned to his box of frames, glancing up at her over the top of his glasses every few minutes. She wiped a framed black-and-white photo of men in striped suits and women in long dark dresses in front of the downtown dam. The next was a copy of a deed for several acres of what was now downtown. With each picture, another historical moment in the Dells was preserved.

"Is this an actual H. H. Bennett?"

She held up a photo of three men wearing dark suits and derby hats, their mustaches curling around their cheeks as they jumped in the air. The image was clear and crisp even though they were in motion.

"Yeah. He was a family friend, if the stories are to be believed."

"You can't hang this here. It should be in a museum."

He took the frame from her. "I want it here. It's in a good frame, and I'll keep it out of the sun."

"Someone will steal it."

"No one will steal it."

She grinned up at him.

"I'm gonna steal it. I could make a lot of money on eBay with that."

He wrapped his arms around her waist and looked into her eyes.

"I'll screw it to the wall." He kissed her, soft and sweet, making her muscles soft and loose. She sighed. "What?" Ray asked.

"Being with you is easy. I'm the most like me." He smoothed her hair with his strong hands, and she set her hands on his chest. "I never thought I could relax with someone who wasn't in my family."

"Well, I kinda like you, too. Even when you talk to yourself."

"I don't talk to myself." Sabrina frowned.

"I've seen you talking to someone, so it's either yourself or someone I can't see."

Ray kissed her forehead and went back to work, but Sabrina didn't move. A tsunami of doubt crashed as if it had been taking shape just out of her line of sight, waiting to slam into her when she thought she was safe, dragging away the comfy lounge chairs and piña coladas. What did he mean? She was so careful; contrary to what he'd just said, she did not speak to Molly in front of people. There had been a few lapses when she'd first returned, but that was because she'd been out of practice. As she reached for the next photo, her hands shook, questions popped into her mind like sulfuric bubbles in a mud bog, and her stomach contracted in on itself. Was she being stupid? She was going to have to tell him her secret at some point. Why was it different if he figured it out? Except she knew that it was, because then she didn't control it. What he learned and how he learned it needed to come from her.

She wiped at a fingerprint on the next frame's glass, then stopped. She couldn't believe what she saw.

"Molly." The words came out as a whisper.

There she was in black and white. Molly beside a handsome man who looked a lot like Ray.

"Molly." She said it louder this time, all pretense of discretion gone.

"What did you say?" Ray asked, but Sabrina ignored him.

"Molly, I know you're around here somewhere."

Then there she was, wearing high-waisted jeans, a red-and-white-gingham shirt, and a bandana around her curls. An adorable Rosie the Riveter. Molly looked confused.

"What's up, doll? You know Ray is right there. Did you finally tell him?"

Her eyes sparkled at the idea. Sabrina held out the photo.

"This is you, right?"

Molly gasped and shifted into the outfit she wore in the picture as she reached for it, her lips forming a silent O.

"Raymond." She whispered at last.

"Raymond. His name is Raymond? Like Raymond Jasper? You knew they were related?"

"You're talking to her, aren't you?" Ray said, looking around the room as he came to stand next to her. "She's here."

Sabrina's throat tightened, the muscles struggling to swallow her panic. What had she just done? Looking at Ray, he didn't look worried, or concerned, just interested. Sabrina held the picture up to him. Nothing made sense.

"Why do you have this?"

"That's my great-grandfather. I'm pretty sure the woman with him was the love of his life, but I can't figure out who she is. That's all I know."

Molly whimpered at hearing him say this about her.

"Why would you say that?" asked Sabrina.

"I have his old journal where he mentions her, and in his will, he requested to be buried with her, but Nana never let anyone else know who she was." His eyes scanned the room. "Pages are missing. I've been trying to find them, which is why I discovered all this. He ended up moving to New York and marrying Nana."

Sabrina's stomach churned. Her worlds were colliding, and nothing made sense.

Ray picked up a different photo.

"See, here he is with my uncle Harry when he came to visit a few years before Raymond died."

"He kept his hair. And still so handsome," Molly said as they both studied the picture.

"Wait, you asked if I was talking to her. What did you mean?"

"Molly. You're talking to Molly. She's here."

"Why would you say that?" Sabrina stepped back. If she put distance between them, maybe they could pretend the last few minutes hadn't happened.

"Sabrina, come on. It all makes sense. You talk to people no one else can see, Rick told me a story about a friend who your mom helped after a grandma died. I've been trying to find out what happened with Number One . . . and it's been leading me to you, but I didn't know it."

Too late for pretending. He knew she was a freak. As her mind reeled at how to keep her secret, Harry appeared, standing next to Ray's keys and shouting, *"Kwee. Kwai. Klee,"* while pointing at Ray's keys. It was too much. Her two worlds crashed with waves hitting her from every direction.

"Harry?" Molly and Sabrina said at the same time.

"Harry? My uncle Harry?" Ray asked.

She held up a hand. He knew. She'd finally let someone in a little, and he'd found out her worst secret. She'd known this was a mistake, all of it. Returning to the Dells, working at the Real Dells Ducky Tours, Ray. She knew what would happen next.

35

MOLLY FOLLOWED SABRINA OUT to her car. So did Harry. Ray stayed where he was, but he didn't know he was now alone. Sabrina sat in her car, waiting until she stopped shaking enough to drive.

"We have to go back. Ray has information about my Raymond."

Sabrina ignored her. Why did everything awful happen to her at this supper club? She couldn't hear anything over the frantic beating of her heart. How could it beat so fast while it was breaking? She began to drive away from The Otter Club.

"Sabrina!" Molly shouted, reaching for her arm but catching nothing, only sending shots of cold through Sabrina's bicep.

Sabrina ignored her all the way home and up to her bedroom, where Molly popped in front of her. Sabrina finally stopped.

"Go back. We need to talk to Ray about what he knows." Molly's voice cracked and her edges shook.

"I can't. I can't. I can't. I can't."

All her thoughts stuttered out in short phrases, stuck on repeat.

"Sabrina Monroe. Right now, it isn't about you. Can you suck it up and be there for me?"

Sabrina curled tighter around her uneasy stomach. She wanted to throw up but knew that wouldn't help. Molly was right. Under normal circumstances, she'd jump at the chance to help her dearest friend. But right now, she couldn't. Her body was gripped around an invisible core, desperately clinging so it didn't fly apart. It killed her that she couldn't be there for her friend after so much time.

She snapped, crying and shouting at the same time. "It's not that simple. I can't breathe. My lungs don't work. My heart races and it hurts. I feel like I'm going to die and the only way to save myself is to hide. I want to help you. But I can't. When you move something, it requires so much energy that no one can see you for a while afterward. *Life* is like that for me. It has to be really worth it for me to expend that effort."

"I'm not worth the effort?" Sabrina had never seen Molly so angry.

"I can't do this."

The yelling had taken the last of her energy. She couldn't help Molly, even a little. Not now. It tore her apart knowing that her greatest weakness was hurting her dearest friend.

"I've waited so long for any information, and now it's waiting there. But you can't handle it? Because you feel overwhelmed? What about how I feel?"

Molly's faint blur took on a vibrant red hue.

"You can't feel anything!" Sabrina knew that was a low blow and regretted it immediately, but even that was too slow. Molly was gone. She was so angry at herself and at life and at Ray, she wanted everyone to hurt like she did. They should feel helpless and confused and broken, just like she always did.

But that wasn't what she wanted. Not really. And she didn't want to be trapped in her room under the covers. Losing time to a panic attack frustrated her. She knew she could manage her anxiety better, but since coming home, she'd stopped trying. It had been months and she knew her stubborn refusal to seek the help she needed was keeping her from living her life and helping those she really loved.

Breathe in.

Breathe out.

Breathe in.

Breathe out.

Five things she could see: Her bed. Hogwarts. Laptop. Dresser. Dirty clothes.

Four things she could touch: Comforter. Pillow. Nightstand. Pajamas.

Three things she could hear: Birds. Mrs. Randolph talking to Mr. Bennett. Her dad in the kitchen.

Two things she could smell: The lilac candle on her nightstand. Her dad's sloppy Joes.

One thing she could taste: Regret.

Breathe in.

Breathe out.

Sabrina sat up on her bed. Her skin still tingled, but her heartbeat had slowed and she could think more clearly. Her phone vibrated with a call from Ray. She needed more time before she was ready to face him. She pulled her notebook toward her and found a business card. Time to take action. Even if she only went once, she needed it. Not taking care of herself had been stupid and had left her unprepared to handle life back in the Dells. She should have known better. Preparation was her greatest weapon, and she'd come home as a blindfolded rat in a maze of hungry cats.

CHILDREN! MOLLY COULDN'T REMEMBER ever being so angry. She popped from location to location. First she tried the waterparks and their noisy chaos. That was no good for thinking. Then the library with its quiet reading space—seemingly good, but lacking in inspirational energy. It's not like she could peruse the books for ideas. Then she went to the cemetery, where she could wander among the headstones reading the epitaphs.

Better. She was in the older part of the cemetery, where people had still used earnest words to express their feelings. There were a lot of biblical quotes and trite sayings. She came to the end of a row and saw Belle a few rows over. As Belle raised her hand, Molly waved in greeting, pleased at this friendly salute. Belle never waved.

Oh, wait. Nope. Belle was not waving at her, but instead displaying a very rude hand gesture. What a cranky old bat.

"Get out of my graveyard, blondie." The voice was deep for a woman.

"Belle, it's been too long," Molly said.

"Not long enough."

Belle wore a long, dark gray wool dress, buttoned up to her throat, where a bit of white lace poked out, the only reprieve from her monotonous outfit. It made her pale skin and tightly wound bun of dark hair look even more severe, like an angry schoolmarm who spared the hugs and loved the rod, paddle, and switch. A dark pipe peeked out from a pocket in her skirts.

"Lovely night."

"I refuse to make small talk with you. Leave," Belle said.

Molly sighed. She'd been trying for almost a century to get Belle to warm up to her. If anything, Belle had gotten more cantankerous.

As a former Confederate spy, she was still angry that she had died on Yankee soil.

Molly turned her back to study the next row, only to be greeted again by Belle with a similar rude gesture involving her arms.

"Is that necessary?" Molly said.

"Yes. You're in my cemetery, and I want you out," Belle said, her dark clothes absorbing the sunlight like a black hole.

"You're impossible."

"I'm not the one who cavorts with breathers."

"Maybe if you did you would enjoy life a bit more."

"That is why I don't. You are not alive. You are just dust below the ground, stuck here forever like me."

Molly didn't need reminding, not when she'd found a morsel of hope that she would finally find out what had happened with Raymond. She was still angry at Sabrina for being so rude, but now that she'd had time to cool off, she could understand some of Sabrina's actions. Molly had been around her long enough to know that when she had a nervous attack, time was the only thing that helped. She'd get there, but Molly wanted her to get there faster, and the best way to do that was to reconcile her with Ray as quickly as possible.

Ray didn't care that she saw ghosts. It was obvious. But Sabrina couldn't see past her panic. She fought so hard to keep that part of her life completely hidden that the effort required ruined the good parts, too. Like the pith in an orange, a little went undetected, letting the sweet flavor take the spotlight, but too much pith made it bitter. The stamina Sabrina used to hide her secret was the pith overpowering the sweetness her life could have. Molly could either stay angry or take action. The answer was obvious.

"I need your help." Belle raised her hand again, but Molly continued before she could complete the gesture. "What if I promised to leave you alone? Stay out of the cemetery?"

"Forever?"

"With exceptions for emergencies."

"Everything is an emergency to you."

"Exceptions for funerals." Belle started to say no, but Molly kept talking. "You can't deny me that."

"Done. Anything to get rid of you."

Molly explained the situation. Belle listened, and when Molly finished, she tapped her fingers on a headstone as she contemplated. Belle's dress shifted to a dark maroon shade with pale pink flowers around her neckline.

"We need Ray to come to Sabrina so they can reconcile, then everyone can get what they need. I'll find out the information Ray knows, Harry can tell Ray where the key is, and Sabrina and Ray can be together. Everyone wins."

"Especially me, because you'll stay away."

Molly huffed. "Yes, I already agreed."

Belled puffed on her pipe.

"You're going to have to move something," Belle said.

"If I move something, then I'm poof for at least a few days."

"Must you say 'poof'? It's not a fun party trick."

Molly ignored her and kept talking.

"Going poof defeats the purpose. I want to know what's happening right away." Molly paced back and forth. "Ray needs to prove to her that the family quirks make her more special to him. Something to show he understands her and accepts everything about her. Something thoughtful and romantic. Where's an airport when you need one?"

"What are you talking about?"

"All the best romantic movies have a moment at the end where one person proves their love to the other, usually by running to their airport gate or singing a romantic song."

"That is the dumbest thing I've ever heard."

"Do you even know what an airport gate is?"

"I am dead, not a moron. This is why I want you out of my cemetery." Belle paced, her large skirts drifting in and out of the headstones. She made no effort to circumvent objects. "Here's how it's going to happen. We will go to Ray's home and play one of those stupid movies that you keep yammering about—ideally to a spot where he'll get the hint. If he doesn't get it, we'll move to plan B."

"What's plan B?"

"Write on the mirror when he's showering. Something like 'Do something romantic, stupid.'"

"That's so cliché—a ghost writing on a mirror. We can't crash his shower."

"Like you've never done it," Belle said with a dismissive wave. "This whole thing is cliché. What do you expect? If you want a happily ever after for those two, then there are only so many ways to get there. You need to enjoy the ride, not just the ending."

Well, who knew? Belle had a soft side for romance.

"When we get there," Belle continued, "tell me what to do. I should be able to move a few things before I disappear."

"I appreciate this, Belle. Really, I do."

"You exhaust me more than moving objects possibly could. I'll enjoy the break. Lead the way."

Molly grabbed Belle's hand, and they popped into Ray's house, where they found him in the study with his laptop open, staring out the window with his elbow on the desk and his hand propping up his chin. Perfect. He was in a good spot.

"You need to type 'YouTube dot com' into that line." Molly pointed at the screen.

Belle nodded and her brow furrowed in concentration. She typed a U.

"No. Not the letter, the word. Y-O-U."

"Then you need to say that." Belle's lips pressed tightly.

"I'll spell it and you type. Y-O-U-T-U-B-E. Then a period." Belle's hand moved to the right spot. "Yep, that's it. Now C-O-M. And press the Return key."

Belle pushed the button, and the screen changed, grabbing Ray's attention. He jumped out of his chair. With his back against the wall, he looked round the room, his eyes wide.

"Molly?" He whispered the words.

"Of course he'd give you credit. What's next? I don't have much left."

"Now, in that spot, type, 'ten things I hate about you guitar.'"

"A movie about my feelings for you. Maybe I'd like it."

Molly pursed her lips and huffed. "Just type. And push Return."

Belle followed her instructions. Ray watched as the words appeared, looking around for the hands creating the words. He didn't look frightened or anxious, only curious and ready. Yes, he would do nicely for Sabrina.

When the search results appeared, Molly pointed to the link she wanted.

"Okay, click on that one."

"Click what?" Belle growled. Her borders trembled like a photo taken with a shaky camera as her nostrils flared.

"Gently put a finger on the rectangle and move your finger until the arrow moves over the video I pointed to."

Belle groaned and moved the cursor toward the right video before she poofed.

"Shit. Shit. Shit," Molly said.

They had been so close! Molly pulled in her focus. She only needed to click the trackpad, and the video should start. She could do it. Belle was a lot stronger than she was, but she could do this one movement. She might not even poof, and even if she did, she'd already waited so long for this information . . . what were a few days more?

As she reached for the trackpad, her hand disappeared into Ray's. He'd sat back down in his chair.

"Do you want me to watch this?" Ray said aloud. "I feel like an idiot talking to someone I can't see. Here goes."

He clicked it. The screen changed to a talking lizard.

Fiddlesticks. It was an ad. Sometimes computers were the most horrible invention. At last, the scene she wanted began to play. It was the girl character reading her poem to the boy. Then, after school, at her car, he surprised her with a new guitar—something they had seen earlier in the movie. Something meaningful. Something that proved he knew he'd made a mistake and appreciated her for who she was.

Ray watched the video, and Molly watched him. When it was done, he played it again. Then again.

He opened his desk and pulled out a pad of sticky notes and a pen and wrote a brainstorming list: flowers, song, dance, trip, dinner.

All of them were awful. Sabrina needed something special.

Ray ripped off the sticky note and stuck it to his desk, then started writing on another. Then another. This time, they weren't gift ideas. They were something so much better.

36

THREE DAYS HAD PASSED since her life had become a jumbled mess, but the pieces were becoming clearer. After one session with her new therapist, they had agreed she should focus on what she could control, like the gala, so she'd moved all the planning materials to her bedroom and worked from there—texting Ray quick questions, which he would respond to equally briefly. She knew she was veering on the overly sensitive side, but knowing he knew her secret left her feeling exposed. Like a cracked tooth when you drank a Slurpee, there was nothing left to protect the nerve from the cold. It was best to keep her mouth shut and see a professional before any irreparable damage was done.

Molly had been ignoring her, too. Ghosts could make it very difficult to apologize to them, since they could disappear at will.

With her arms full of boxes containing advertising for the Goodbye Gala, Sabrina left the printers and stepped onto the sidewalk, heading toward her car. Even though it wasn't even noon, nearby

Main Street was already filling with tourists roaming in and out of the various stores.

"Watch where you're going," said a nasally voice that Sabrina recognized instantly. She moved the stack of boxes away from her face so Erika would see it was her. "Oh. I should have known."

In Erika's arms, a stack of slippery dry-cleaning bags revealed layers of bright-colored dresses and dark suits. Sabrina waited for the usual dread and angst to roll through her body, but nothing happened. Erika's face became more pinched as she waited for Sabrina to respond, and the longer the moment stretched, the more certain Sabrina was that she had nothing to say. This woman, who had bullied and hurt her in more ways than there were to cook a chicken, didn't matter anymore.

Sabrina didn't go to school with her anymore. They didn't share friends. And she most certainly didn't have to work with her anymore. Sabrina never had to talk to her again. There was nothing Erika could do to hurt her.

It was liberating.

Sabrina stepped around her and continued to her car, leaving a stunned Erika standing on the curb.

"Wait, Sabrina."

She kept walking and popped open the trunk of her car with her key fob.

"Please," Erika said.

Well, holy shit.

Sabrina set the boxes down before finally responding. "Yes, Erika."

Still clutching the plastic bags, Erika tottered over to her, one of the bags sliding down the front of her body, finally landing on the street when Erika stopped. Erika looked down at it, then up at Sabrina, expecting her to pick it up for her. Sabrina didn't. Since Erika couldn't let go of the rest of the bags or they would all end up in a heap on the dirty street, she did her best to squat and lean forward to grab the hanger, her fingers not quite reaching.

"Oh my God, stop." Sabrina bent over to pick it up, hanging it on Erika's entwined fingers. "What did you want from me?"

Erika's nostrils flared, and she collected her thoughts.

"You may not know this, but Ray has banned us from The Otter Club . . ."

"I know."

"Our parents don't."

Sabrina understood. Given the pile of fancy clothes, she could see where this was headed, but she was going to make Erika say it.

Erika let out a huff.

"Will you talk to Ray so we can go to the Goodbye Gala?"

Part of Sabrina wanted to say no, and it was not a tiny part. Thinking about all the parties and dances and sleepovers that Sabrina had been excluded from because of Erika, one gala seemed like more than a fair price. Sabrina imagined Erika having to explain to her parents why she and the Boy Wonder wouldn't be attending. Mrs. Hendricks's lips would purse, just like Erika's did now. It didn't matter that Sabrina wasn't talking to Ray at the moment—Erika didn't need to know that.

Sabrina took a breath. Perhaps there was a way that everyone could win.

"I'll talk to Ray if you and Bobby agree to buy a table."

"My parents already bought one, so done."

"No. You and Bobby will buy a separate table and fill it with people who will bid big on the auction items." Erika's lips thinned.

"The only table left is the school district's Angel Fund. Imagine how generous everyone will think you are."

"Fine. We'll buy it."

"Great. Do you want to pay for it now or drop a check off at my house later?"

Erika looked down at the bags in her arms. "Later."

"I'll text Ray immediately." Sabrina held up her phone.

Erika nodded and walked to her car, losing more bags when she opened her back seat.

"You're welcome!" Sabrina shouted at her.

She paused as she was about to text Ray. It had been three days since the photo incident. He'd tried to call a few times, then had stopped. Had he given up? Should she call? Her feelings about Ray knowing the truth flashed from terror to hurt to shock and back again, but she also loved him. That didn't go away. Good thing she had a therapy session in an hour.

She'd text him for now.

> I gave Erika and Bobby permission to come to the gala. They bought last 😬 table.

The dots appeared immediately.

> As long as you're okay with it.

She was.

> I'm good. Dropping off auction items later.

> K

That was it?

She checked her list. She had a few more stops before her appointment.

How could he go from a declaration of love to "K"?

:ᘓᘜᘔᘖ:

SABRINA AND HER MOM sat on the front porch in the sagging and chipped wicker furniture, complete with squashed and faded striped cushions and more than a few dried leaves from years past ground into the crevices. They didn't often have time together, just the two of them alone. Molly and her dad were always hovering about, or the grandkids, whom her mom would let move in if her brothers would allow it. Mom was never happier than when surrounded by family.

When it was just the two of them, her mom would let a curtain drop. Not that she was harboring secrets, but more that Sabrina was the only one who might understand. They were the only two Monroe women. She knew there were other women like them scattered around the world, and they were probably related if they traced it far enough up a vast ancestral tree, but they weren't family.

She held her mom's hand, soft and warm, but with skin thinner than it once was and more spots and veins. They were the hands of a grandmother, a young grandmother to be sure, but definitely a grandmother. Sabrina didn't like to think about it, but her mom would not be around forever, and she was sure to not leave behind anything unfinished.

Sabrina set her head on her mom's shoulder.

"I'm staying."

It was the first time she'd said the words out loud. She had expected a weight to lift because she had finally made the commitment. The deal was done, the contract signed. But she felt the same.

"Not what you expected?" her mom said, reaching her arm around Sabrina's back so she could rub her shoulder. She would never be too old for her mom's comfort, and it hurt deep inside knowing that someday it wouldn't be there, even if that day wouldn't arrive for many years. A person couldn't grow up in her family without an intimate relationship with death. Sabrina had always accepted that time was finite on this plane of existence. She just never wanted to be on a plane where her mom wasn't.

"Staying feels like accepting that someday you won't be here."

"Can you picture me and Belle hanging out in the cemetery?" Her mom chuckled.

"Of course not. I fought the idea of staying for so long, I expected a bell to ring or wild animals to bring me baked goods now that I've finally accepted my destiny. Instead, I'm worried I'll fail like I do at everything else."

"You aren't a failure. But this isn't something you can be good or bad at. It's like breathing. There's no wrong way to do it."

"My panic attacks say otherwise."

"You know what I mean. What we do is an extension of who we are. We might approach a problem differently, but the end goal is the same—to help people. It's a burden, but you already knew that. I only wish I'd prepared you better."

"I'm prepared."

"I don't mean now. I mean when you were younger. There had to be something I could have done."

"You couldn't protect me from Erika and her friends. Not really. I have a gift for bad timing."

Her mom kissed the top of her head.

"What we do isn't easy, Sabrina. People will say you're strange at best. Often they'll call you delusional, and maybe even dangerous.

It's human nature for people to be uncomfortable with death. And then we appear when they're at their most vulnerable and reveal that the world is nothing like they thought.

"On one hand, we help a soul find peace. I don't think there's a more honorable task than that. At the same time, we're intruding on a family's grief. We need to be sensitive to that, too. And sometimes situations are ridiculous. Those are the days I come home and laugh about it with your dad. Other times, it'll feel like climbing Denali barefoot and backward.

"Remember, you're there to help the recently deceased. The living will have time to sort out their problems. The dead shouldn't have to. What we do is weird, and people are going to notice. At the end of the day, we need to surround ourselves with people who love us for everything we are. The rest doesn't matter."

Sabrina and her mom stared out at the quiet street while the sound of cars driving nearby interrupted an owl hooting in the tree above their heads. Fireflies sparkled in the hostas, and the scent of a neighbor's backyard fire made her crave roasted marshmallows. The world that mattered to her had shrunk and slowed, and instead of feeling trapped, she finally felt free to be herself. Living with her parents for a while meant she could make her student loan payments. She'd find another job—maybe talk to Mr. Garnham at the funeral home. If she was going to commit to the dead, she might as well help all the recently deceased, and not just the ones with unfinished business.

The air filling her lungs was sweeter already.

"I'm glad you're staying," her mom whispered.

31

MOLLY WAS FLITTING THROUGH the house, peeking out windows and humming. It was really annoying. Molly had ignored her for days, and now she couldn't be quiet. Sabrina roamed from room to room, collecting her belongings and shoving them into drawers. She was finally unpacking. If she was going to scrape out a living, she'd find a job she liked, something that would put her love of office supplies and organization to good use. And after her call to Mr. Garnham, she had a lead.

Molly's whistling should have clued her in that something was about to happen, especially when she added dance steps to her music. To top it off, even though it was a ninety-five-degree September day, Molly was wearing an emerald-green wool suit jacket and skirt, matching green Mary Jane heels, and a fox fur stole around her shoulders. Looking at her made Sabrina's temperature rise.

"Could you stop? I thought you were mad at me."

Molly shrugged.

"Sometimes good people make mistakes, and if given an opportunity, they make amends. The bigger person would realize that, forgive them, and give that person another chance, because maybe life needs a little more empathy and forgiveness."

"What are you talking about?"

Molly pointed out the window, the incoming breeze not moving her hair. "Well, well, you have a visitor."

Sabrina pulled back the curtain to find Ray leaning against his car, looking up at her window. Ray held up his phone and tapped the screen. A ping from Sabrina's phone sounded almost immediately.

Please listen.

Next came a sound file, followed by another.

With headphones. 😊

"What did you do?" Sabrina asked Molly as she pulled her hair into a knot on top of her head and checked her shirt to make sure there weren't any obvious stains. Sabrina fought a smile, not wanting to admit how thrilled she was to see him outside her window.

"I don't know what you mean." Molly smoothed her fox and gave its head a little pat. "Belle helped."

"I'm going to need to hear that story."

Sabrina found her earbuds and plugged them in, staying by the window so Ray could see her. She pressed Play. The effect of his voice was instant at the base of her head, like a warm neck pillow.

"Sabrina. I'm sorry it's taken me a few days, but I needed time to think about the best way to express my thoughts. Please forgive me the delay, but I hope you find the wait worthwhile.

"First, you are wondrous, and learning your family's secret only adds to that. I could tell you over and over again that I love you exactly as you are, but I understand that might not be enough right now.

"Instead, I'm sharing ten embarrassing and odd things about myself that no one else knows. You are now the keeper of my secrets.

"One. I put ketchup on steak and eggs. Only when I eat them together, but there it is.

"Two. I really like waterslides. Like, an embarrassing amount. I love them so much. The day we met, I had dragged my sister with me so I wouldn't be the creepy single guy in a waterpark.

"Three. Anytime I'm on the subway, I plan at least two different escape routes in case shit gets real. I pay attention to where doors are located, spot side tunnels, and plan how to get through the crowds like a trained spy.

"Four. I participated in a dance battle against an eighties TV star and lost. If you get me drunk, I might tell you the entire story.

"Five. I believe in bigfoot. For real. Have you seen how big Canada is?

"Six. I met Keanu Reeves at a cocktail party and said 'Be excellent,' played the air guitar, then ran.

"Seven. I never step on sidewalk cracks, ever.

"Eight. I love the word 'epic,' but I rarely use it.

"Nine. All through middle school, I referred to myself in the third person. Sometimes when I'm alone, I still do it.

"Ten. My Tamagotchi is still alive and its name is Tamagotchi Hanks."

She played it again, her hand covering her mouth. This man, who stared at her from across the yard, who liked D&D (she noticed that wasn't on his list), understood her, maybe even more than she understood herself. Sabrina bit her lip to keep from smiling as she went outside to meet Ray. As she stepped out the back door, he walked up to meet her, both of them failing to hide their grins.

That meant something. Their mutual eagerness, the meeting half-way, the trust. They had nothing left to hide from each other.

Ray's hands shook, one of them carrying a bouquet, the other he rubbed on his pants. Sabrina recognized anxious hand sweats—another thing they had in common.

"Epic list," she said. Ray's grin widened.

"Sabrina." He took a deep breath. "I don't know how to tell you how sorry . . ."

She shook her head. "No. What were you supposed to do? Accuse me of seeing dead people? That sounds nuts. I know that."

"I don't want to lose this new part of my life—it's something I didn't think I'd ever find. My every decision until I came to the Dells was always determined by what would benefit the family most. Then there's you. You do everything for everyone else for no reason. You're too good, but I want you in my life anyway."

"Ray, when I found out you knew . . . about the ghosts . . . it left me exposed. I couldn't control what you thought of me anymore. I do nice things for me, because it makes me feel like a part of the world rather than a sidelined observer. It's purely selfish. Don't put me on pedestal—I'm afraid of heights."

"Then the world needs more of your selfishness."

Not sure how to respond, Sabrina pointed at the bouquet.

"Are those for anyone special?"

He handed it to her.

When she looked in the brown paper wrapping, she realized it wasn't a bouquet of real flowers, but dozens of tiny paper blossoms in pale yellow, blue, and pink.

"Are these made from the sticky notes?"

Each of the blooms was crisply folded and perched atop a green stick. It must have taken him hours.

"I have an alarming number of paper cuts. Post-its are tiny razor blades of death, but totally worth it."

Tucked in the center of the bouquet was one note with writing on it. She pulled it out to read the words "Kiss Me."

"Is this the one from the dining room?"

Ray nodded.

"You kept it?"

"Our second kiss. I can't throw out the best move I ever made."

Here was a man who had been on his way to massive success, and he'd chosen to live in this small, silly town and fall in love with her. Her heart melted.

Sabrina stood in front of Ray, who saw her for everything she was, and she stuck the "Kiss Me" note on her forehead.

He did. If her heart hadn't already melted, it would have surely burst into flames. Breathless, she stepped back.

"Maybe we could go to your house? Mine is a little crowded."

She raised her eyebrows, hoping he understood her meaning.

He did. "You sure?"

"Yeah. Now, please."

Ray didn't make her ask twice. They were both buckled in his car faster than Mr. Bennett could escape through a hole in a screen door.

As Ray pulled out of the driveway, he turned to Sabrina.

"I do have one more secret to confess," Ray said. "My family is coming into town for Labor Day, and they want to have a cookout with your family."

:⟨҈⟩:

"WHAT NOW?" SABRINA ASKED, sitting next to Ray in his car.

Ray gripped the steering wheel with one hand while lacing his other fingers through hers, grateful she didn't pull away. She wasn't upset, only surprised.

"Mom wants to meet you."

"How does she even know about us? *I* barely know about us." ·

Unsure how to explain his mom's domineering ways without terrifying Sabrina, he trusted she could take it and told her everything, from the matchmaking to worrying that Sabrina was after his money to holding the Jasper land over his head. Sabrina nodded as he spoke.

"Why does she want to meet my family?" Sabrina said.

"With everything you know about her now, do you really need to ask? Family is everything, and she wants to know who your people are. But don't worry. Lucy will be there to help as a buffer."

Sabrina frowned. *Oh no.*

"I get the impression you expect me to be worried about meeting your family, but I think it's the other way around. The Monroes aren't easily intimidated."

She had a point. A little East Coast snobbery wasn't going to faze Jenny and Doug Monroe. He laughed.

"Your family is a tour de force."

After the short drive from the Monroes' house to his, they entered his kitchen. The silent home, so different from her family's, underscored their seclusion. They were alone.

"Wine?" Ray asked, grabbing two glasses and an opener, studying her under his lashes for any sign of regret or trepidation.

"Yes, please," Sabrina said.

With easy movements, he uncorked the bottle of red he had on the counter and poured them each a generous glass.

Sabrina gulped down half her wine.

"Sabrina." Ray set his glass down and stepped close to her. "We don't have to do anything. We can take our wine into the backyard and start a fire. When it gets dark, we can listen to the whip-poor-will and stare at the stars."

She closed her eyes as she took a deep breath, her hands on her stomach, her lips forming an O as she exhaled. When she opened them, her usual warm eyes crackled with syrupy heat as she stepped closer to him, and her hands were confident when they caressed his face.

"I want this, but that doesn't mean I'm not nervous."

She touched her mouth to his, soft and feathery, ending with a nip on his lower lip. With a soft growl, Ray buried one hand in her hair while looping his other arm around her back to pull her body tight to his, her curves fitting neatly along him like they were two halves of a broken whole that had finally found their way back together.

"Unless you want the raccoons watching, we should take this upstairs," Ray said between kisses.

Sabrina nodded and blushed. "I'm not on the pill or anything. Do you have protection?"

"I do."

He led the way up to his bedroom, setting the necessary condom on the nightstand, but he didn't plan to use it for a while. In many ways, this was Sabrina's first time, and he intended to make sure she enjoyed it in every possible way.

When he turned, Sabrina stood in front of him, her hands slowly unbuttoning her shirt.

"Let me," Ray said. His hands trembled as he undid the first button. It had been a while for him, too, and he had never needed anyone as much as he needed Sabrina. Somewhere on the way to his bedroom, want had become need. He struggled to keep his pace slow, wanting to savor every second. With each button, Sabrina's breath grew shakier, until they both trembled as he released the last one. He lightly pushed her shirt off her shoulders, leaving Sabrina in a simple tan bra and jean shorts.

"Beautiful," Ray whispered as he tugged each sleeve over her hands.

"My lingerie might need an upgrade."

Ray shook his head.

"It's perfect—you're perfect."

He held her face between his hands, trailing kisses along her brows, across her cheeks, and under her jaw, her skin heating under his lips. He continued down her neck, across her chest, his hands skimming the sides of her body, barely touching, but memorizing every curve that he planned to kiss before the night was done.

When his hands met the top of her jeans, he knelt, unbuttoning her shorts and sliding them over her round hips to reveal her purple underwear. After helping Sabrina step out of the shorts, his hands trailed a path up her legs, then over the soft cotton. She moaned softly, and Ray nearly lost himself.

"Ray," she whispered, her hands in his hair.

He stood slowly, letting their bodies graze each other until they were face-to-face again, breaths ragged, though they'd barely touched each other.

She reached for his shirt, slowly pulling it over his head and tossing it aside. She looped a hand into a belt loop and pulled him close, crushing her lips to his, her hands racing over his skin while he fumbled with the back of her bra, at last freeing the clasp. They broke apart long enough for her to shrug the straps off her arms, while he lost his shorts. He barely maintained enough control to intentionally keep his boxers in place.

Picking her up, he laid her on the bed and covered her with his body, skin on skin. Touching her surpassed anything his imagination could have invented, better than a dream because he could taste and smell and hear every tiny sigh each time he discovered a new sensitive spot. He throbbed with need when she moaned, but stayed on course, tossing her underwear off the bed, and smiled into the sweetness of it all.

:⊙⟩⟨⊙:

"So . . . HOW ARE YOU feeling?" Ray asked, his chest still rising and falling at a rate that matched hers, his arm bent over his head as he lay on his back. Sabrina wished she could bottle this feeling—right now, nothing could cause her anxiety to spike.

"That was . . . so much better than I remembered. I wouldn't have waited so long if I'd known sex would be that great."

Her heavy limbs sunk into the soft covers, exhausted and well-pleasured. Her tangled curls flopped when she moved her head. Three times she'd orgasmed. Three times. The first time, she'd worried she would crush his head with her thighs. He'd kept finding new places that came alive with his touch.

"Oh, it's only like that when it's with me. I'm magic that way."

Sabrina laughed and rolled over so she was tucked into the curve of his arm.

"Are you implying you have a magic penis?"

"Are you implying I don't?"

Ray kissed her forehead.

"Tha—" Sabrina started to say, but Ray put his finger over her mouth.

"If you are about to thank me for having sex with you, I will have some strong words to say to you when I get my energy back."

"How about a kiss, then?"

"Anytime."

Sabrina stretched to reach his lips, her own feeling tender and sensitive. She traced a finger across Ray's chest, finally looking at the room around her. It was fairly big, with dark-wood wainscoting and burgundy wallpaper that was dated and peeling in places.

Next to the bed, Harry materialized.

"Harry! What the hell?" Sabrina gasped, and Harry had the nerve to laugh. She didn't want to know how long he might have been around. "Ray, did your uncle have a pervy streak?"

"Is he here? Now?" Ray pulled the sheet up higher over Sabrina.

"Yes, right there." She pointed a thumb in Harry's direction.

"*Kleeeee*," Harry said.

"Shit. I'm sorry. I've been distracted, but I'm on it now," she said to Harry, then spoke to Ray. "Did you find a key in Harry's desk, by chance?"

"Yes. I thought it was for the desk, but it didn't fit."

"It's for a safe-deposit box. Whatever it contains, he wants you to have it." Sabrina needed to come fully clean. "I've known for a while, but I didn't know how to tell you how I knew. I was hoping to find it and point you in the right direction. I'm sorry."

"No need to apologize. I understand," Ray said.

"I was apologizing to Harry. He's had to stick around longer than necessary because of me. Do you have the key?"

Ray slid out of bed and into his boxers, then dug the keys out of his shorts pocket. Once he found the right key, he held it up toward the area Sabrina had pointed to earlier. "Is this it?"

Harry nodded, and with each head bob, he became brighter and brighter, and then suddenly he was gone. Harry had moved on. Sabrina always expected to hear angels sing or a bell chime when a spirit disappeared, but it was more like the absence of sound, a tiny black hole where something once was, but now there was nothing.

"He's gone," Sabrina said.

"Did he leave?"

"He's gone wherever they go once their unfinished business is complete. You have the key, so he can be at peace."

"Huh. It's a bit like he's died again. Even though I couldn't see him or talk to him, it was reassuring that he was still around."

"Did you love him? Have good memories?" Sabrina asked.

Ray nodded.

"Then he'll never be gone."

Ray wiped at his face and sat back on the bed.

"Want to go find out what's in the box?"

38

THE FIRST BANK OF the Dells closed at five o'clock sharp, and not a minute earlier or later. When Sabrina and Ray walked in at 4:59 p.m., Faith Garnham, Mr. Garnham's daughter, could do nothing but help them with a smile, even if her teeth gnashed together so tightly she could have cracked a tooth.

"I really appreciate this, Faith," Ray said. "I promise, we'll only be a moment."

Faith led them to a room filled with tiny boxes, each with two locks.

"May I see the key again?" She wrote down the number on a form, then inserted her key into the corresponding box's lock and turned. Ray used his key to do the same. Faith pulled out the box and set it on the table.

"I'll be outside if you need me."

"What do you think is in it?" Sabrina asked.

"It had to be something fairly important, right? Why else would he have hung around and kept it here?"

"What if it's the map to One-Eyed Willy's treasure?"

"That's my girl. Goonies never say die."

He kissed her quickly and thought about stretching it out, but the curiosity was too strong.

"Ready?" he said.

Sabrina nodded, and Ray opened the box. He had hoped he would find the journal's missing pages, but instead it contained one sealed envelope, barely thick enough to contain a piece of paper. *That's it?* Ray opened it and pulled out the single-page document. It was short, but it changed everything, starting with the first, most important line.

I, Harold Jasper, being of sound mind and body, leave all of my be-longings, including property, accounts, and possessions, to Raymond Harold Jasper IV.

It was signed, notarized, and dated a month after Ray had moved to the Dells, when Harry had been sick but still in his right mind. This paper meant he was completely free from his parents, and the relief overwhelmed him. He had to sit to let the truth of it sink in. Harry had left everything to him. The house, the properties in town, Harry's portion of the supper club . . . all his.

The future he had wanted was finally happening. The restaurant, the house, the Dells, and Sabrina, who was sharing this moment with him. The realization that he had full control over his fate rooted him in the moment. How he chose to grow his life from here was all on him.

:᠕᠊᠊᠊᠊᠊᠊᠊᠊᠊᠊᠊᠊᠊᠊᠊:

"RAY, SORRY IT TOOK us so long. There was a minor emergency over whether pink or yellow sprinkles were the right color for cupcakes," Sabrina said as she stepped through the patio door off his kitchen, immediately followed by Arabella, Lilly, and Oscar.

"We went with both, of course," said Arabella.

"Hello again, Arabella," Ray said, holding out his hand for her to shake. She took it and delivered an impeccable curtsy, then ran off with the other kids.

"She's in a royalty phase. We drew the line when she insisted we only refer to her as 'Her Highness,'" Cal said, shaking Ray's hand. "Thanks for having us. Where do you want this?" He held up the tray of purple-frosted cupcakes, generously coated in pink and yellow sprinkles.

Ray pointed to the table already loaded with food and introduced his family to Sabrina's. They were still sizing one another up when Oscar ran up to Ray's mom and stopped. His head tilted as far back as it could go so he could see her face.

"Can you see Molly? Grandma says she's looking in the windows over there, but I can't see her."

Almost as one, Sabrina's family leaned forward to stop him, but Ray's mom knelt down in front of him.

"I don't know. Why don't we go over and check?" She took him by the hand and walked past Ray. "How cute, he has an imaginary friend named Molly." They stepped off the patio and peeked into his office windows.

Ray turned to Sabrina and whispered, "Is she here?"

"Yeah, but I don't know what she's doing."

He had a newfound appreciation for the discretion Sabrina's family had to practice every day.

"Ray, is that urn what I think it is?" his mother asked. "How did he get here?"

Ray looked down at Sabrina. "Busted."

A frown wrinkled Sabrina's brow, and she stepped toward the house, then stopped.

"Huh. That was weird. Molly looked sad, then poofed." Sabrina paused, tapping her lip. "Is that her Raymond in there?"

"Oh. It is. I didn't even connect the two. I've been so preoccupied with—well, you."

"It's okay. He's not going anywhere. I have to come back with Molly so we can find those pages. She has some ideas on where to look."

Ray's dad and Doug had pulled two chairs under a tree and sipped beer while Sabrina's brothers, Cal and Trent, helped the kids fill water balloons from the hose. After dinner, if they were good, they had been promised a water balloon fight of epic proportions—Sabrina's words, and he loved her for them.

"Jenny, your grandkids are just darling. You must be so happy." Ray didn't miss his mother's sideways glance at him as she spoke.

Lucy stood next to him and snorted. "Notice how she didn't look at me."

"Should I do it now?" Ray asked. He had told her about Uncle Harry's new will, but he hadn't mentioned it to his parents. He was going to share it today.

"Wait, let me get a chair, I want to be comfortable as I watch this," Lucy said.

Sabrina laughed. "I like her. A lot."

Lucy winked and settled awkwardly into a bag chair.

"Everyone, could I have your attention? I have some information I'd like to share," Ray said. Everyone turned toward him except the children, who had found a toad in the flower bed and followed it as it hopped between the hostas. "While cleaning the house, I found a

key to Uncle Harry's safe-deposit box, which contained a more recent will."

Ray watched his parents—he didn't want to miss their reactions.

"It left all his property to me. I have it in the study if anyone
would like to look at it. I checked with my attorney, and it's valid."

His parents didn't flinch, but the Monroes erupted in congratulations and handshakes.

Lucy stood. "A toast to the Wisconsin Dells' largest landowner,"
she said.

Everyone raised a glass, but the moment was broken by a squeal.

"No, Lilly, I don't want to hold it!" Oscar screamed, running from
Lilly, who held the toad in both hands.

"He won't hurt you. He's nice," Lilly said.

Trent and his wife, Becky, jumped up in unison to chase after
their children, and the moment was broken. His parents still hadn't
reacted. Ray didn't understand.

"You don't seem very surprised, and Dad isn't that good of an ac-
tor," Ray said.

"We knew ages ago, Ray. Harry called us when he decided to
change his will."

"Then what was the bullshit with having to prove myself? Holding The Otter Club over my head."

It was just like his parents to play games like that. Sabrina rubbed
his back, but it didn't help his irritation at his parents.

"We wanted to make sure this was what you really wanted. The
will would have surfaced eventually. We couldn't believe you thought
we'd actually sell this land. Now that we know you're serious about
staying here, we're confident you'll do the family proud."

"Holy hell." Ray threw his hands in the air and walked away for a moment, then returned. "Do you have any idea what kind of stress this caused me? I'm trying to get a business off the ground and plan my first Goodbye Gala, and you put this giant hoop in my path. Who does that?"

His mom sniffed, then said, "Good parents."

Sabrina grabbed his hand, and it calmed him. Was this what it felt like for her when he calmed her? If so, it was very effective.

"Regardless," Sabrina said, "you would be very impressed with your son. The Goodbye Gala is going to be the best we've ever had. You should come back."

Ray's mouth dropped open. What had she just done?

"We'd love to, dear. How thoughtful of you to invite us, since it must have slipped Raymond's mind on account of all his newfound responsibilities." His mother put her arm around Sabrina and drew her away. "Tell me, where do you stand on children? Two, three, six?"

Sabrina's face whitened.

Lucy walked past and whispered in Sabrina's ear, "Run."

39

"**Ready?**" **Sabrina said to** the space next to her. She and Ray were in his kitchen, presumably with Molly, but Ray couldn't see her. "They might not be here, Molly." Sabrina listened for a moment, then rolled her eyes. "I don't know where you pick up these sayings. They sound ridiculous coming out of your mouth. They're worse than when Dad mashes up textspeak."

Ray watched the one-sided conversation, thrilled he was now privy to this part of Sabrina's life.

"Where should we start?" Ray said, looking around his home with fresh eyes.

Sabrina nodded. "Yes, this is tedious, but it's how it has be."

Ray raised an eyebrow.

"She's annoyed that she has to wait for me to tell you what she says. That it's taking too long. And she said she'll know it when she sees it and we should follow her."

Sabrina grabbed Ray's hand and pulled him after her as they roamed slowly from room to room on the main floor, spending extra time in the library, where they emptied all the cupboards so Molly could see the contents.

"Well, I don't know, do I?" Sabrina's words came out clipped. She turned to Ray. "Are these all the books and files you found?"

"Yeah, I've been through them all, even shaking out all the books. I suppose it could be in a binding, but that seems like a lot of effort to hide some journal pages."

Sabrina listened and nodded. "Did you check the throne room?"

Ray's brow scrunched, and Sabrina threw up her arms to indicate she was only the messenger.

"You've swallowed the red pill now. This is what life is like with a Monroe woman."

Ray laughed and nodded. "That I have." He took stock of all the rooms in the house to see if any could be considered a throne room. His best guess would be the office, but that was clearly not it. "We don't have a throne room."

Pause.

"It's under the main staircase." Sabrina walked in that direction.

"The bathroom?" Ray asked.

"Exactly," Sabrina said. "Molly's words, not mine."

They walked past the large six-foot-wide staircase, and Sabrina opened the door to the small room that contained only a toilet and a small pedestal sink.

"Harry wanted me to look in here, too." Sabrina stepped in, then stepped out again to look at the steps. "Don't you think the room is too small given the giant staircase it's under?"

"I never thought about it, but there *were* rumors the house had a secret hideaway." Ray saw it now, and Sabrina was right. The bathroom should have been larger.

Sabrina looked at Molly.

"How do you know about this?" Sabrina studied the light fixture above the sink. "Never mind, I don't want to know why you were sneaking around with Raymond in the middle of the night in his house." She pushed the center of a flower, and they heard a soft click. A crack appeared in the corner of the room, and they pushed it wider.

Sabrina and Ray lit up their phones and stepped into the dark room. Sabrina shivered.

"I'm sorry. It's a tight space, and you keep moving." Pause. "Fine, we'll stay put so you can look around."

Ray stayed where he was as Sabrina moved her light around the small space, presumably where she was told. He used his to look where he wanted. A little larger than the bathroom, the tiny room contained a dusty love seat, a table with a gas lamp, and shelves Shelves full of books. A lot of books.

"The family used this space to hide booze during prohibition, and apparently to read and have illicit affairs. Molly and Raymond spent some time . . ." Sabrina trailed off, then pointed to a dark-green book. "This one?" She pulled it off the shelf, looked at the cover, and laughed. "*The Canterville Ghost.* Come on, that's super ironic." She handed the book to Ray. "You want to do the honors?"

He took it. The cover was a dark-green cloth with gold text in a serif font, and a black silhouetted castle and white moon were pictured behind a spectral figure in gold—presumably the titular ghost.

"Why this book?" Ray asked.

"Molly gave it to Raymond as a gift the night before he went away. He loved Oscar Wilde, but it was also a joke. Her last name is Cantor. She spent a lot of money on it. Books were more expensive back then, relatively speaking."

Ray slowly opened the book. Inside was an inscription from Molly.

Never love anyone who treats you like you're ordinary.
—*Oscar Wilde*

> *All my extraordinary love,*
> *Molly*

Also in the book was a pack of folded papers, one side torn where they had been ripped from a book—a tear that matched the tooth-shaped edge in the journal. The missing pages at last. Ray's hands trembled as an icy shiver ran through him.

"Molly, give him some space," Sabrina said.

"Let's go where the light is better," Ray said, and they filed out of the tight space.

He spread the pages on the kitchen island so they could read the faint script.

"Why don't we let Molly read them first?" Ray said. Sabrina nodded. He watched her face as she watched Molly's. At one point, her eyes began to tear up, and she covered her mouth. Occasionally Sabrina would flip over one of the pages so Molly could read the back. He could only imagine how heartbreaking this was for her.

"She's gone. I think she needs a bit of time. Maybe you could let us have the pages for a while. I'm sure she'll want to reread them."

"She can keep them," Ray said.

Now it was their turn to read.

> *October 14, 1931*
> *A train in Illinois.*

My heart aches and I owe my Molly the greatest of apologies. I will spend the rest of my days making up the hurt I have caused her.

312

My family, those small-minded fools, have sent me away upon discovering our engagement. My mother uncovered my deep feelings and intentions to marry by reading this diary, which I had kept hidden in my room. For many years, they have desired a mutually beneficial match with the Hendricks family, one in which I was loathe to participate, even before I knew Molly's beautiful heart and buoyant charms. But once we met, my soul had found its match and no other would suffice. I want to spend every day until the end of days by her side, and even that will not be enough.

My older brothers forcibly took me to the train station and boarded a car bound for New York. I did not leave willingly and have the blackened eye to prove it—with my one to their three, I made a good showing, but could not overpower them. Alas, being outnumbered and not wanting to cause permanent injury, I was rendered unconscious, and I woke to the tall buildings of Chicago blocking my view of the lake in a rumbling train car. Each mile that separates us stings my soul like salt on cracked skin. My plan is to get away at the earliest chance and return home. While I have no money on my person, my accounts are still mine. I will return to Molly and take her away, where my family cannot interfere.

For now, I've decided my best course of action is to go along. Travel to New York, let them think I'm acquiescing to their will, then leave once they let up their observances. It may take more time than I would like, but I will not give up. I hope to mail a letter, but I'll have to wait until my family isn't watching.

I pray my Molly waits for my return and does not doubt my steadfastness. She has my heart until we can be reunited.

He'd written several paragraphs outlining his attempts to leave that were hampered by his interfering family. The last entry was the most heartbreaking.

November 22, 1932
Wisconsin Dells, Wisconsin

I have returned home, but it is no longer such. It can't be. My heart will never find a home again, and I'm enraged over the loss. During my unintended and unrequested absence, the worst has happened; my dearest Molly has perished. Gone too long, I have failed her utterly. In speaking with her former employer and landlord, I learned she grew ill in early October, and it worsened quickly when Mr. Oliver had to fire her. He could no longer afford employees after closing Hiawatha's. Without work, Molly had no one and no income. She stayed in her apartment for weeks. Mr. Oliver refused to tell me what happened when my beautiful Molly was discovered—too late and dead several days—but my imagination, it treads paths so dark and gruesome the truth would be a relief, I'm sure.

I will never forgive my family for taking me away from her. Had I been here, I know she would be alive, healthy, and blushing as my bride. It pains me to think she waited for me to return and I did not come. I pray she didn't die hating me. I could not bear that, knowing I held her trust and failed to keep her safe. I can never tell her I'm sorry or beg for her forgiveness or even begin to make amends, let alone enact all my plans of making her smile every day.

They buried her in the back of the cemetery with a small white stone that would have faded and eroded with time. I had it replaced with one more befitting her cherished role in my life. It pained me to leave her last name as Cantor, so the world will never know the place she will always hold in my heart. I may as well be buried alongside her, as all is now flat and gray. I cannot stay here a day longer. Every corner bears memories that drag me down. If I'm to carry on, then I have to leave, but not forever. I will come back in death to be with her. There is room on the headstone for my name, too. We couldn't be together in life, so we will be forever together in death. My mind is firm on this, since that is all I have left of her.

Tomorrow I return to New York with my parents and brothers. We have a house near the large park. I will follow my family's wishes and marry the woman they have chosen, a distant Vanderbilt cousin. I will work where they tell me to. It matters not anymore. I'm only biding my time until I'm reunited with my Molly. Then I can live again.

Ray's throat tightened as he held Sabrina close to his side, needing to touch her. His parents had their issues, but he couldn't imagine them forcing him away from the woman he loved. He would make sure his great-grandfather was laid to rest where his heart already resided.

40

"YOU AREN'T CREEPED OUT at all?" Ray asked, walking closely by Sabrina's side as they weaved between the gravestones. The heat of the day was already gone, and Sabrina wished she'd worn a sweater over her T-shirt. "Surrounded by all these bodies?"

"Of all the things I'm afraid of, death is not one of them." She reached back to squeeze his arm, careful not to bump what he was carrying. "There's nothing here that can hurt us."

Ray banged his shin on a low headstone he couldn't see in the dark. "Ow."

"Except your shins. You should watch out for those," Sabrina said.

"That's going to leave a bruise," Ray said.

"I'll get you some ice when we're done. Follow me and you won't bump into anything."

"Why did we have to do this at night? Without flashlights?"

"Even though we have permission to be here, it's easier if we don't have to explain anything to the police. The moonlight gives us enough light."

Ray grumbled something Sabrina couldn't hear.

"Almost there, chickadees," Molly said, leading the way, with Sabrina following Molly, and Ray following Sabrina. They stepped around a large granite cube to stand in front of one of the largest headstones in the cemetery—a giant block of white marble with a dramatically draped weeping angel. The headstone read:

MARGARET CANTOR
THE LOVE OF MY LIFE
"AND LOVE IS STRONGER THAN DEATH IS."—OSCAR WILDE

"Wow, subtle," Sabrina said.

"It's a little ostentatious for my taste," Molly said, but she looked pleased.

"Your name is Margaret? How come you never told me that?" asked Sabrina.

"I don't have to tell you everything." She set her hand on the stone. "Besides, I didn't care for it much. Molly suited me. I'm not sure why Raymond chose to put it on the stone. He knew I hated it."

"We would have connected dots a lot sooner had I known your real name." Sabrina touched the cool stone. "Why have I never been to your grave before?"

Molly's mouth dropped in shock. "That's morbid. Why would you want to? I come to you." She sniffed, then ran her fingers over the words. "He really did love me. We would have been so happy together."

Ray joined them at the headstone, pulling the silver urn from the bag he carried. Molly's eyes brimmed with tears.

"There he is." She reached out to touch it. Sabrina's eyes started to tear up because Molly's face shone with such love. It was heart-rending.

"What's happening?" Ray said.

"Molly's touching the urn. It's the closest she's been to Raymond in a long time."

"She could have visited the urn at the house."

"I don't wander around homes unless invited," Molly said, still touching the urn.

Sabrina raised an eyebrow, knowing for a fact that wasn't entirely true, but now was not the time.

Ray looked down at the urn, squinting to try to see Molly's hand.

"Hi, Molly," he said.

"Hi, Ray," Molly whispered.

Sabrina passed it on.

"He really does look like my Raymond. That hair. Don't you just want to grab it and pull his face to yours and kiss him till you can't think straight?"

"Molly!"

"What did she say?" said Ray.

"Things I am not planning to repeat."

"Don't act so shocked. I've been around you kids long enough. I've picked up on how you speak," Molly said.

"It's worse than my mom talking like that. It's disturbing."

"So what are we supposed to do?" Ray asked.

In front of the stone was a hole, a few feet deep and a foot wide. A shovel was propped against the side of the grave next to a small pile of dirt. Sabrina had called to have it set up this way so they could have a private moment without anyone watching them.

"Put him with Molly so they can always be together."

"Give me a moment first," Molly said.

She set both her hands on the urn and closed her eyes. After a few moments, she gave it a gentle kiss.

"I wish I could go with you, my love," she said at last, and nodded to Sabrina.

"Ray, set him in the grave, and I'll fill it up," Sabrina said.

Ray knelt on the ground, gently lowering the urn to the bottom, and Sabrina shoveled. It didn't take long to fill the small hole. She tamped down the earth and propped the shovel back where she had found it.

"The caretaker will plant some fresh grass on it tomorrow. By next year, it will blend right in."

They stood in silence for a moment.

"Molly? Is that really you?" In unison, Sabrina and Molly lifted their heads to see a new figure: an older man with thick white hair and a bespoke gray suit. He stepped toward them, his hair gradually darkening, his skin smoothing out, until a young man stood there.

"Raymond." Molly closed the distance between them. "How?"

He looked around himself. His eyes settled on Molly's headstone, then turned back to her, his eyes drinking up her face like a man dying of thirst.

"I . . . I don't know." They both glowed with a soft white light. "I was in New York. The last thing I remember doing was pulling my journal off the shelf so Ray would find it." He pointed at Ray. Sabrina covered her mouth with her hands.

"What. Is. Happening?" Ray asked.

"Your great-grandfather is here. The last thing he remembers is yanking the journal off the shelf so you'd find it."

"You tried to get back to me? After all this time?" Molly reached for his hands, and when they connected, the glow increased, pulsing like a firefly.

"What is that?" Ray said, pointing to where Molly and Raymond stood.

"You can see it?" Sabrina asked.

"How could I miss it?"

"Molly." Sabrina's alarm bells went off. All Molly had ever wanted was to see Raymond's face again, find out what had happened to separate them. They had found the journal, and here he was. And Raymond had wanted to be buried with Molly. Done and done. "Molly?"

"Sabrina, you have to meet my Raymond." The light increased. Molly beamed at Sabrina. "Raymond, this is Sabrina, my dearest friend. You're going to love her."

"Molly." Sabrina said it softly. "It's time."

"Time for what, hon?"

"Your unfinished business isn't unfinished anymore." Sabrina's words started to clog her throat. Molly's eyes widened, and the glow increased again until it was as bright as a car's headlight.

"I can see them," Ray whispered, his eyes wide and unblinking, not wanting to miss anything.

Molly turned to Raymond, and he nodded. Molly came to Sabrina and reached her hand out to touch her cheek. They both gasped as her fingers made contact with Sabrina's face.

"I can feel you," Molly said. Sabrina clutched at the hand that was as real as Ray's, warm like it had spent hours soaking up sunlight. She squeezed it, then pulled Molly into a hug, her bouncing curls hiding the tears that sprang to her eyes. The silk of Molly's dress whispered under her fingers as she held her tighter. Sabrina could feel her heart beat against Molly's still chest.

"My dear girl," Molly said.

"You're going, and it's too soon. I know that's selfish."

Molly hugged her tighter.

"My dearest girl. I don't have long. I can actually feel the pull—it's fascinating. I thought I would be here forever. You were my friend, and you made it bearable—more than bearable, delightful. I don't know where I'm headed, but I know it will be less because I can't watch movies with you or gossip with you." Sabrina rolled her eyes and smiled. "But I promise, I'll never forget." She let go of Sabrina and held up her pinky. Sabrina took it with her own, gasping to keep the tears in check, then finally letting them fall freely.

"What will I do without you?"

"You'll figure it out. You're not alone anymore." She looked over her shoulder at Ray.

"Neither are you." Sabrina let her hand go and nodded toward the spot where Raymond waited. Ray stepped up beside her and grasped her hand. "You've both waited long enough. Go get your happily ever after."

When Molly took Raymond's outstretched hand, the glow became incandescent, and then they were both gone. Her own Ray pulled her tight as her shoulders shook with each sob.

A voice spoke from behind a puff of smoke. Sabrina couldn't see the face, but she knew who it was. She couldn't mistake that raspy voice for anyone other than Belle.

"Finally, I might get some quiet around here."

41

WITH ONLY A FEW days before the Goodbye Gala, the wall in front of the dining room table was covered in sticky notes, but this time for something else, something bigger. Sabrina had pushed the dining room table against the wall so she could read the sticky notes while she worked, occasionally stopping to add a new one to the arrangement.

In front of her was her laptop, open to a blank document, where the blinking cursor flashed like a beating heart. She'd stared at thousands of blinking cursors, all waiting for her to tell someone's story. But now the blinking cursor waited for her story, which felt right. Sabrina lived with one foot in a fantastical world, rich with tales of love and hate, betrayal and revenge, greed and kindness.

She wanted to tell Molly's story first. That of a lost love, found again because they never gave up on each other, even though it took death to bring them together. It was a beautiful story of hope, and Sabrina wanted to share it.

She typed the title:

An Absolutely True Ghostly Love Story

Ray tiptoed in and set a grilled cheese sandwich next to her.

"You've been in here awhile. I thought you could use some nourishment."

He kissed her head and had turned to leave when Belle popped into the room. By her side was an older woman wearing a hospital gown and fuzzy socks, her short gray hair squashed in some places and sticking straight out in others, the telltale glow blurring her edges.

"Here's another one," Belle said, releasing the woman as if she were throwing her in a jail cell.

"Hi, Belle," Sabrina said. Ray perked up and looked around. He still tried to see the ghosts when they arrived.

"I caught this one wandering on Highway Twelve."

"Thank you for bringing her to me, Belle." Sabrina turned to the woman. "What can I help you with, Ms. . . . ?"

"Ally is fine." She looked at Belle and Ray with wide eyes.

"Do you understand what's happening to you, Ally?"

"I'm dead, right?" She sucked on her teeth. "I was real sick."

"I'm sorry to say you're right. You're here because you need something done before you can feel fully at peace. I'll help you with that." Sabrina smiled at her. "You just have to tell me what you need done."

Ally looked at Ray.

"Don't worry about him, he can't see you, though he likes to think if he squints hard enough he can."

"That's my cue." He walked out of the room. "Bye, Belle. Have fun, Sabrina!" he shouted from the kitchen.

Belle pointed toward the doorway.

"As far as breathers go, he's okay." She looked at Ally. "You have this."

Then Belle was gone.

"Okay, Ally. It's just us. You can tell me anything. I've heard it all." Ally's entire aura pinkened.

"There are some items I have hidden that I would prefer my husband or children didn't find." She looked toward the kitchen door again and whispered, "Adult items. I don't think they would understand."

Sabrina blinked and covered her mouth with her hand to hide her smile. She hadn't heard it all.

"No problem, Ally. Come with me, and we'll take care of this. With any luck, your family is still at the hospital and we can be in and out before anyone knows."

Ally looked relieved. Some secrets were best taken to the grave.

42

"TASTE THIS," RAY SAID, holding a bite-size morsel in front of Sabrina. He set it in her mouth. It was a ball, lightly breaded, and when she bit down, it was rice—no, risotto—with sharp cheddar and a chunk of brat with a light bitter finish of malty beer and tang of sauerkraut.

"Did you make your Wisconsin risotto into arancini?"

Ray grinned.

"I want to eat them all night long. That's brilliant."

"It's the only one of my ideas Rick approved, but even that's an achievement."

"Look at you, inventing delicious foods."

She reached up to straighten Ray's bow tie, even though it didn't really need it. She just wanted a reason to touch him, and even though she didn't need an excuse, it was nice to have one. He wore formal wear like he was born to do it. He looped his arm around her waist, careful not to crush her gown, which was patterned with leaves against a dark-burgundy background. The one-shouldered dress had a full skirt that whooshed out when she spun.

"Shall we check on our guests of honor?"

The two of them wove their way through the growing crowd, stopping to chat along the way, with Ray doing the majority of the talking. At last they made it to the porch where three Dine with a Dog tables were set, each for seven people and one pooch. Already at his table, the very handsome and bow-tied Frank waited with Gabby at his side.

"Look at this handsome man!" Sabrina said, scratching Frank's soft black ears. "We have the best-looking table."

Ray nodded.

"Not just that." Ray gave Frank a treat from his pocket. "But this guy is going to be my new roommate."

"Really?" Sabrina asked.

"Frank has been tough to place because he's so big," Gabby said.

"You're not too big, are you, boy?" Ray got close enough to get some kisses. "He's also going to be our poster pup. He'll come to work with me and always be here for snuggles with our guests."

"How has the program been going?" Sabrina asked Gabby.

"In a month, we've found two forever families and one possible. Plus Frank. Donations are up, too."

Sabrina bent down to look at Frank, his dark eyes swimming with canine adoration.

"We're going to be seeing a lot of each other." She smooched him on the forehead.

"Sabrina."

Sabrina turned to greet Ray's mother.

"Claire, I'm so happy you and Raymond could make it."

"Everything is stunning. You and our Ray went above and beyond. You'll have to come plan some parties for me."

"Only if you have them here. Mr. Garnham has hired me at the funeral home. I start next week."

Claire made a face. "That's an unusual choice."

"It's a better fit then you might think," Sabrina said. Ray squeezed her arm and smiled. "Plus, Ray has conned me into some party planning gigs. I've told him he can't afford me, but he doesn't listen."

"He rarely does."

Lucy stepped between them, forcing Claire to either move out of earshot or get licked by Frank.

"Hey, lady." She kissed Sabrina's cheek. "Love that dress on you. Mom wouldn't stop talking about you on the way here." Lucy nodded over her shoulder toward her mom. "You're in now. She's never letting you out of the family."

"I'm not *in* the family."

"You are in the way it counts. You're her best shot at grandkids in the next decade. The rest is a formality—one she'll want to spend a lot of money on, but a formality nonetheless. Gird your loins."

Sabrina laughed, pleasantly surprised that the idea of children didn't send her spiraling. Her new anxiety meds must be working.

"I'm glad you're here, and I know Ray is, too," Sabrina said.

"Funny, it's not that hard to get to the middle of nowhere. And these are growing on me." She held up a brandy old-fashioned and shook the glass to clink the ice against the sides. "Who is that?" Lucy pointed at Gabby, who was luring Frank onto his special seat with bacon. Gabby's hair was tied back in a ponytail, with the tail dangling over a gold sequined top, leather pants (probably faux, knowing Gabby), and dark chunky boots. Gabby looked up and noticed

Lucy staring, then smiled back before returning her attention to Frank.

"Let me introduce you," Sabrina said.

After Sabrina saw that Lucy was settled in the chair next to Gabby, she wanted to make one more round before dinner to make sure everything was prepared. In the kitchen, she hoovered two more rice balls as Chef Rick reassured her everything was on schedule. But if she wanted snacks, she could get them from the waiters on the floor because he wouldn't let trays with empty spots leave his kitchen. Sufficiently reprimanded, she checked that the bar had enough ice and the silent auction items were all getting bids. A few had even surpassed the inflated value listed at the top—a major win since all the items were donated.

She pulled her list and a pen from the pocket of her dress—yes, it had pockets—and checked off the last few items. There was nothing she could do now but enjoy the evening. The lights flashed to signal that dinner would be served, and she turned in the direction of her table.

In front of her stood Erika, her hair high on her head, making it impossible to miss the pebble-size diamond studs in her ears and the matching necklace, which she made sure to trail her fingers across in case anyone's eyes weren't already dazzled by their sparkling. The black dress hugging her body made the short trail of toilet paper sticking out the bottom all the more noticeable. Two young boys behind her pointed and giggled.

"It looks like you managed to not embarrass the town," Erika said. Sabrina opened her mouth to remind her that she wouldn't even be here if it weren't for her, but Sabrina's mom appeared at her elbow and gently squeezed her arm.

"What lovely diamonds," her mom said.

Erika was instantly distracted, like a child being shown candy. "They've been in the family for years. Grandmother wanted me to have them."

"Yes, I know, dear. Madam was so certain she'd live into the triple digits that it never occurred to her to tell anyone where she hid them. It would've been horrible if I hadn't been there so she could pass on that very specific information. I doubt anyone in your family would have found the loose brick in the attic."

"How *did* you know?" Erika asked.

Jenny leaned in to whisper. "Make sure to write down where you decide to hide them. You never know when the Monroes will tire of helping the Hendrickses."

Her mom patted Erika's cheek and turned Sabrina away.

"That felt really good," her mom whispered, but Sabrina stopped and went back to Erika.

"What is it now?" Erika said. She really made it hard to be nice to her.

"Lift up your left foot."

Sabrina squatted, her dress ballooning around her, and unhooked the toilet paper from the spike of Erika's shoe.

She stood and held it up for Erika to see.

"Got it," Sabrina said, crumpling it in her hand, and didn't wait for a thank-you that would never come. Some people were incapable of change.

After the dinner and the auction, when all that was left was drinking, dancing, and raiding the candy buffet, Sabrina and Ray surveyed their success. She no longer tracked how long it had been since she'd last spoken to someone, not because she'd found a hidden extrovert inside herself but because it no longer mattered. She was who she was, and the right people loved her for it. It didn't matter if she hid

329

in her room or organized a grand party, she would be true to herself. Striving for perfection and worrying what others thought about her only ever led to unhappiness. The flaws were what made life interesting, like the uneven wood grain and sporadic knots in a beautiful wood floor.

Ray led her to the dance floor, circling his arms around her waist. Sabrina scanned the crowd, at first not realizing who she was looking for, until it hit her that she wouldn't find the bouncing curls or dimpled smile. Molly. She would have loved this night, dressed in some elaborate gown, or maybe changing every hour for fun, eavesdropping on the different tables of guests, and sharing the funniest stories later with Sabrina.

If Molly were here, she'd tell Sabrina how this was the perfect end to her love story. The villain had been defeated, the couple was together, and there was a party with fancy clothes and good food and plenty of music. But happily ever afters in real life were very different from the movies. The pain and loss and difficulties didn't disappear. With every joy came the reminder that someone wasn't there to share the moment. Real happily ever afters were flavored with bitter and sweet. With Ray by her side, Sabrina wanted to taste it all.

Recipe

WISCONSIN-STYLE BRANDY OLD-FASHIONED

We make old-fashioneds differently in the glorious dairy state. There are many different stories about how the Wisconsin version came to be, most dating back to the Chicago World's Fair in 1893, when the California-based Korbel brought a case of brandy, and Wisconsinites loved how it reminded them of their Germanic (and brandy-loving) roots. After that it gets murkier until post-prohibition, when brandy old-fashioneds and supper clubs emerged inseparable. A Friday-night fish fry wouldn't be complete without one. With the following recipe, you can enjoy the Wisconsin tradition for yourself.

Makes 1 in a cocktail tumbler

- ½ ounce of simple syrup (Boil equal parts sugar and water until the sugar dissolves, then cool.)
- 2 cherries, plus a little of the juice from the jar and extra cherries for garnishing (Maraschino cherries work, but if you can find brandy-soaked, high-quality cherries, use those instead.)
- 2 orange slices

10 dashes of bitters (Angostura bitters are traditional, but feel free
  to experiment.)

1½ ounces brandy (Korbel is traditional, but any brandy will work.)

Ice

Soda (Use 7UP for a sweet version, sour soda for a sour version, or
  club soda.)

Add the simple syrup, 2 cherries plus juice, 1 orange slice, bitters, and brandy to the cocktail tumbler, then muddle.

Add ice and stir.

Fill the rest of the glass with soda.

Garnish with the other orange slice and cherry.

Acknowledgments

I'm so grateful for the many, many people who make my life and career possible.

Rachel Ekstrom—my best interests are always your best interests. You roll with my silly ideas and never-ending random questions about every corner of the publishing industry. I'm so thankful we're doing this together. Thank you to the Folio team, especially Maggie Auffarth.

Kerry Donovan—from our first conversation I knew you understood the kind of books I wanted to write, and you've helped me make them a reality! Thank you!

To everyone at Berkley who embraced me with open arms, but especially Diana Franco, Jessica Mangicaro, and Mary Geren. Also, Vikki Chu for the perfect cover design, Stacy Edwards, Craig Burke, Jeanne-Marie Hudson, and Claire Zion. Copyeditors have a thankless job. They basically tell authors the hard truths—like how we don't know how to use commas or our timelines have eighteen days in a week. Abby Graves, thank you!

Acknowledgments

Writing a book is a major accomplishment, but it's much more meaningful when people actually read it. Thank you to Kathleen Carter for helping spread the word to the world. Danielle Noe, you are a Facebook sorceress.

Melissa Marino—my partner in crime and research, you helped me muddle through this story in the early days when it was trying to be fifteen things at once. Kelly Harms and Kristin Harmel for sharing their wisdom with me.

Early readers are crucial for knowing if a book makes sense. Thank you to Carla Cullen—our breakfasts mean so much to me—Sarah Cannon, Gail Werner, Anne Siess, and Heather Webb (and our four-hour wine-soaked video chat to discuss it in the middle of a pandemic). My girls—Karma Brown, Colleen Oakley, and Nicole Blade—our daily texts keep me sane and our mutual love of *The Vampire Diaries* restores my faith in the world. Team Damon forever.

The internet is great for research, but sometimes you need real people to fill in the details. Thank you to Kiki Rodriguez—you know who you are. Lynette and Terry Gunville—not only are you both amazing supporters of my books, but your insight into the struggles and treatment for anxiety brought life to Sabrina. Any mistakes are my own.

My family—for months at a time I'm half-aware of what's going on. Thank you for being patient and making up the difference. Mom, Sandy, Pam—for always helping when I'm in over my head. Daisy, the majestic floof and ultimate writing companion. My children, Ainsley and Sam, you are my world. My Johnny Reichert—you support me completely.

Lastly, to all my readers who reached out to say how much they wanted more books—it means so much to know that strangers like the way my brain works.

The KINDRED SPIRITS SUPPER CLUB

Amy E. Reichert

Questions for Discussion

1. The women in Sabrina's family can see ghosts and have used their gift to help the recently deceased with their unfinished business. It has become a family vocation that everyone gets involved in. Have you and your relatives ever adopted a family cause? If not, what might be something that would interest you?

2. Sabrina suffers from an anxiety disorder. Approximately 18 percent of the population suffers from anxiety, be it caused by genetics, brain chemistry, or life events, yet this isn't often discussed openly. In what scenes did you feel particularly empathetic toward Sabrina due to her anxiety?

3. Sabrina chose to study journalism. Do you think that was the right career choice for her? Why do you think she felt drawn toward journalism?

4. Food and drink play an important part in *The Kindred Spirits Supper Club*, helping to capture the local culture. Have you traveled to any places where the food and drink was an equally important part of

the location? Which specific mentions of food or drink in this story stood out to you?

5. Sabrina's experience with Bobby in the parking lot of the Goodbye Gala was a pivotal moment in her life that changed her perspective forever. Have you experienced any life-changing moments that changed things, for better or for worse? How did they change your perspective?

6. In what ways did you notice Sabrina and Ray changing throughout the story? How did your opinion of them change?

7. Was there a character you related to the most, and what was it about them that you connected with?

8. The title of the book uses the phrase "kindred spirits." What does this phrase mean to you? Do you have any kindred spirits in your life?

9. By the end of the book, Sabrina is no longer bothered by Erika and her bullying. What changed? What did you think about Sabrina's attitude toward Erika at the close of the book? How would you have handled things in Sabrina's place?

10. What did you think about Molly and Belle and their unfinished business? They have chosen very different ways of handling their purgatory. Did you have any favorite moments from Molly's story line?

11. At one point in the book, Sabrina refers to her kindness as selfish. Why would she say that? Do you agree or disagree? And do you think instances of kindness can be very impactful in someone's life?

Photo by Kelly Johnsen

AMY E. REICHERT is an author, wife, mom, Wisconsinite, amateur chef, and cider enthusiast. She earned her MA in English literature and serves on her library's board of directors. She is a member of Tall Poppy Writers.

Ready to find
your next great read?

Let us help.

Visit prh.com/nextread